Not without
Your
L♥VE

Not without Your LOVE

New York Times Bestselling Author
LEXI RYAN

Cover and cover image © 2021 by Sara Eirew
Interior designed and formatted by

emtippettsbookdesigns.com

For Kim Jackson, mama to the *other* Jake Jackson

Other Books by
LEXI RYAN

Orchid Valley

Every Little Piece of Me (Brinley and Marston's story, includes their prequel novella)
Every Sweet Regret (Stella and Kace's story)
Every Time I Fall (Abbi and Dean's story)
Every Chance with You (Savvy's story, coming in 2022!)

The Boys of Jackson Harbor

The Wrong Kind of Love (Ethan's story)
Straight Up Love (Jake's story)
Dirty, Reckless Love (Levi's story)
Wrapped in Love (Brayden's story)
Crazy for Your Love (Carter's story)
If It's Only Love (Shay's story)
Not Without Your Love (Colton's story)

The Blackhawk Boys

Spinning Out (Arrow's story)
Rushing In (Chris's story)
Going Under (Sebastian's story)
Falling Hard (Keegan's story)
In Too Deep (Mason's story)

LOVE UNBOUND: Four series, one small town, lots of happy endings

Splintered Hearts (A Love Unbound Series)
Unbreak Me (Maggie's story)
Stolen Wishes: A Wish I May Prequel Novella (Will and Cally's prequel)
Wish I May (Will and Cally's novel)
Or read them together in the omnibus edition, *Splintered Hearts: The New Hope Trilogy*

Here and Now (A Love Unbound Series)
Lost in Me (Hanna's story begins)
Fall to You (Hanna's story continues)
All for This (Hanna's story concludes)
Or read them together in the omnibus edition, *Here and Now: The Complete Series*

Reckless and Real (A Love Unbound Series)
Something Wild (Liz and Sam's prequel)
Something Reckless (Liz and Sam's story continues)
Something Real (Liz and Sam's story concludes)
Or read them together in the omnibus edition, *Reckless and Real: The Complete Series*

Mended Hearts (A Love Unbound Series)
Playing with Fire (Nix's story)
Holding Her Close (Janelle and Cade's story)

OTHER TITLES

Hot Contemporary Romance
Text Appeal
Accidental Sex Goddess

Decadence Creek (Short and Sexy Romance)
Just One Night
Just the Way You Are

Chapter One

VERONICA

I read a lot of romance novels, but until Colton McKinley came into my life, I never understood what the authors meant when they talk about the hero *growling*. What is he, a bear?

After some quality time with the tall, sexy jackass who's also sorta-kinda my boss, I consider myself enlightened.

Colton has two kinds of growls: the panty-shredding *I'm taking you right this minute* hungry rumble of a man about to do some serious ravishing, and the *I should really fire your ass* angry snarl of an employer to his delinquent employee.

While I might actively—and frequently—fantasize about the former, my life is brimming with the latter. Especially this morning when I push through the door, harried and hands full, and the first words out of his infuriating wet dream of a mouth are "You're *late*."

"Thank you, Captain Obvious." I juggle my purse, coffee, planner, and notebook as I pull the keys from the front door and kick it closed behind me.

"A *half-hour* late."

Shit. I plop my coffee and my purse on the front counter and glance at the clock, praying he's wrong on this. *Alas . . .* I give him my most innocent smile. "You must've been *so worried.*"

His eye twitch tells me he's not amused. "I need you to be on time or I'll find someone who will be."

My hackles go up. When I was scrambling to get out of the house this morning, I was mentally reciting the apology I'd give him, but now that he's gone and growled at me, I don't want to give the self-righteous ass the satisfaction. "You keep saying that, and yet here I am."

"Don't push me."

Oh, but I want to. I spend way more time than is healthy imagining what it'd be like to finally push equal parts asshole and hottie Colton McKinley over the edge. As my friend Star likes to say, God puts the biggest assholes in the hottest packages. It's the only way to preserve their species.

Colton folds his arms and glowers. "What the fuck am I supposed to say, Veronica? I literally can't do my job if you aren't here to do yours." He rocks back on his heels and looks me over with the slow, thorough appraisal of a guy who's mentally cataloguing all the reasons he wants to take a girl home. But I know better than to think he takes any enjoyment out of his visual perusal. We had one night together before either of us knew the other well enough to understand we're vinegar and oil. One night that was impulsive and reckless and *So. Fucking. Hot.*

Until, suddenly, it wasn't.

Colton hates me as much as I hate him.

His gaze lands on my coffee before flicking back up to meet mine, and murder lurks in his eyes. "Now I have a guided ATV expedition that's going to start late because you thought putting on makeup and getting coffee were more important than *my* business."

I could tell him that neither the coffee nor the makeup played any part in my tardiness, but why should I reason with a man who assumes the worst of me and can't be bothered with basic decency? Propping a hand on my hip, I bat my lashes and give him my best pouty mouth. "Maybe if you didn't stare at me all day, I'd do a better job remembering my appearance isn't supposed to be a priority."

"No one here cares what you look like, Veronica. Next time, choose punctuality over the smoky eye." He turns on his heel and strides into his office. I take the opportunity to ogle the muscles stretching the back of his white T-shirt. After seeing him work on the boats, it's obvious those things aren't just for show. He has the kind of strength necessary to throw a woman over his shoulder and carry her to his bedroom. Or throw her on his desk and have his way with her. Not that I've imagined such scenarios. *Much.*

He slams his office door, yanking me from my fantasy and making the walls shake.

They say Colton used to be this wild thrill-seeker, but the guy I know has a stick up his ass and lives to remind me of my shortcomings—of which, let's be fair, I have *many.*

I watch the door and wait for him to remember he's supposed to be washing the ATVs for this morning's guided trail tour.

He reemerges after three seconds, and I flash him a smug smile. "Have fun!" I call after him, resisting the urge to show his back my middle finger. When it comes to Colton McKinley, I'm shamefully immature. Except for what he does to my libido. That is definitely more *mature*.

I walk around the front counter and sink into the chair at the desk stationed behind it, shoulders sagging. The phone blinks with messages, and there's a stack of paperwork waiting for me.

I really, *really* don't like being late, but it turns out that along with the other thousand reasons sharing a bedroom with my almost-three-year-old isn't ideal, I need to add "Jacks can now climb out of his crib" to the list.

He's never done it before, but this morning he somehow managed while I was sleeping. And since he loves buttons, it's not even surprising that he turned off my alarm. I can't be mad at him—not when he woke me up with kisses on my cheeks, whispering, "So pitty, Mommy. So pitty."

How could I be mad about anything that gave me that moment?

I'm firing up the computer and pulling out my notepad when Amelia wanders in from the docks, her dark hair twisted into two shoulder-length braids and her light brown skin glowing from a morning fishing expedition.

"Back already?" I ask. The sunrise tours usually stay out another hour.

"City folk. They got a couple of good ones and were done." She shrugs, accustomed to the various kinds of clients who use the services of Heartbreak Bay Adventures. "Who pissed in Colton's Wheaties?"

I raise my hand. "Me. As always. I just got here, so he's late preparing the ATVs for his booking."

She glances at the clock and cringes. "Again? Girl."

I sigh. "I *know*. Trust me."

"What happened this time?"

"I don't know for sure, but when Jacks woke me up, he was out of his crib, and the alarm was on the floor with all the settings changed. He must've climbed out and played with the buttons." *And now I need to figure out the logistics of moving him to a toddler bed.*

"Did you tell Colt that?"

I grimace. "Are you kidding? It's the single-mom version of *the dog ate my paper*. I'd rather he believe yesterday's makeup and this coffee are behind my tardiness." At the reminder of the makeup, I pull a baby wipe from my purse and rub it under my eyes. I fell asleep at the computer last night, and when I realized I needed to drag myself to bed, I couldn't be bothered to wash my face.

Chuckling, Amelia props her elbows on the counter. "Why don't you just tell him you drop your kid off with Star at the coffee shop? Why let him think you stand in line for coffee even on the days you're running behind?"

"Because it's none of his business. He's the one who assumes the worst. That's on him." I toss the wipe in the trash and reach for my lip gloss. I caught a glimpse of myself in the mirror when I brushed my teeth this morning, and it's downright *insulting* that Colton believes I took time on this look.

"You sure push his buttons."

"Understatement of the century," I mutter. There's not much

about me that doesn't piss off Colton. "I'm pretty sure he would've fired me by now if he weren't so worried about staying in the Jacksons' good graces. Hell, *I* would've fired me already."

"The guys won't let him. You're too valuable to fire, and they'd kick his ass if they lost you because of his temper. He knows that."

"If you say so." Colton and his friends are all equal owners in Heartbreak Bay Adventures, but while I know the other guys might appreciate me more than he does, Colton could make a hell of a case against me if he wanted.

Because you can't seem to get your shit together and you sabotage everything good in your life, the old familiar voice in my head reminds me. I slam the door on that bitch, take a deep breath, and focus on my work.

I click through emails, clearing out the spam and forwarding the messages that Colton or his business partners need to handle to their respective addresses.

"You look tired," Amelia says, watching me work. There's so much worry in her voice that I can't be offended. "Another late night writing papers?"

I nod, my attention half on an email inquiry about weddings on the lake. "At least this one was interesting. The correlation of abstinence-only education and college dropout rates among women. I could've aced it, but the student was aiming for a B."

"If they're paying so much for a paper, don't they want an A?"

I shake my head. "The perfect paper makes instructors suspicious."

Amelia makes a sour face. "I hated writing papers in school. You couldn't pay me to write someone else's essay."

"It's not so bad." I have more issues with the ethics of my side hustle than I do with the work itself. I have a teaching degree, for goodness' sake. I believe students should write their own damn papers, not use their trust funds to pay a desperate single mom two hundred bucks a pop to crank them out for them. But ethical high ground is a lot easier to stand on when your nine-to-five pays the bills. "And it's something I can do from home while Jacks sleeps. Win-win."

"I still think you're paying too much for that tiny room," she says. "Wasn't the whole point of renting a room from June that it'd be a small fraction of the cost of your own place?"

"It still is. Even after her rent hikes." I've lived there less than six months, and she's already raised the price for my room twice. The dark side of living without a lease. It's overpriced, but so is everything in Jackson Harbor, and at least our place is safe until I can find something better for me and Jacks.

"But it's temporary, right?" Amelia asks, worry pulling at her fine features. "You're saving money to get a place of your own where you can have some privacy for once?"

I frown at the computer, unwilling to meet my friend's eyes and let her see how stuck I am. "That's the plan."

"Thank God. You need to be able to bring a guy home and get yourself a little something for once."

I scoff. "I wouldn't know what to do with a guy in my bedroom. I'm in such a dry spell that even my vibrator has abandonment issues. Hell, at this point I'd settle for fifteen minutes alone to get reacquainted with her."

Crosley emerges from the garage that's tucked behind the reception area. He's drying his hands on a shop towel, but streaks of motor oil are smeared across his forearms. He props the swinging door open with a jean-clad hip. "Reacquainted with who?"

"It's *with whom*," Amelia tells her brother.

Crosley rolls his eyes at his sister, and I bite back a smile. I've always liked Amelia and Crosley, but I might feel a special connection to them because, like me and Nic, they're twins. "Reacquainted *with whom*?" He draws the words out with a fake British accent.

"No one," I say at the same time as Amelia says, "Her vibrator."

"Thanks for respecting my privacy, Mele," I mutter.

Crosley wipes his cheek on his shoulder, grinning. "Your vibrator is a *her*?"

Amelia props her hands on her hips and glares at her brother. "Why are you still lurking?"

"I work here." He turns to me. "Explain, please?"

"Variable speeds means she's adaptable. She always gets the job done and never asks for anything in return?" I turn up my palms. "Obviously female."

Crosley cringes. "Damn. What kind of lame-ass man gave you that impression?"

"All of them," Amelia and I say in unison.

"That's tragic," he mutters.

"And you're not part of this conversation, so go away," Amelia says, shooting him a glare before turning her attention back to me. "You need more than a vibrator. You need a *man*. Or a woman, if you're into that." It's officially been so long since I've seen any action that Amelia, one of my best friends, isn't even sure of my sexual preference. Maybe she has a point. "But, you know, actual human lovin.'"

"And when would I find time for this? Between bath time and writing freshman comp essays for cheating college kids?"

Folding his arms, Crosley rocks on his heels and looks back and forth between us, clearly not intending to leave anytime soon. "I could swing by about then," he says.

"Ew, Cros. Stop." Amelia elbows her brother in the side, and he doubles over, laughing.

"I think I'll pass on screwing my boss," I say, winking at him, because as equal owner of HBA, he's my boss as much as Colton is. We all know he's just joking anyway, but if casual hookups were still part of my life, I might've had to consider taking him up on it.

Crosley's a hottie—tall and strong, with big hands and an excellent sense of humor. He's got the jaw line of a Greek god and intense brown eyes, but it's the unexpected *cuteness* of his curly hair that somehow pushes his hotness over the edge.

Alas, the last time I tried to do casual, I ended up with my dress around my hips and Colton's dirty words in my ear, his hands cupping and kneading my breasts until I shattered in the best orgasm I'd had in . . . ever.

All things considered, it wouldn't have scared me off casual hookups—if he hadn't ruined it.

"You work too much," Amelia whines, pulling my thoughts out of my secret memory. "Please tell me you're still coming out with us tonight."

"Where?" Crosley asks.

"Girls' night," Amelia tells her brother. "We're finally getting Veronica out of the house."

He grins. "Girls' night?" He shifts his deep brown eyes to me.

"Will Star be there?"

"It's her birthday," I say, ignoring Amelia's pointed glare in her brother's direction.

"I'll be there," Crosley says with a broad grin. Despite his playful flirting with me and every other single female in town, his crush on our friend Star is the worst-kept secret in Jackson Harbor, which is saying something.

"You're not invited," Amelia says. "Stay away from my friends."

"You'll put in a good word for me, won't you, Veronica?"

"Every chance I get." I wink at him, but we both know nothing's going to happen. Star is a single mom like me, but unlike me, her kid's thirteen. Last I checked, she's not interested in bringing anyone into her daughter's life.

"So . . ." Amelia says, pressing her hands together. "Please say you got a sitter and can come. Don't make me beg, V."

"I'm coming, I'm coming," I say, laughing.

"If I had a nickel for every time I heard that," Crosley says.

"You still wouldn't be able to afford a piece of gum," Amelia says.

Crosley ignores her and points his attention to me. "So, what'd you do to piss off Colton this morning?"

I duck my head, truly uninterested in rehashing this again.

"She was late and made him run behind," Amelia says.

"Why didn't you call?" Crosley asks. "I could've covered for you."

"Because I was sleeping and didn't know I'd be late."

"And she's too fucking proud to explain what happened," Amelia says, "so Colton thinks it was for bullshit reasons."

"Late is late," I say, grabbing my planner and jotting notes for the day in it. "I'm not here to make excuses."

Crosley drags a hand through his curls. "You ever think maybe you two just need to fuck and get it over with?"

Been there. Done that. I hide my cringe. "First, you offer yourself, and now you're trying to get her to do the deed with Colt?" Amelia smacks his chest with the back of her hand. "You can't *say* shit like that, Cros."

He holds up both hands and bites back a smile. "I'm sorry, but you know you've thought the same thing. There's *tension* when they're in the same room, and it's not the kind of tension I feel when I'm around folks I hate."

"Just because you think it doesn't mean you have to *say* it. Anyway, as Veronica's already pointed out, she's not dumb enough to sleep with her boss."

I watch them from the corner of my eye but keep my head bowed. "That's one on the very short list of mistakes I've managed to avoid." Because Colton *wasn't* my boss when we slept together. No, I didn't start working here until later—after the coffee shop cut my hours and my sister asked Colt to give me a job. Of course, I didn't know at the time it was a pity hire. I thought he truly wanted me to help with the new business.

There aren't many secrets in Jackson Harbor, and yet somehow Colton and I have managed to keep ours. For now.

"Would you two get to work so I can catch up on these messages before the day turns crazy?"

"Yes, ma'am," Amelia says.

It's tourist season, after all, and come ten a.m., it seems like the phone never stops ringing. They both head out to the garage, and I put my head down and work, but a few minutes later the door whooshes open again. I look up as Crosley squeezes my shoulder.

"I forgot why I came in here to begin with. Will you have time to confirm tomorrow's fishing expeditions before you leave?"

I tap my pen to my planner. "It's already on the list."

"You're the best." He hesitates for a beat then says, "You want me to talk to Colt about this morning?"

I force myself to exhale and smile up at him. Crosley's a good guy, but I don't want to be a wedge in his friendship or partnership with Colton. "If you're going to talk with anyone, I'm pretty sure it should be me. I was the one who was late. Again." I swallow. Time to be a big kid. "I wouldn't hold it against you if you wanted to hire someone else."

"What? Are you kidding me?"

"You have a business to run. Colton's right. I don't expect special treatment just because—"

"Just because we need you? Just because you save our asses on a daily basis, and we'd sink without you?" He shakes his head. "Veronica, you've been late a few times, and it sucks. We're a small business, and if one person is missing, the rest of us feel it. But it *happens*. I'm not going to fire you, and I'm not going to let Colton fire you. Hell, you might push his buttons, but he needs you as much as the rest of us do."

I scoff. "Sure. If you say so."

"I *know* so."

I draw in a deep, shaky breath. "I'm still hoping to get a teaching position for the fall, so if you *could* put up with me for a couple more months, that'd be amazing." When I imagine trying to find another full-time position for the summer while also trying to get in with the school corporation *and* keeping up with the side hustle and trying to be a halfway decent parent to Jacks, I feel myself breaking out in hives.

"I'm just happy you're looking for a job that'll keep your summers free," he says. "We *need* you for high season."

"Maybe have a chat with your business partner before inviting me back for next year," I say, looking pointedly toward Colton's office.

Crosley's always-smiling face goes solemn. "He does care about you. He just acts like a hard-ass because he doesn't know what to do about it."

"You're a busybody. Get back to work." I force a smile as he retreats. He has no idea how wrong he is.

Colton doesn't care about me. He can't stand me.

Chapter Two

COLTON

When my office door is open, I have the perfect view of the Heartbreak Bay Adventures reception area. At first, this was by design: I'd keep an eye on reception and take care of any walk-in traffic between dealing with the contracts, bookkeeping, and endless paperwork involved in running a business. Since we offer everything from sunset cruises to ATV rentals to winery tours, the "paperwork" side of things got overwhelming fast. I had to quickly find someone to cover the front so I could get anything done at all. I gave the job to Veronica Maddox as a favor to her twin sister, Nic. And now I have the perfect view of the only woman who's ever gotten under my skin this way.

"Maybe if you didn't stare at me all day, I'd do a better job remembering my appearance isn't supposed to be a priority."

I can't even scoff at that because she's right. Most of the time when Veronica's around, I have trouble looking anywhere else. This whole arrangement would be easier if my irritation with her weren't matched by a borderline obsessive attraction.

I never should've followed her away from the crowd at the Jacksons' cabin last summer. I never should've kissed her. Definitely shouldn't have touched her or made her come. I'm fucking *haunted* by the sounds she made and the way her eyes fluttered closed and her head fell back as she came apart.

Crosley slaps the back of my head. "You're staring again."

I wince, rubbing my scalp and glaring up at him from my desk chair. "That hurt, asshole."

"Sorry. Next time I'll kick you in the balls instead."

I make sure Veronica isn't looking our way before I add, "And lower your voice."

His lips twitch. "Is it a secret?"

I shove the contract at him, shaking my head. "Is that all you need?"

He takes the stack of papers and nods. "You okay?"

"Yeah, why?"

"I hear you were in a mood this morning. Made our receptionist think she needs to be job hunting."

"She was late." But hell, it wasn't her fault I was so on edge. My mood was less about my late departure from the office and more about the call I got on my way to the office. I've been sober for two and a half years, but learning an AA friend relapsed always sucks. Not only am I worried sick about Mike, but something about seeing him fall off the wagon makes me feel vulnerable as fuck. It's an unwanted reminder that I'm just one bad decision away from losing the life I've had to fight so damn hard to build after destroying my old one.

"Shit happens," Crosley says. "And Veronica has way more on her plate than the rest of us. You need backup in here, pick up the fucking phone. If I'm not in the shop, I'm upstairs and I'll cover."

I give a casual shrug. He's right, of course. When we bought this place, we debated renting out the run-down apartments that sit over the office and garages. We decided we'd be better off living upstairs ourselves—we'd renovate them as our budgets and schedules allowed and eventually charge what the bay-view apartments are really worth. It also meant we'd be right on site when extra hands were needed and could run upstairs to clean up between excursions. I know all this, and yet when it comes to Veronica, I lose my goddamned mind.

I was a dick this morning, and I owe her an apology. I'll swallow my pride and make sure she knows I'm not planning to fire her. Maybe I'll even ask if we need to adjust her schedule. She's a single mom juggling a lot. I'm a compassionate guy under normal circumstances, but there's nothing normal about how I feel when Veronica is around. "I'll talk to her and fix it."

"Good," Cros says. "Coming out with us tonight?"

I arch a brow. "We're going out?"

"Jackson Brews after work. What do you say?"

"Sure." My first year sober, I avoided bars like the plague, but Jackson Brews is low-key, and their new selection of nonalcoholic beer makes going feel like a treat instead of a test. Especially when I get to drink it while kicking Crosley's ass at pool. "Rematch?"

"We'll see," he says, grinning and backing out the door. "I'm heading upstairs. I need a shower, but I'll meet you there."

"Good deal," I say, turning my attention to my computer.

Only when Crosley's gone do I realize I forgot to tell him to close the door.

My gaze drifts to the reception area again. To Veronica. She's wearing a little white sundress that seems to be one of her favorites. It has skinny straps that slip off her shoulders all day, and the hem barely reaches mid-thigh. And if she forgets a sweater, which she usually does because she's a hot fucking mess most of the time, her nipples get hard in the cool air conditioning, and the dress is too thin to disguise it. That fucking dress haunts my dreams.

She leans on the counter, helping a customer scroll the iPad we keep loaded with details and pictures of our services, and I have the perfect view of the curve of her ass and the exposed backs of her thighs. If she leans over just a little more, I might get a glimpse of her panties. Are they the same silky fabric as the ones I stroked between her thighs last summer? *The ones I took home and still haven't returned.*

I'm dying to know, and I fucking hate myself for it. I don't want to be that creepy coworker who puts his eyes where they're not welcome. I don't like to think of myself as her boss. That just makes this whole situation even more fucked up.

The guy at the counter says something I can't quite make out, and Veronica's full laugh fills my ears. His gaze drifts down to her cleavage, and I want to kick the asshole right out the door. Even if the impulse makes me a fucking hypocrite. Maybe *because* it makes me a hypocrite.

I force my attention back to my computer, and within a few minutes, I'm lost in preparing new contracts and mapping out future expeditions.

The day gets away from me again, and it's not until I hear Veronica closing up that I realize how late it's gotten. We have a private party going out with Wes tonight, and I needed their signed contract yesterday. Veronica promised she'd get their signatures today.

"Do you have the Hammish contract?" I push out of my desk and stride toward reception. I should've asked earlier, but, truth be told, I was avoiding her.

Veronica locks the front door and turns the sign instructing people to go online for reservations or try back tomorrow. All the while, she doesn't spare me a fucking glance. Why should she? I'm just her boss. Just the asshole with the temper who didn't bother asking if she was okay before letting loose on her this morning.

But it doesn't change the fact that I need that paperwork. I soften my tone. "Veronica? The contract?"

She sighs. "I put it in the shared drive like you told me to."

"I didn't see it there."

"Are you sure?" Her full lips pull into a grimace, and the urge to kiss it away fuels my shitty mood.

"I just refreshed." I sound like a dick, but we shouldn't be working together. She makes me fucking crazy. I focus my glower on the wall behind her head while she circles back to the computer to check. I'm trying really hard not to use the moment to get another look at her thighs.

Most days I can't decide if I want to fight with her or fuck her, and, yeah, even if she didn't hate my guts, it's not a good look. I'm not that guy anymore.

Just the fact that I want her pisses me off, and I grit my teeth as she leans over the desk to get a closer look at the monitor.

"Shit," she whispers, and if I didn't know better, I'd think that was embarrassment in her tone. "Here. I'll move it now." She clicks her mouse a few times before closing the laptop and straightening, no trace of chagrin on her face as she meets my eyes and lifts her chin. "It's there now."

"You want a parade? I asked for it by lunch." I pointedly shift my gaze to the clock. Five p.m.

Her cheeks flush a pretty pink. "Don't be a dick," she snaps.

"I hired you as a favor," I say, all plans of apologizing out the window. "You're here to make my life easier, not harder."

Her jaw drops, and I hear the words I just said. I'm an asshole. I'm a *horny* asshole who apparently can't handle keeping his hands off Veronica Maddox without turning into a raging dick. But hell, this would be easier if I didn't know how good it feels to be inside her. It would be easier if I didn't remember the sounds she made when I scraped my teeth over the swell of her breast.

Creep.

"What exactly do you think I do out here for eight hours a day?" she snaps. "My nails?"

Of course I know she works hard. That she even has to ask proves that I'm screwing this up. I grimace. "I didn't—"

"Never mind." Veronica steps away and doesn't spare me a glance as she opens my office door. "I have to go pick up my son." She grabs her purse off her desk and shoves out through the front door. And I watch the swish of her hips with every step.

VERONICA

Sometimes life as a single mom feels like a series of ticking clocks. I wake up in the morning and I'm on the clock. Shower, dress, wake Jacks—if he somehow isn't awake yet—to change and feed him, and hustle out the door. Don't forget our lunches or Jacks' blankie. I drop him off with Star at Ooh La La! because preschool doesn't officially start until nine, and she can walk him across the street on her break. Once I leave Jacks with my best friend, I rush to get to work on time. There, I work against the clock again, trying to reply to as many messages from our email and social media accounts as possible before turning on the phones and opening the doors for the day. At lunch, I'm on the clock again—rushing to the preschool to pick up Jacks and take him to daycare for the afternoon. Then I get back to work to finish my day. If I leave on time, I have an hour between when I leave work and when I pick up Jacks. Seems like plenty of time, until that hour becomes your only opportunity to take care of errands you need to do alone. Christmas and birthday shopping are a must without Jacks, but half the time, I'm squeezing in a run to the store for this or that.

Tonight, I'm using my precious hour to shower and get ready for a rare night out with the girls. Normally, I pass when Amelia and Star try to get me to go out with them. I just don't have the kind of life that lends itself to regular evenings out with friends. My sister would be happy to watch Jacks, but I try not to ask very often. Tonight, however, is an exception. It's Star's birthday, and all she wants is a night out with her girls at Jackson Brews. How could I say no? I only do this a few times a year.

No one takes a shower as fast as the mother of a toddler, so in record time I'm clean, dry, and exiting the bathroom with a towel wrapped around my body and another around my wet hair. A glance at my phone tells me I can spend nineteen minutes on my hair and makeup.

"Damn, girl. Look at you."

I grip the top of the towel more tightly and bite back my cringe. Landon, my roommate's boyfriend, is standing in the hall.

Mostly, I like living with June. Mostly, I feel safe here. But then there's the week every month or so that her boyfriend's around.

He works on an oil rig in Texas most of the time, and when he's in town, he spends more time here than I anticipated. He's not slimy—not exactly. But any time June's not around, his glances in my direction turn to leers. I've made it a habit to never be alone with him. But today, I forgot. "Hey, Landon."

He drags his bottom lip through his teeth and stares so hard at my towel that I wonder if he's attempting telekinesis or something.

I sidestep him, headed to my room, but he blocks me, standing in front of my door.

"I think it's time we talk."

"I'm in a hurry." Dread makes the hairs on the back of my neck stand up. I stare at his chest, unwilling to back down but uninterested in seeing what lurks in his expression. "I have to get dressed and pick up my son."

"Ask June to do it. You know she would, and that would give us the time we need." He lifts a hand, taking a stray lock of wet hair between two fingers.

I jerk back. "We don't need time, and I have to get my son. We have plans."

Landon chuckles low. "Come on, now. We both know you're not scared of me. Stop pretending." He licks his lips then follows my gaze to my bedroom. "If you were my girl, you'd have more than a little room to live in. I'd take real good care of you."

"You're with June," I say, as if the reminder will do any good.

He lifts a shoulder in a lopsided shrug. "We're casual. She knows I'm not too serious about her. Knows I'm keeping my options open."

Bullshit. I squeeze my eyes shut and give myself until the count of three to be upset about this. This isn't my first rodeo. The silver lining of a bumpy life is becoming a pro at recognizing garbage humans. Landon is trash, and part of me has always known that if anything screwed up my arrangement with June, it'd be him. When I open my eyes, he's smiling, like my moment of weakness was some sort of win for him.

This time, I meet his eyes. "Get out of my way."

"Sure." His smile grows. "If you drop that towel."

Garbage human. "No." I set my jaw. "Get out of my way so I can get dressed."

"Come on, Ve-ron-i-ca." He pronounces the four syllables of my name as if they're each their own word and closes the distance between us with each beat. I swing around him, lunging for my room and slamming the door behind me.

"Your loss, bitch," he mutters in the hall.

I bite my lip, knowing anything I shout in reply will only drag this out.

A quick look at my phone tells me I have seventeen minutes

before I need to get out of here.

I should call June. I should tell her what happened.

My gut clenches as I look around the little bedroom Jacks and I call home. It's not much, but it's a lot more than my sister and I had for most of our childhood. What if I tell June about what just happened and she blames it on me? What if knowing that her boyfriend came on to me is too much for her to handle? Nic would take me and Jacks in, but any space we'd have in her house would never be ours. We'd be visitors. Imposing. I don't want to ask that of her. I spent most of my life dragging her through the mess I made. I'll never drag her down again.

With a deep breath, I shove down the worry and lock it away. Sixteen minutes now. Sixteen minutes to do my hair and makeup and get dressed. The clock is always ticking.

Chapter Three

VERONICA

"May I have a hug before I go?" I call to Jackson, who's already chasing his cousin Lilly into the living room.

He changes course, races back to me, and gives me a quick leg squeeze. I barely land a kiss on his forehead before he's out of my grasp and turning toward the living room again.

"He'll be fine," my sister says, one hand on her growing belly. "Have a good time tonight. You deserve it."

My son loves to spend time with his aunt Nic and her family, but I still struggle when I have to leave him. I know he's fine. I know the time apart is good for both of us. But I also know that I'd do anything to make sure my kid knows he's loved. That I'd do anything for him and give up anything to keep him in my life. Nic and I never had that.

I drag my bottom lip between my teeth and stare toward

the living room, where Jacks has disappeared. "Call if you need anything at all. If he's homesick or gets cranky or . . ."

Nic squeezes my shoulder. "He's going to be fine."

"Hey, Veronica," Ethan calls from the top of the stairs, heading down. "Thanks for bringing Jacks over. Lilly's been asking when she'd get to see him again."

I cough to cover my laugh. That is such a typical Jackson thing—to do me a favor while somehow pretending I'm the one doing them a favor. There's a reason I named my son after this incredible family—even if their perfection is a little hard to swallow sometimes.

"She's doing the thing," Nic tells her husband as he wraps his arms around her from behind.

"The thing?" he asks, sweeping a kiss across her neck.

"The guilt thing."

"The *mom* thing," I say.

"You'll understand soon enough," Ethan tells his wife, grinning down at her.

They're so cute it's sickening. Not only is their financial position enviable—they live in this amazing house but are in the middle of construction on their forever home—their marriage is the stuff dreams are made of. Love and lust and friendship all braided together in this unbreakable bond most of us can only imagine. Until I saw it for myself, I didn't believe relationships like that existed outside of novels.

"Yep," I say, backing toward the front. "Bye, you two. Call me if you need anything."

"We'll see you in the morning," Nic says.

I force a smile before slipping out the door and jogging to my car.

I am so happy for my sister and the life she's built with Ethan, but sometimes I long for what she has so badly it hurts. I'll never have someone who looks at me like that. I'll never have an equal partner in bringing up my son.

My sister's been amazing since I moved to Jackson Harbor. I didn't deserve her forgiveness or her help, and she gave it anyway, but that doesn't change the fact that at the end of the day, it's just me and Jackson. All I can do is hope like hell that I'm enough.

By the time I park behind Jackson Brews and make my way inside, the other girls have been there for over an hour. I could've made it earlier, but I wanted more time with Jackson, so while the girls ate their greasy bar food, I treated my son to dinner at McDonald's and let him burn off his excess energy in their play area.

When I walk into the bar, I spot Star in a booth at the back. She's impossible to miss with her big, curly red hair.

I didn't have anyone when I came to Jackson Harbor. I was running. Running from my baby's father, Marcus, and his demands, his rules that made his house feel more and more like a cage. The only people I knew here were my sister, Nic, my college friend, Teagan, and Kathleen Jackson, who once interviewed me for the job as Lilly's nanny.

That was more than three and a half years ago, when all I cared about was finding somewhere safe and getting my sister back, but life in Jackson Harbor became lonely pretty quickly. I didn't want to insert myself into Nic's new life, so I tried to stay on the periphery of her friend group, and I wasn't sure I'd ever find friends to call my own. Luckily, Star adopted me.

She spots me and jumps up to greet me with a hug.

"Happy birthday," I croon, squeezing her tight.

"Thank you. I'm so glad you made it!"

"I promised I would." I glance toward the empty booth, then the table and the miscellany of empty glasses and appetizer plates. "Where is everyone else?"

"Amelia and Juliette ran over to Howell's for a minute."

I pull a face. Howell's is the other major brewery in town, and most of the Jacksons consider it a personal offense when their friends patronize the place. "Why Howell's?"

"A guy Amelia is talking to is hanging there tonight." She waves it away, clearly uninterested in the intricacies of Amelia's dating life. "How'd drop-off go?"

"Too easy," I say. "He doesn't need Mama anymore. I'm afraid I'll blink and he'll be moving out on his own and go weeks without calling."

Star throws her head back and laughs, taking her seat again. "Don't worry. God gives us teen years to make that transition easier to swallow—take it from someone who's living it."

I slide into the booth across from her. "I'm such a cliché, but I don't even care. I want time to slow down for a minute. My baby is growing up so fast."

"It's not all bad—them growing up. Just imagine, soon enough, he'll be able to wipe his own butt and dress himself for school."

"Oh, he already wants to dress himself," I say. "On Tuesday,

I was making breakfast, and he came into the kitchen with his Spider-Man shirt on one arm and his Captain America undies over his pajama shorts."

Star presses her palm to her chest. "Gah! Never mind. Don't let him grow up. Find the science to stop time, and do it fast."

"I *know*. Like, right now he gives slobbery cheek kisses and thinks I'm the prettiest girl in the world, but in twenty years? He could be . . ." I scan the room and immediately spot the guys from work. I yank my gaze away before it can linger too long on Colton but vaguely gesture in their direction. "He could be one of those bro dudes, plotting the fastest way into a woman's panties."

Star snorts. "Okay, first of all? Your sweet Jackson will *never* be a sleazy dude bro. We're raising that boy to bring down the patriarchy. Second? The Heartbreakers don't need to plot their way into panties when women are so busy throwing them at their feet."

I snort-laugh, letting my gaze return to the guys for a moment. "Please don't ever let them find out you call them that. They'll be insufferable."

She gapes at me. "They're already insufferable. You think they don't know? They're fine as hell and charming as fuck. I'm not saying anything groundbreaking over here."

I take a minute to survey the group. They're built and tan from working in the sun all day, and she's right. They are nice to look at. My gaze snags on Colton. *Especially him.* His back's to me now, so I take my time admiring his ass as he bends over the pool table to line up a shot. The man's delicious. Tall, tatted, and powerfully built, he's a walking advertisement for testosterone.

Unfortunately for me and my libido, I know exactly how good

those muscles feel pressed against my body and how skillfully he can use his hands and mouth when he puts his mind to it. The trouble is, while I may have found the brooding, growly asshole shtick hot as hell the night I indulged in the fantasy and let him between my legs, it's not nearly as charming in real life.

Tonight, he's wearing a pair of faded jeans and a white T-shirt. His beard and dark hair are neatly trimmed, and as he stands again, my mouth goes dry at the memory of that night at the Jacksons' cabin—of that hard body under my palms, his fingers brushing where I ached for him.

I'd cut my tongue out before I admitted it, but I wanted Colton from the first time I saw him. I like to blame the contact high from all that testosterone oozing off him. Colton is hot. The kind of hot that turns smart girls dumb. Like, abs-for-miles, smoldering-eyes, exploding-ovaries, don't-bother-with-the-panties *hawt*. And anytime he turned that too-rare smile on *me*, I was no better than the next girl. I'd giggle. Probably batted my fucking lashes, too. I cringe to imagine it.

The thing about Colton is that he *isn't* just some dude bro. Until I started working with him, I actually *liked* him.

A few years ago, Colton's life hit rock bottom and he went into rehab, cleaned up, and came back home to start a new business and a new life. He isn't just another hot guy with a charming smile—he's this amazing human who's given himself a second chance. Something I've secretly always wanted for myself. He's proven himself even after those closest to him believed the worst.

Across the table from Colton, Crosley catches me staring and points in my direction as he says something to his buddies. Embarrassment warms my cheeks. *Busted.*

When Colton turns, I don't try to hide that I was looking. I hold his gaze and arch a brow.

"What is going on between you two?" Star asks.

I grunt and shift my attention back to my friend, where it belongs. I pretend I can't still feel Colton's eyes on me and shrug. "Not a thing."

"You're telling me you're not hot for boss?"

So hot. "He pretty much hates my guts. And I'm not a fan of his, either." *Except when he's touching me.*

"Mm-hmm," she says. "Tell me another one."

"What? I'm serious."

"Well, if not McKinley, then how about the other guys? I've caught Wes checking you out more than once."

"Wes is just a friend. And, frankly, I'm not looking to date any of the guys at work."

Star grunts. "Fair. But maybe it's time to date *someone*?"

"What is with you and Amelia both coming at me with this today?"

She cocks her head to the side. "What's with your two best friends noticing you're lonely and wanting better for you?"

She's not wrong, but I thought I hid it better than that. I blow out a long breath. "You know what's frustrating about dating as a single mom? There's this assumption that I'm looking for a daddy for Jackson."

She coughs on her beer and nods. "Girl, you're preaching to the choir. But Jackson's young. Hear me when I say it only gets more complicated when they get older. My daughter has *opinions* on every-fucking-thing. Can you imagine what Katie would do if I actually brought a guy home?"

"She'd quiz him on his political views and make him feel like trash for every time he shopped at Walmart." I shrug. "There are worse ways to filter the guys you date."

Star chuckles. "God forbid I actually *like* someone. She'd recite all his flaws the second we were alone." She wrinkles her nose. "But, hell, wouldn't it be worse if she didn't? I swear, the only thing that scares me more than disappointing this kid is that she'll stop talking to me."

"She's amazing, and so are you. I'm not even worried about that."

She waves a hand. "Regardless. Jacks will only find your dates lacking if they somehow reveal they don't like Spider-Man."

I mock gasp. "The horror."

"Right. The kid has to have *some* standards, but who doesn't love Spidey? I'm saying get out there while you still can."

"I don't know. I might eventually want to try, but sometimes a girl just wants her needs met. It's like going to the dealer for an oil change and having them assume you're there to invest in a whole new car."

Star chortles. "So Colton thinks you want to buy the car when you're really just looking for some service?"

"I don't pretend to know what Colton thinks. I try not to speculate. What about *you*?" I ask. "Is it time for you to get back on that horse?"

She bites her bottom lip and waggles her brows. "I might be contemplating a dusting off of the old riding muscles."

"Crosley? I know he's been waiting to drop to his knees and worship you like the goddess you are."

She rolls her eyes. "*Not* Crosley. That boy wouldn't know

what to do with me. I've been testing the waters with someone more . . . mature." She winks.

I smack the table. "I need *details*, bitch."

"Nah. I'm not about to jinx it by talking about it too soon," she says. "Hey, look who's back!" She nods to the door, where Amelia and Juliette are standing, laughing with the bouncer.

I scoot over in the booth to make room and wave to the waitress to take my order. I'm ready to have a little fun.

COLTON

*I*t isn't all that uncommon for the guys and me to meet at Jackson Brews for a drink after work, but now that we're here, I realize what they *really* wanted to do was be at the bar while Amelia and her friends were out. Crosley's got a thing for Star, and the other guys? Well, they just like hot women in general, and that group is smoking.

It's not that I mind coming out with my friends. They're actually great. No one gives me shit about my NA beers or tries to get me to take shots. A striking improvement over the people I surrounded myself with in my former life. Back before my *second* round in rehab, the only person who gave a shit about keeping me out of trouble was Levi. Sure, there were times when Levi was the start of the trouble, but I blame myself for that. I was the bad influence. I was the inspiration behind every bad decision.

Those days are behind us now, and I'm grateful Levi turned

out okay despite me. He took a sales position with his family's brewery, and I cleaned up and bought into Heartbreak Bay Adventures with Crosley, Wes, Miles, and Brady. Between the five of us, we had enough capital to get the bank to give us a business loan. We bought the neglected bay-front business and some new equipment—well, new to us, at least. This shit's expensive. We all traded everything we have for the opportunity to work our asses off and carry more debt than I like to think about.

So far, it's been good. Better than good. I get to spend part of my work week outside, on the water, or leading tourists on ATVs, and the other part putting to use the only worthwhile thing my asshole father ever gave me: my brain.

"You gonna talk to her or not, Cros?" Wes asks, tipping his beer back to his smiling lips.

Crosley eyes Star from across the bar and shakes his head. "I'll get around to it. Just mind your business. I'm playing the long game here."

"The long game?" Brady asks.

"Hell yeah," Crosley says. "It's the only way to make a woman like that give you a chance."

Miles wrinkles his nose. "I don't get it. Star's fine as hell, but you get with her and suddenly you have a teenager." He shudders. "No pussy's worth that."

Crosley smacks the back of Miles's head—*hard*, judging by the way Miles flinches. "Don't reduce women to their parts, you juvenile man-child."

Miles rubs the back of his head, messing up his perfectly styled dark hair. "Jesus. I didn't mean it in a bad way."

"What about Veronica?" Wes asks, glancing toward the girls.

"Her kid's, what, three?"

Every muscle in my body locks up. "What about her?"

Wes shrugs. "I just wondered if anyone knows if she's interested in, ya know, getting out there again."

"What is this, seventh grade?" Brady asks. "If you're interested in V, just tell her. She'll give it to you straight."

Crosley groans. "Or . . . *don't*. Do you want to make shit awkward at work?"

My shoulders loosen and I make a mental note to do something nice for Cros, since he spared me from having to say something myself.

"Yeah," Miles says, frowning at Wes, "you're technically her boss, and that shit's shady."

"She's only there for the summer. And anyway, I'm only her boss in the sense that I'm part owner," Wes says. "Really, Colton's her boss more than anyone."

Just like that, I scowl again. "No more than you," I mutter, and Crosley eyes me curiously. And I get it. Objecting too much is *real* subtle.

Wes shrugs. "I know I'm not the only one who's noticed her, so don't pretend like you're a bunch of saints."

"We're not saying we haven't noticed her," Brady says. "We're just requesting that you proceed with caution. Do you forget your track record with women?" He ticks off examples on his fingers. "The one who keyed your car, the one who threw your shit in the street."

"Let's not forget the one who climbed into *my bed* in the middle of the night to try to piss you off," Miles says.

Wes turns up his palms. "So I attract the crazies. Veronica's not like that. She's chill."

I choke on my drink, and Crosley smirks at me.

"You don't *attract* the crazies," Brady says. "You turn them crazy."

Everyone laughs, even Wes, who can't deny it.

I look Veronica's way again and catch her watching me. *Again.*

She yanks her gaze away quickly, but a guilty little flush creeps up her cheeks. What's she thinking about? And fuck, why do I hope she's as haunted by that night as I am? I hope she thinks about it when she touches herself. I hope she'll touch herself tonight and remember all the dirty details. The thought's enough to make me half-hard standing in the middle of the damn bar.

The next time I look Veronica's way, she holds my gaze for a beat longer than strictly necessary, and the heat in her eyes makes something go tight in my gut. Her girls are chatting and so are my guys, and the rest of the bar falls away as our eyes lock.

It's so damn hot in here that it's impossible not to think of our night together. Of sweat-slicked skin on leather seats. Of how fucking perfectly we fit.

"You two ever talk about it?" Crosley asks.

I'm so lost in my memories that I freeze for a panicked beat, thinking he's asking about what happened last Fourth of July. *Of course we didn't talk about it. She turned into a raving bitch the next day, as if I were the world's biggest ass when all I'd done was fuck her the way she begged me to fuck her and make her come so hard I had nail marks in my back for a week.*

"What happened this morning?" he asks.

I clear my throat, still unable to pull my gaze off Veronica. "I didn't get a chance."

"Didn't get a chance, or your pride was too big to swallow?" he asks. He grumbles under his breath, "You're gonna go postal if Wes pursues her, aren't you?"

My head snaps to the side so I can see Crosley's face. "What?"

He shakes his head. "Figure your shit out. I don't need my business partners fighting over a woman, even one as good as V."

Wes might not have a clue, but to Cros, I'm transparent. "You don't have anything to worry about," I promise, but it feels like a lie.

Chapter Four

COLTON

4th of July, 11 months ago

I've spent more July Fourths at the Jackson family cabin than I have at any single other place, but I don't know why I agreed to come this year. I'm not part of this big, happy family, and I never will be. Guys like me don't get families like this one. Not for real. I'll always be on the outside looking in, always be a spectator on the sidelines of their incredible lives.

Most of the time, I'm okay with that. After all, these people are my sister Ava's family now. Her daughter, Lauren, will grow up a Jackson. And because of that, when she's a teenager looking for trouble, it'll never be because anything sounds better than going home. It'll never be because she needs them to prove they'd still love her at her worst. So, yeah, maybe it's okay to be a spectator when it means seeing her grow up. When it means seeing my sister so damn happy.

But being here also means seeing another happy couple. Ellie and Levi. I wish I could say it's easy to tear my eyes off them as they sway together by the beachside fire. The sight of the love of my life dancing with my lifelong best friend pulverizes something in my chest that used to pass for a heart, but who needs that organ anyway?

Levi is better equipped to give the woman I loved the life she deserves, and I'm happy for them. But I'm also a fucking masochist for agreeing to come this weekend, and there's no denying that.

Ellie tilts her face up to Levi, and he touches his forehead to hers. They're losing themselves in each other's eyes, and I can't fucking look away.

I could leave. Unlike almost everyone else, I haven't had a drop to drink, so I'd be perfectly safe driving home. And yet I sit here. Torturing myself because I don't want Levi to know how much this shit fucks with me. At least they're all boozy enough to forget to make polite conversation with the outsider.

"Seems like you could use some company," Veronica says. She sinks into the chair across from mine. She smiles softly, looks me over, then leans forward and whispers, "Don't tell me if it's not true. I just got my son to sleep and I desperately need a minute with an adult who isn't trying to fix everything that's wrong with me."

I chuckle. I don't know much about Veronica other than she's Ethan's wife's twin, but I know Nic well enough to recognize the truth in Veronica's words. Nic is a fixer. She wants to make everyone's life better, and I'm sure her twin isn't exempt. "Make yourself comfortable."

She lifts her beer to her lips and stops halfway, grimacing. "Do you mind if I drink this?"

Ugh. I might not know much about her, but apparently she knows some key details about me. Colton, the addict. My reputation precedes me. *Fucking fantastic.* "Not even a little."

She considers her beer for a minute before standing halfway and launching it into a nearby trash can. "I'm too cold for a beer anyway," she says, and maybe it's a lie to make me more comfortable or maybe it's true. She's wearing a tank-style dress, and her arms are covered in goose bumps.

She settles back into her seat and shivers delicately, rubbing her hands together as she looks out toward the beach.

Veronica and Nic are identical, and when I first met them I had a hell of a time telling them apart, but then I realized the trick: there's something about Veronica that always strikes me as hotter. Maybe it's the way she carries herself or the look in her eye that tells me she carries a chip on her shoulder too. Or maybe it's just the psychology of knowing she's available. Whatever it is, I take advantage of her diverted attention and use the moment to check her out—her silky light brown hair, her plump pink lips, the freckles on her shoulders, and the swell of her tits. Her hard nipples. The sight of her makes me feel alive in a way I haven't in too long.

"I don't know why I come to these things," she says. She closes her eyes and rubs her temples. "Scratch that. I come for my son and for Nic. But I guess I don't know why the loneliness always takes me by surprise."

Veronica is the only other person at this party who's

welcomed by the Jacksons but not really one of them. Her words are so close to my own thoughts that they startle me a bit, and I immediately want to defend my surrogate family. "If you go down to the fire, they'll include you. They wouldn't invite you just to make you feel ignored."

She cuts her eyes to me and smirks. "Says the guy who took a spot on the patio instead of joining them on the beach."

I shrug. Kathleen and the kids are all tucked into beds inside the cabin, which means the couples have all paired off down by the water. Veronica and I are the only single folks here. I could take a blanket down to the waterfront and join the others, but I'd rather take a stick to the eye. "I'd go down there if I wanted to. I just . . . don't want that tonight."

She smiles, but there's a sadness in her expression that unsettles something deep in my gut. "Me neither. Some days I can pretend I'm okay being on the outside, but tonight I'm feeling raw."

I arch a brow. "Any reason?"

"Foster kid baggage. Old regrets." She tips her head back and closes her eyes. I can practically see her getting lost in the memory. "I used to pull all my tricks, thinking if I was bad enough they'd send me home. And maybe it didn't work, but at least it meant we never had to stay anywhere long. But this one time we were placed with this woman who had the patience of a saint, who made a real good home for kids." She blows out a breath and opens her eyes. "I ended up screwing that up too, but the Christmas after we were kicked out, I walked to her house and hid in the bushes to watch her and her charges through the window. I sat there for an hour in the cold, so jealous of how happy they all looked and so angry with myself for screwing up my chance to be part of it."

My childhood was pretty shitty in a lot of ways, but her story makes me realize how much of it I took for granted. It's not just her words, but the look in her eyes that tells me she had it rough, and I'm surprised by how much I want her to share more. "I'm sorry. That must've been really hard."

She shakes her head. "It's . . . whatever. But as much as I love the Jacksons, as grateful as I am for them, sometimes being around them all makes me feel like that little girl hiding in the bushes."

I swallow hard and nod. "I get that." More than she realizes, I'm sure. It's always been somewhat that way for me. I'm just on the outside of their family. Levi and I have been best friends since we were kids, so I grew up with them, but I was always acutely aware I was part of the group without being one of them. More so now that Levi and Ellie are together. "Is there anything I can do to help?"

"If only you could." She closes her eyes, and her tongue darts out to touch her bottom lip. "You ever want to get out of your own head for a minute? Like you just want to escape your own thoughts?"

She has *no idea.* Since I don't party anymore, my thoughts can feel like a bigger prison than ever. But all I say is "Sometimes."

She bites her bottom lip and meets my eyes. "Is there a trick?"

I huff out a laugh. "I used to get drunk and high, but now that those options are out, all I have left is . . ." I shake my head. "Well, you know, my other vice."

She arches a brow. "Which is?"

I honestly don't know if she's being coy. "Fucking."

Pink rushes into her cheeks. "Sex is a vice?"

I drag a hand over my face, memories flashing through my mind. The clubs, the parties, the women. Blacking out and waking up next to a pretty face I'd never seen before. I was such a shit boyfriend when I was using. I'm glad Levi's a fucking saint who worships Ellie. She deserves nothing less after what I put her through. "Not for me anymore, I guess. But it can be."

She tips her head back and sighs. "It's been a long time since I've used that particular method of escape. Too long."

"Why?" I ask before I can stop myself. *Curiosity killed the cat.*

She bites back a laugh. "His name is Jackson and he's two. Doesn't leave much time for finding a guy to fuck my brains out." The way she says it—so matter-of-fact and unapologetic—sends blood rushing to my dick.

"No time to search for Prince Charming?"

This time she doesn't stifle her laughter, and it rings across the backyard. "I'm not interested in Prince Charming." She leans across the table and whispers, "I thought I found him once, and he turned out to be an entitled ass."

I wave toward the beach, where all the Jackson brothers are hanging with their wives and girlfriends. "Not a believer even after meeting this family?"

"I didn't say I wasn't a believer." Her gaze drops to my mouth. "I said I wasn't interested. Maybe when my kid's older, but I have more important priorities right now."

"But a mind spinning with haunting thoughts nonetheless."

Her gaze lingers on my lips for a few beats longer than is socially acceptable, and more blood rushes to my dick. "Shame there's no one who can help me with that," she says, then walks away.

Does she think I'm going to follow her? Does she want me to?

The answer was in her eyes. In the way she looked at my mouth. I don't make it a full minute before my chair screeches against the concrete and I'm following the path around the house in the direction she disappeared. Part of my brain whispers that messing around with a Jackson relative—even one by marriage— is a bad idea. The other part says it's been too damn long since I've indulged in something good.

I find Veronica at the side of the house, her head tipped back, studying the stars. "Are you sure you know what you're doing?" I ask.

She grins without looking at me. "I have no idea what I'm doing."

We're so tucked away back here—just off the stone path that wraps around the house and hidden between overgrown evergreen bushes. "Then why did you lead me here?"

She finally drops her gaze from the stars and sighs. "My son is two, and I don't know how to do this anymore. Hell, I'm not even sure all the requisite parts are in working order."

I fight back a smile. "Do . . . what, exactly?"

She drags her bottom lip between her teeth and looks me over before laughing and shaking her head. "Point proven."

I step closer, ignoring the warning bells blaring in my head and loving the thrill of it. She's trouble. She's a bad idea, but I'm a moth to a flame. "You're looking for some . . . entertainment? Distraction?"

"I'm no good at games," she says. "Actually, I hate games."

"Then don't play." Another step closer, and her smell fills my nose. She smells like summer. Like lavender and sunshine. It's been too long since I've been close enough to a woman to smell her perfume. And if my body wasn't aware of Veronica as a *woman* before, it would be now. "Tell me what you want. No games."

She answers in the way I hoped she might—sliding a hand behind my neck and pulling my mouth down to meet hers.

Fuck yes. It's been more than a year and a half since I've tasted a woman. I've missed it.

Veronica moans, and my already thickening cock hardens the rest of the way. I slide my hands around her, finding her ass and hauling her body against mine. Her grip tightens in my hair, and she tugs my head to the side to get a better angle and deepen the kiss.

I am such a sucker for a woman who knows what she wants, and Veronica isn't messing around. I tear my mouth from hers, dragging it down her neck while I stroke my hands up her sides. When I reach her breasts, the weight of them feels so fucking good in my palms that I instinctively press the length of my erection into her stomach. "This what you wanted?" I ask against her neck, teasing her pebbled nipple beneath my thumb. "Did you drag me back here because you need this?"

"Yes," she breathes, arching against my hand. She twists her fingers in my hair. "Please."

Lust floods my bloodstream at that word, at the way her desire wraps it into one long, breathy syllable. "Since you asked nicely." I dip my head to her breast and press my open mouth against the tank of her dress, sucking on her through the fabric. I'm breathless and already so hard that my cock strains against the fly of my jeans.

Now that I've had a taste of her moans and her desperate *please, God yes, please,* I'm greedy for more. I slide my hand between her legs and up, cupping her sex through her panties. *Christ.* So warm. And already wet. "This all for me?" I ask, stroking.

Her breath catches. "I caught you watching me today. In the lake. I liked your eyes on me. Liked how it made me feel. Thought about it all day. Almost went to my room to think about it more while I could still be alone."

"You were gonna touch yourself thinking about me?" I stroke her again, but I'm dying to pull her panties to the side and feel that slick flesh on my fingers.

"Maybe."

Fuck, that's a sweet image. Veronica in bed, her hand between her legs and her thoughts centered on me? "Not tonight. Tonight, this is my job." I scrape my teeth along the neckline of her tank and across the swell of her breast. "You good with that?"

Her shaky inhale skates the line between anticipation and desperation. "Just tonight. I'm focused on my kid. I can't get involved with anyone."

I chuckle into her neck. "Good. Because tonight is all I have to offer. Now take these off." I snap the string of her panties against her hip, and she gasps, hesitating only a beat before shimmying them down her hips and stepping out of them. I sweep them off the ground before she can. I'm not sure what kind of untapped fetish has me shoving them in my pocket, but I don't overanalyze it. I can't. Not when my mind is so zeroed in on her needy breaths and the instinctive sway of her body toward mine.

"Lean back," I whisper, guiding her away from me to lean against the side of the house. She obeys, and it takes seconds for me to drop to my knees, shove her dress around her waist, and bury my face in her pussy.

Part of my mind registers how fucking crazy this is. Ten minutes ago, Veronica was the off-limits honorary Jackson, and now I don't want anything as much as I want to feel her come against my mouth. I'm too far gone to care.

The second I touch her clit with my tongue, she whimpers and bucks against me. "Yes."

I nudge her legs farther apart and guide one over my shoulder, ready to lick and suck until she comes apart. God, I need this. I need to forget my own pathetic thoughts for one night. Need to lose myself in the only one of my vices I'm still allowed.

"Colton." Hands in my hair, she tugs gently. I don't know if she wants me to stand or give her more, so I pull back and lift my gaze to hers.

Her eyes are hazy, and she's staring down at me like she can't quite believe this is happening. That makes two of us. A lock of hair falls in her face. The house light several yards away makes her eyes glow and illuminates her parted lips, swollen from my kisses.

"You're beautiful." Turning my head toward the leg I hiked over my shoulder, I press a kiss to her inner thigh. "You want me to stop?"

She takes my shirt in both fists and tugs, dropping her leg back to the ground and pulling me up. I'm faintly disappointed that my time between her legs was cut short, but I don't get to think about it for long before she's unbuttoning my jeans and palming my dick in her hand.

Fuuuuuck. That's good. Too good. My hips jerk forward, greedy for her touch. It's been too long, and she's . . . hell, I don't know what to make of Veronica Maddox half the time, but right now? Tonight? She's perfect. She's exactly what I need.

I tug down the top of her dress, faintly aware of the sound of popping stitches but focused on baring her to me. I pull aside her bra and lower my head. I circle her nipple with my tongue while she strokes me. It's so damn good.

I could come right here. All over her hand. It would be hot and it'd feel amazing—that intoxicating combination of pleasure and the forbidden I've always loved so much—but I want more than that from tonight. "Tell me what you want," I say, already tugging at her dress again so my hand can return to that sweet heat between her thighs.

"Want?"

I circle her clit then press down lightly with my thumb. "You want this." I slide a finger inside her, and she moans. I love the sound so much, love the way she rocks against my hand and squeezes. I slip a second finger inside her, and her grip tightens on my dick.

It's my turn to moan. "This what you want? Maybe all you need is my hand tonight." I'm trying to keep my mind straight. When I put my mouth between her legs, she pulled me up like she didn't want that. I don't want to inadvertently rush onto something else she doesn't want. "I can make you come like this." I bite her neck then flick the bite with my tongue to soothe it, working my fingers in and out of her. "I'd like that. Feeling you on my fingers, watching your face as you fall apart."

She shakes her head and shoves my hand down and away. "Come on."

I barely have time to tuck myself back into my boxers before she takes me by the wrist and leads me to the side door of the garage.

She pulls me to the family's classic Mustang and opens the passenger door, tilting her head to the side to indicate I should take a seat.

I freeze, memories washing over me. Ellie in a soft pink dress a few Easters ago. We came out here for Easter with the Jacksons, and seeing the way Levi looked at her all through dinner, I found myself needing reassurance, needing the reminder that she was *mine* and no one else's. We found that place in this garage. In this old Mustang. She rode me, and I kissed her hard and deep until we were both sated and sweaty.

This is the last place I want to fuck another woman.

Veronica pulls her bottom lip between her teeth. "There's no worry about someone walking in on us here," she says, and when I don't reply, she drops my wrist. "Never mind. It's dumb."

"Hey." I close the distance between us and slide one hand into her hair. I don't know this woman. Not really. But if my only job tonight is to wipe that vulnerability and loneliness from her eyes, I want to do it. I lower my mouth to hers and kiss her gently before sucking her bottom lip between my teeth. "Not dumb at all."

"Maybe this is a bad idea."

Maybe. Or maybe it's a good one. I don't ever want to lose the memories of my days with Ellie, but it's past time for me to make new ones. That's what Veronica's offering me—a chance to give myself a new memory.

"If you want it, I want it," I murmur against her lips, my greedy hands already searching for the slick heat between her thighs.

"I want it," she whispers. She frees my cock from my boxers again, squeezing and stroking. Pleasure builds at a furious pace at the base of my spine, and I don't want anything as badly as I want to drive inside her.

I back away, breathing heavily, and slide into the bucket seat. She straddles me, her hand returning to stroke my dick between our bodies.

"Condom," she says between hungry kisses.

Our hands fumble as we work together to shove my jeans down. I grab the condom I keep in my wallet, and she takes it from me, rolling it on with a desperation that only makes this whole thing hotter.

Then she's easing herself onto my dick, her hands gripping my shoulders, her lips parted.

"You feel so good." I shake my head in wonder. There's no way she could understand how much I needed this tonight. "So fucking good."

I yank down a strap of her dress, revealing a perfect breast covered by thin white lace. Cupping her, I lower my mouth to the stiff peak of her nipple, sucking her through the lace. She curls her nails into my shoulder blades, riding me harder. Faster.

It's hot in the garage, and it's not long before our bodies are slick with sweat. Old memories flood me—Ellie riding me like this. Here. Ellie whispering she loved me and smiling as she looked into my eyes. Ellie's heart, her goodness, how desperately I wanted to be the man she deserved, how terribly I failed.

My angst and grief have no place here. I grip Veronica's hips, willing my mind to focus on this moment, this woman. This night.

"More," she pleads, and I'm more than happy to give it.

I return my mouth to her breast and am rewarded with a whimpered *yes*. I tease her nipple with my teeth, and she clenches around me, her movements and pace turning more desperate. I toy with her breasts—flicking her nipple with my tongue before pulling it into my mouth and sucking almost savagely—until she turns frantic, until she throws her head back and stifles a scream, until her orgasm is milking my cock. Hot and wet and tight and so fucking good, so fucking sexy.

I let my hands roam up and down her sides as I urge her to keep fucking me, to take all the pleasure she can. I murmur dirty words in her ear, and when my orgasm bears down on me, I bury my face in her neck and come harder than I ever have in my life.

When I can think clearly again, I realize Veronica is stock-still on my lap. I pull back and see shock in her eyes, in the rounding of her lips. Shock or . . . hurt? *Shit.*

I cup her jaw. "Are you okay? Was I too rough with you?"

She bats my hand away and wiggles off my lap and out the door we never bothered to close. "Not at all. I'm not that fragile." She pulls the strap of her dress back into place and smooths down the skirt. When she meets my eyes again, whatever I saw before is gone, replaced with a hard, unreadable expression. "I appreciate your discretion about this," she says, turning away and heading to the door.

I hop out of the car, confused. "Veronica, wait. Talk to me. Tell me what's wrong. Are you hurt?"

She stops but doesn't turn to look at me. She tips her face toward the ceiling and shakes her head. "I'm not hurt. And you gave me exactly what I asked for."

"You don't seem happy about it."

She pulls in a deep breath before turning to me. "Sorry. If you wanted pillow talk and snuggles, I'm not your girl."

And with that, she walks out into the night.

I don't see Veronica again until the next morning, despite watching for her on the patio and even subjecting myself to the couples at the lakeside fire just in case she was hanging with them.

We're all halfway through our breakfasts when she finally comes to the table and is forced to take the seat beside me.

We eat in silence for a few minutes before she releases an exasperated breath and leans in to whisper in my ear, "Let me tell you a secret."

I arch a brow, hoping she's about to explain her strange behavior last night. "What's that?"

"You aren't fooling anyone," she said. "And the sad puppy-dog eyes are a little pathetic."

"What?"

She nods across the table to where Ellie is practically in Levi's lap. "You're transparent, and you're depressing the shit out of everyone here."

She's speaking right to my deepest fears. I'd been feeling this all weekend—up until she pulled me away from the group and let me touch her. I tighten my grip on my coffee mug. "How do you figure?"

"Nobody wants to see the sad-schmuck ex. So maybe you have a hard-on for your best friend's girl, but the time to do anything about that has officially passed. Get over it."

What a bitch. I'm speechless, but it doesn't matter. Because she's grabbed a muffin and left the table. Again, she's walking away from me, but I can't shake the feeling that I'm the one who screwed up, and I wish I knew how.

Chapter Five

COLTON
Present day

All night, my gaze returns to Veronica. On the one hand, I'm irritated with myself—for wanting her, for this fucking *craving* I can't seem to get past. On the other, I like being able to keep an eye on her, and I'm enjoying seeing her relax and cut loose with her friends—something she rarely does. I enjoy it, that is, until some ass steps up to her table and blocks my view. I vaguely recognize him but can't quite place him. That happens a lot when you live in a small town.

I wait patiently for her to tell him to fuck off, but instead, she lets him pull her out of the booth and to a small area between the tables. Veronica sways on her feet, and the guy steadies her as he pulls her body close to his. He settles his hands on her hips, and she grins up at him as they begin swaying to the music.

Next to me, Crosley coughs, and I drag my gaze off Veronica to look at him. "You're staring again," he says under his breath.

"She's drunk."

Cros arches a brow, and I know what he's thinking. *How's that our business?* But dammit, there are some serious assholes in the world. I'd know. I used to be one of them. Maybe I never took advantage of a drunk woman, but I knew every seduction trick in the book.

"What the fuck does he think *he's* doing?" Wes asks, coming up behind me.

"You two are ridiculous," Crosley mutters.

"She's drunk," I tell Wes.

"I don't think she's *drunk*. Maybe tipsy," Crosley says. "But not our business. Let her be."

Wes sighs, nods, and returns to the game.

But I can't let it go. They're barely swaying to the music, and every so often, Veronica stumbles. A decent guy wouldn't be making his move right now. He'd be calling her a freaking cab.

I try to stop fixating and focus on the conversation around me. Brady's talking about test-driving the new electric F-150, and normally, I'd have all kinds of questions, but half my attention is still on Veronica. Just enough so that I see when the guy buys her another drink. Just enough so that I notice when she tries to go back to her table, and he grabs her by the wrist and leads her to dance with him again. Just enough so that I notice when her smile's gone.

"Come on, V," I say under my breath. "Tell him to get lost."

I curse every drop of alcohol she's had. *Sober Veronica* would tell this heavy-handed, enterprising ass where he could shove it.

Wouldn't she? Or is she only like that with me? That possibility makes me feel pretty damn small.

This time when he takes her by the hips, he pulls her body flush with his. Veronica squirms, putting a little space between them. He laughs it off, relinquishing the position but not letting her go. She might be drunk, but now she looks really uncomfortable. Surely she's going to kick him in the balls if he tries to grope her ass again.

I glance toward the table to see if her friends are going to intervene, but Star and Amelia are the only ones left, and they're deep in conversation and probably too drunk to notice Veronica's predicament.

I make myself count to ten. By the time I get to six, Veronica's face relaxes. *I need to mind my own fucking business.* Then he pulls her close again.

I shove my pool stick at Brady. "Take this. I'll be right back."

My strides are long and purposeful as I cross the bar, and I know I look pissed. She'll probably give me endless shit for this at work on Monday, but I don't even care.

"Hey, V," I say, stepping close like I'm approaching two people casually talking and not a couple dancing. "You promised to be my partner the next round, remember?" I nod to the pool table.

Veronica's eyes go wide and her mouth forms a circle. "What?"

Come on. Play along. "Crosley's talking shit," I lie. "Saying you're chickening out."

She blinks at me. Is she too buzzed to get what I'm doing here? Or did I read her all wrong?

The guy twists his face up in disgust. "Read the room. We're busy."

55

"No." Veronica steps back. "He's right. I promised. And Crosley will never let me live it down if I forfeit."

Thank you, sweet baby Jesus, for her little remaining bit of sobriety.

The guy curls his lip, but his hands drop to his sides. "You know where to find me when you finish."

"Probably not tonight." Her smile doesn't reach her eyes. "I promised my friends I'd spend it with them." She steps closer to me then swallows as if she's losing her nerve. "Thanks for talking to me, though. I hope we can chat about it more later."

His smile is as sincere as a snake's. "Of course. Any time."

She nods and turns toward the pool table, striding on unsteady legs.

"Veronica!" Wes calls. "Finally joining us?" He offers her a pool cue.

She starts to take it, then shakes her head. "I need a minute."

I keep an eye on her as she strides toward the bathroom.

"What did you do?" Crosley asks.

I shake my head. "I'll be right back."

There's a long line outside the bathroom, and Veronica's a few spots away from the door, her face tipped toward the ceiling. As if she senses me, she tenses and blows out a long breath before stepping out of the line and striding toward the exit.

I can't tell if she's pissed or embarrassed or something else altogether, but I follow her. Once I know she's okay, I'll go back to my friends and leave her alone.

I find her in the alley, leaning against the building, eyes closed. Something in my chest clenches at seeing her like this—unguarded and vulnerable.

"You don't want to miss a second of my humiliation, do you?" The defeat in her voice makes me pause. Did I make her feel like that, or the idiot in the bar?

"You don't have anything to be embarrassed about. He was being pushy." I pause a beat, shoving my hands into my pockets, still not confident I did the right thing. "You pissed at me for getting involved?"

She doesn't open her eyes. "No. You're right. He was getting handsy, and I didn't know how to get out of it."

I take the spot beside her, leaning a shoulder against the wall so I can watch her. "That doesn't seem like you."

She coughs out a laugh. "And you know me so well?"

Maybe. Or maybe I just want to.

The realization should come as a surprise, but it doesn't. I've been curious about this hidden side of Veronica since our night together. Since the night she told me that the Jacksons' big family get-together made her feel lonely. "What happened to her?" I mutter.

She opens one eye. "What?"

I swallow. Sometimes I hate the animosity between us. "What happened to the girl from the lake last summer? The one who admitted she was lonely? The one who kissed me like I was exactly what she needed?"

She turns to face me, mimicking my posture. Just when I expect her to sneer at me, her gaze drops to my mouth. "She gets me in trouble, so I don't let her out much."

"That's a shame." I inch closer. Her intoxication must be contagious, because I haven't had a drop of alcohol and have no excuse for being this honest. "I really liked her."

"Yeah, right."

I frown. Have I been that much of a dick? "I'm serious. I thought I'd found a kindred spirit."

She tilts her face up and shakes her head. "Don't do that. Don't rewrite history."

I frown. "I'm not. I . . ." How many moments have I had the opportunity to be vulnerable with Veronica and chosen not to? And how many times have I wished she'd be vulnerable with me? "I really liked you, but after you just ran away, and the next morning . . ." I release a dry laugh. "The next morning, you were kind of a bitch."

She leans toward me. And she smells like heaven. Lavender and sunshine, just like last summer. It's a fresh scent I can all too easily imagine on my pillow. "Only because you deserved it."

"Why are you always so determined to piss me off?"

"Because you're so uptight it makes my head hurt. Because you watch me like you want to screw my brains out but don't have the balls to so much as touch me."

My jaw drops. "Why would I after the way you acted last time?"

She spins around and walks toward the door. I move fast, grabbing her by the hips before she can get far. I don't know what's gotten into me, but the second I feel the swell of her hips under my fingertips, I can't bring myself to regret it.

She leans back into me. Barely. As if she wants to resist but can't. *Fuck*, she smells good. I graze my nose over the shell of her ear. The scent of her makes blood pump to my dick. And the feel of her under my hands? Goddamn. She's perfect.

"You're the one who's always picking fights. I think *you're* scared of this chemistry, and this is your way of keeping distance between us." I skim my lips down the side of her neck. "I think you've been scared of what's between us since the first time I touched you."

She leans her head to the side, making room for my mouth to explore her neck. "Maybe I just think you're hot when you're pissed."

"I think it's both." I slide my hands around to her stomach. I sneak one up, my thumb grazing the underside of her breasts, and the other down, the tips of my fingers finding the top of her panties through her dress. God, this is a terrible idea, but I want her so damn much. "Tell me to stop."

"Don't tell me what to do." I think she meant to sound snappy, but the words come out on a sigh, and she presses into me as if she wants our bodies to be as close as possible.

"Then tell me what you want."

"It's such a shame you can't figure it out for yourself," she says.

I spin her around, pressing her back against the building and stepping forward until her breasts are pressed to my chest and my leg is between her thighs. Still not close enough. "You're full of shit. You know exactly how well I can figure it out. You remember, don't you?"

Her eyes flare. "Maybe I need a reminder."

Not until she's sober. I ache to cup her breasts in my hands and suck on the sensitive spot at the top of her shoulder, but I won't cross that line tonight.

That doesn't mean we can't talk. "What happened that night? Why did you run away from me?"

"No one likes being a stand-in for the real thing, Colt. I may be a bitch, but I do have some standards."

What is she talking about? Just how drunk is she? "Why would you think you were a stand-in? For whom?"

"If you're fucking someone else to forget your ex, you should at least try not to call out your ex's name in the heat of the moment." Straightening, she steps around me. The click of her heels echoes through the alley as she walks away.

VERONICA

I'm that fuzzy kind of drunk where I still feel like I'm in control of my decisions, but the whole world blurs around the edges. Until Jim Moody decided to use his leverage with the school board as an excuse to grab my ass, I was having more fun than I'd had in a long time. Dancing with Jim was even okay at first.

"All I have to do is make a call, and I can guarantee you'll get an interview."

I thanked him, and then he let his hands drift to my ass, making his message clear. Jim doesn't do anything without getting something in return. Fuck him. I can get my own interview. Even so, I'd rather not start my career with the school corporation with an enemy on the school board.

Having Colton—of all people—rescue me was just mortifying.

Now, more than anything, I want to go home and shower off this night. That's my plan, until I get back to the table and Amelia's paying her tab.

"I've gotta head out," she says. "Early expedition tomorrow. But you'll keep the birthday girl company, right?"

"Of course." I give her a quick hug and make sure she has a cab coming before sliding into the booth across from Star.

"What exactly were you and Colton doing out there?" Star asks once Amelia is gone.

I shake my head. "Nothing."

"He's been watching you all night. Looking at you like he wants to eat you up." She waggles her eyebrows. "Maybe you took him outside to give him a chance?"

Been there, done that.

Star squeals and claps her hands like a delighted toddler. "I knew it!"

I smack my hand to my mouth. *I just said that out loud.* "I'm cut off." I shove my unfinished beer toward the back of the table.

"I always said there was too much sexual tension between you two for there to be no history."

Cringing, I look around the bar. "Would you keep your voice down? No one knows but me and Colton, and I'd like to keep it that way."

She bites her bottom lip but is unsuccessful in trapping her smile. "When did this happen? And how was it? And where— Oh my God, please tell me it happened at work in the middle of one of your stupid fights."

I scowl *hard*. "I do not appreciate how amused you are right now."

She presses a hand to her chest. "Can you blame me? This is epic. God, I've personally been on Team Fuck Already since you started working there, and you know it."

"Team Fuck Already?"

"Yup." She sips her beer. "We have T-shirts."

I wad up a napkin and hurl it at her chest. "You do not."

"Okay, I don't, but Amelia and I discussed the possibility."

I slouch at the mention of my friend and coworker. "You cannot tell Amelia. Seriously, I don't want anyone we work with to know. The fact that we turn each other into bickering children is bad enough."

She presses her index finger and thumb together and draws a line across her lips. "Sealed. I promise. Now spill."

I take a deep breath. "It was the Fourth of July out at the Jackson cabin."

"It's been almost a *year*?" she screeches, and several heads turn in our direction, some expressions curious, some annoyed. "A year, and you haven't told me?" she asks, more quietly this time. "I feel a little betrayed."

"I didn't tell *anyone*. It was a huge mistake. I didn't want to talk about it."

She cringes. "Was it bad? Is he a selfish lover? A minute man?" She studies me, unfazed by my lack of response. "No, if it had been that bad, you two wouldn't fight like you're trying to hate-fuck with words."

I close my eyes. "Hate-fuck with words," I mutter. "I don't even know what that means."

"It means you don't look at him like he was disappointing in bed. So what was it?"

I lean across the table and lower my voice even more. That night made me feel like a fool, and sharing the story makes it all come back. "It was really good, okay? Until it wasn't. He . . ."

Star stares at me expectantly, and when I can't make myself finish that sentence, she tugs on her hair. "Bitch, I swear if you don't start talking, I'm going to waltz over to the guys and make *Colton* give me the dirty details."

"He called me by another woman's name." I glare at the table. Saying it out loud is even more mortifying than the experience was. "His *ex's* name."

Star gasps. "He called you *Ellie*? They were engaged, though, right? And together a while before that?"

I deserve a medal for not growling in response. "That doesn't make it okay."

"When did it happen? Like, in the middle of things? What did you say? God, he must've been so embarrassed."

"He said it as he was . . ." I circle my hand in the air to indicate *finishing.* "I didn't say anything. I climbed off him and got out of there."

"So you're walking around all butt-hurt because he called you by his ex's name in the middle of sex *a year ago* when you didn't even know each other very well, and you don't have any reason to believe he's even aware he did it?"

"No worries. I just let him know while we were chatting outside." Do I really have to go into work on Monday? Maybe I'll quit and skip town and never have to look Colton in the eye again.

Frowning, Star narrows her eyes on something at the bar. I follow her gaze. "Do you know that woman?"

I study the line of people waiting for drinks, none of whom I immediately recognize from the back. "Which one?"

"The one in the pink shirt and— She's turning around now."

The woman looks right at me and gives me a tentative smile and a wave. She has blond hair and rosy cheeks, and after a few beats of me trying to figure out who she is, she abandons her spot in line and heads toward our booth.

"No idea who that is," I whisper, trying to keep my smile in place as the stranger weaves through the crowded bar and closer to our booth. "Should I know her?"

"I don't know, but she keeps looking over here like she knows *you*."

"Maybe she thinks you're cute," I say.

Star shrugs. "But she only has eyes for you." Then we both shut up, because the stranger is getting closer.

"Hey," the woman says, shoving her hand toward me. "Veronica Maddox, right?"

Star and I exchange a look before I take the woman's offered hand. "Yeah."

"It's so nice to meet you. I'm Kristi—with a K, no C, with an I. Know why? Because my mama spelled it that way!" The Southern lilt to her words reminds me of home, but I still have no clue who this woman is. "Get it? *No Y*, as in the letter, but also *know why*, as in the question?" She laughs at her little pun and shakes my hand gently before pulling away.

I force a smile. "It's really clever." *Who are you?*

"You're probably wondering why I came over here."

"The curiosity is killing me," Star says, but her tone says she just wants this woman to leave us alone. Not me. I don't like mysteries.

"I'm from Jeffe, just like you."

Even though the possibility occurred to me, given her accent, my hackles go up. I escaped more than a controlling man when I left Jeffe. I escaped a reputation and a past loaded with hardship, drama, and bad decisions.

"You don't know me," Kristi-with-an-I says, "but obviously I know who you are."

I arch a brow and try to keep the distress off my face. I don't like the idea of anyone dragging what they think they know about me up here from Alabama. "Is that so?"

"I was four years behind you in school, but I had a big brother—Kyle Kerman—and he told me about all the trouble you got into back then." She chuckles softly. "Oh, my mama hated you."

Kyle Kerman. I vaguely remember him from high school. He was just one of the many boys who was happy to treat me right just long enough to get in my pants, but the second we were around his friends from school, he wouldn't have anything to do with me. I was trash, good only for one thing. "How is your brother?" I ask, kind of hoping karma's caught up with him.

"He's good. Working at Putnam Lake Insurance, just like Daddy. He's kind of a big deal there. Go figure!"

"I'm sure." My smile is so tight that my face might crack. "So, what brings you to Jackson Harbor, Kristi?" *Why are you in my favorite bar? Why are you even talking to me?*

"My husband and I recently moved to Grand Rapids. I'm just in Jackson Harbor for the weekend on some personal business. Looking into a few things." She scans the table, eyeing my friends' empty drinks. An assortment of martini, pint, and shot glasses

Amelia likes to keep on the table until the end of the night to "keep us honest." With just me and Star sitting here, I can't deny it looks bad, but I refuse to explain myself or my friends to this virtual stranger.

"Well," I say, "have a nice trip."

"Sure. I'll let my brother know I saw you. And that it doesn't look like much has changed."

I refuse to justify that low-key cattiness with a response, but Star snaps, "What the fuck is that supposed to mean?"

Kristi shrugs. "Party girl doesn't change her stripes, am I right?"

Star looks like she's ready to scratch out eyeballs. "Veronica isn't—"

I hold up my hand, stopping her. There's no reason we should sit here and explain who and what I am to this woman. "Did you need something, Kristi?"

"Just one thing. Smile!" She taps on her phone screen a few times, and then, before I realize what she means to do, she holds it up and takes a picture of me and Star and our messy table. "Thanks."

"What. The. Actual. Fuck?" Star says.

I shove down the apprehension brought on by that odd interaction and roll my eyes. "Can't fix petty."

If Jim's roaming hands didn't ruin my night, I'm not going to let some weird reminder of my past do it.

Chapter Six

VERONICA

I haven't been hungover in years, but I'm paying for last night. I'm at the park with Jackson because the day is too pretty to waste, but I'm feeling rough. My hair's in a sloppy bun, and a pair of giant sunglasses are my only defense against the vicious things the sunlight's trying to do with my headache. I didn't even bother to change out of the yoga pants and T-shirt I slept in. One of the many awesome things about kids is they don't care. Jackson doesn't need me to look like a perfect suburban soccer mom. He just needs me to show up. Sometimes showing up is what motherhood is about. Today, that means hiding my mild hangover and pushing my giggling boy on the swing, watching him go do the same little slide one hundred times and stepping back as he climbs the ladder to the twisty slide because "do it myself" are his three favorite words.

He's making the ascent for the twentieth time when a familiar syrupy Southern drawl calls my name.

"It *is* you, Veronica!"

Jacks reaches the top and waves to me. I wave back before turning to Kristi-with-a-know-why. "We meet again." I don't bother trying to sound happy about it.

"Yeah, we do! I wasn't gonna leave town without sayin' bye to my new friend." Her smile falls away as her eyes land on Jacks. "That's him." She presses both hands to her chest and screws her face up like she's being presented the sash for Miss America. "He's so precious."

"Excuse me?" I ask. Jacks is waiting impatiently behind two more kids for his turn to go down the slide.

"It must be so hard for you," she says, staring at my son intently. "A single mom with no parents to lean on. Trying to get by and do what's best for him."

My spine locks up, and all thoughts of my headache and queasy stomach fade away as my instincts tell me to put up my guard. "We're fine."

"For now, maybe, but a boy needs a father. And never mind your own history. Apple doesn't fall far from the tree and all that, but I'm sure you want to give this sweet little man a better childhood than your mama gave you." She shakes her head. "In and out of foster care. Must've been a nightmare."

Why is she talking about shit that's none of her business? "I managed all right," I say through clenched teeth. I typically don't have the patience to bother with people like her, but I'm afraid if I outright ignore her, she'll make a scene in front of Jacks.

"I bet you'd do anything to spare your boy from that." There's something desperate in her eyes that makes me want to grab Jacks and run away. She swallows. "He looks just like his daddy."

Dread is a clawed beast climbing up my throat.

Before I can figure out how to respond to that, Jacks gets his turn at the slide. He cruises down, and at the last second, Kristi lunges forward to catch him at the bottom.

"Gotcha!" she says, picking him up by the waist.

Jacks shrieks, his arms flailing and his head snapping to me.

I hold my arms out for him and force myself to smile so he won't be more alarmed than he already is. *She didn't just do that.* "I'm right here."

For a terrifying, painful moment, I'm not sure Kristi's going to let go of my child. I imagine chasing after her and ripping him from her arms, imagine shouting at the top of my lungs that someone's trying to steal my baby.

But as fast as the moment began, it's gone, and she's handing Jacks over.

His bottom lip quivers and he clings to me, only cutting his eyes toward Kristi for a second before burrowing in my chest again. He's shy about strangers *looking* at him, and this one just had the audacity to pick him up. "Who she?" he asks softly.

"I know your daddy," she tells Jackson, and I gasp.

I have no idea what goes through his mind when he hears the words *your daddy.* He knows he has a father. I've never pretended otherwise, but we don't talk about it much, and I'm pretty sure it's still an abstract concept to him.

"She's no one, baby." I glare at Kristi and turn toward the parking lot. Once Jackson realizes I mean to take him home after only thirty minutes of playground time, I'm gonna pay, but that

LEXI RYAN

woman put her hands on my child and then mentioned a father Jackson's never met before. A tantrum is a small price to pay.

"I am *too* someone," Kristi calls behind us. "I'm your stepmom. And trust me, your mommy needs to talk to me."

For one blissful moment, I dismiss her words as the ramblings of an unwell person.

"Marcus is my husband," she says, as if she can see I don't believe her.

My feet freeze in place, torn between conflicting messages from my brain as I realize my logic isn't sound. *Run. Talk to her.* I need to get him away from her. I need to know why the hell she's here, why she thinks it's okay to put her hands on my child, and what it is she has to say.

This is what happens when your baby's father isn't in your life. You forget that he's connected to your child in any way.

I wildly scan the playground for a familiar face. I know some of the parents here casually, but there's no one Jackson would willingly go to. No one I'd trust to distract him while I take care of this.

I slowly force myself to turn to her. "If you want to talk, meet me at the coffee shop downtown in fifteen minutes. Jackson doesn't need to be part of this conversation."

Her painted lips press into a thin line, as if she's disappointed my almost-three-year-old won't be hearing what she has to say, but then she nods. "Okay. I'll meet you there."

My hands shake as I buckle Jacks into his car seat and shake harder when I call Star to let her know what's going on. She has today off, but she and her daughter live in the apartment over her coffee shop, and as I suspected, she's happy to watch Jacks while

70

I deal with Marcus's wife.

Fifteen minutes later, Kristi and I are seated across from each other at Ooh La La! with fresh cups of coffee.

"I bet you feel pretty rough after last night," she says, giving me an appraising once-over.

"What do you want?" My voice is as cold as ice. My whole body is tight with dread.

"I'm not your enemy, Veronica."

"You're not my friend, either. And I don't know why no one's told you this before, but you can't just pick up strangers' children."

"Like I said, I'm not a stranger," she says, all wide-eyed innocence. "We're connected in one of the most important ways I can imagine."

My head pounds, and my stomach threatens to eject the toast and coffee I managed to choke down for breakfast. "Marcus never mentioned you." Not that we talk often, but still.

"We got together about a year ago. It was a bit of a whirlwind, but it's true. I'm Jackson's stepmom."

It always is with Marcus. "For Jacks to have a stepmom, he'd have to have a dad. And he doesn't."

"And do you think that's fair to either of them? Marcus is sick about it. His boy—his *only child* taken from him." Her eyes go watery, and I realize she believes every word she's feeding me.

Marcus didn't give a shit about the baby when I left. He's never so much as met his son. He didn't even inquire about him until a year ago when Marcus had a health scare and contacted me because he wanted Jackson to be a beneficiary in his will. At the time, I worried he wanted something from me—wanted to be in Jackson's life somehow—but he assured me he didn't want to do that to Jacks. That maybe they could have a relationship later when Jacks was old enough to understand the distance between Jackson Harbor, Michigan and Jeffe, Alabama. He didn't want to form a relationship with his son, only to have to go months at a time without seeing him.

I knew it was too good to be true. Marcus never coming after me, never insisting on having rights where Jacks is concerned. Being so damn amenable to everything when he had me sign those paternity papers last year. "I'm going to ask you again. What do you *want*?"

"I just want to see my stepson," Kristi says. "Marcus wants to see his son."

"Marcus sent you here?" God, I should be grateful. I'd probably be losing it right now if *he* was the one saying these things to me. It would make this whole thing feel too real.

"He's busy. Such a hard worker—always providing for his family. He wants to provide for Jackson. He said you refused child support no matter how much he tried to convince you."

And when I told Marcus as much last year, he seemed *relieved*. Not like he was determined to talk me into it. "I don't want his money. Jackson is fine. We are fine."

Child support terrifies me. It feels like it gives Marcus some sort of right to my child. Though I've educated myself on the basics of my parental rights, part of me irrationally clings to the belief that if I never take his money, he'll never be able to take Jacks away.

Kristi sighs. "I did this all wrong. It's not like I'm expecting you to hand the boy over to me. We just want to help make your life a little easier. You know Marcus makes a good living, and I have some money too. We want to help. For Jackson."

"In exchange for what?"

"It's not like that."

Bullshit. No one wants to give out money for free. "What do you want?"

She blows out a breath. "Visitation. A couple of weekends a month."

The vise wrapped around my stomach notches tighter. "I can't do that. He doesn't even know you, and you want me to send him away with you? Never."

"We wouldn't be strangers for long. We'll start by coming to town and spending a couple of afternoons with him, and then do one overnight and work our way into the full weekend."

I open my mouth to explain how unrealistic her plan is, given the distance between us, when I remember what she told me last night. "You moved to Grand Rapids *with Marcus*."

"Yes. The Lord gave us the opportunity to be closer to Jackson, and we took it. Marcus's new job was an answered prayer."

I swallow hard. "You've really thought this through."

"We've talked to a lawyer," she says, and my stomach heaves. "He said we can take you to court if it comes down to it, but we don't want to do that. Jackson is better off if we all work together. He's better off if this is resolved amicably."

"It's been three years. Why now?"

Kristi shrugs. "Marcus felt like he couldn't ask. He's wrecked about the way everything happened with you and your sister and what a mess he was through that time in his life. His guilt kept him from asking for a relationship with his child, but that doesn't mean he never wanted one."

My instinct is to hide Jacks. To tell her no again. Absolutely not. But deep down, I know that's my own selfishness rearing its head.

Mom was selfish. She was always fighting to keep Nic and me, even though anyone could see we would've been better off in another home.

I push away from the table and stand. "I'll think about it. Tell Marcus I'll call him when I have an answer."

"We don't want to do this the hard way, honey. Just let Marcus see his boy."

I grab my full coffee and toss it in the trash. "I have a right to some time. It's been three years."

She nods solemnly, and I turn for the door.

I make it three steps before I spin back to her. "Why didn't you talk to me about this last night? And why did you take that picture of me?"

Her eyes go big, too innocent. "You were in no shape to have this conversation last night. So, once I introduced myself, I decided to wait until you weren't so"—she looks around, as if she's about to say something scandalous—"*inebriated*. I wanted to show Marcus that I tracked you down." She shrugs. "And that you're doing okay. He worries."

Liar. "I'm a good mom. No judge is going to take my child from me because you took a picture of me having a drink with my friends."

She presses her palm to her chest. "Oh, my." She shakes her head. "Marcus said you'd assume the worst of us. I should've listened."

I can't look at her one more minute—this perfectly manicured woman with her sleek hair and designer clothes. She's the picture of the suburban soccer mom. She's everything I'll never be, represents everything I'll never be able to give my son, and I can't take another moment remembering that.

Star rubs her temples and shakes her head. "Wait. So you're saying your baby daddy used to be engaged to *Nic*?"

I hide my face in my hands and groan. "I know. I know. Worst sister ever. Trust me, I know."

"Aww, that's not what I was thinking."

I peek at her between my fingers. "Really?"

"I mean, I was thinking it a *little*." When I scowl, she laughs. "I'm joking. Seriously, Nic's married to hot Dr. Jackson now. She's so happy it should be illegal. Meanwhile, you're a struggling single mom whose baby daddy's been MIA for three years. I'm pretty sure you did her a favor."

I drop my hands and sigh. "I like to think of it that way. It was such a mess, but I never meant to hurt her. I just . . ." I shrug. "I was an idiot."

"Hey, I ended up knocked up at sixteen. I'm not judging. We've all made bad choices for good"—she glances toward Jacks, who's playing on the floor, and clears her throat—"appendages. Good appendages can make us forget ourselves."

I snort. "His name was *Henry*."

Star frowns. "I thought you said his name was Marcus."

"No, Marcus's"—I gesture to my crotch—"*appendage*. He

called him Henry."

She cocks her head to the side. "And that wasn't a giant red flag?"

"It should've been, but I'm an idiot and was too drunk on all the pretty words he fed me to think twice."

"Apparently."

I grab a pillow off the couch beside me and hurl it at her.

Star chuckles, but then her face goes serious again. "And after three years he wants to be part of the little man's life, huh? Did he give you any hints this was coming?"

"He drove up here last summer and asked to put his name on Jackson's birth certificate. He was okay with Jacks keeping my last name, but he'd had a health scare, and he was drawing up an estate plan. He said he wanted to make sure there'd be no question that Jackson would get his due should something happen."

"Well, that's downright decent of him. Unless you think it was a con to get his name on the birth certificate?"

"I don't think so. After a little Google research, it was pretty obvious that if I didn't agree to put Marcus down as Jackson's father, Marcus could've filed for paternity anyway. As his biological father, he has rights, so it seemed futile to fight it."

"But he wanted his name to be on a form. That's different than wanting to be in Jackson's life."

"I know." I give a shaky nod. "I can't really say no now, can I?"

"I mean, you could, I suppose, but then he could take you to court and all that."

The room sways.

"Don't get me wrong," she continues. "It's totally worth fighting if that's what you need to do to protect your son. The questions is, do you trust him?"

"As a boyfriend or husband, not as far as I could throw him. We didn't part on great terms. Mostly because he wanted to control me, and once he realized he couldn't, he wanted my sister back more than he wanted to be a father to his baby. It was all for the best, though. I settled in Jackson Harbor and can't think of a better place I'd like to raise this guy." I smile down at my oblivious little boy. "But trust him as a father?" I shake my head. "I don't know. I don't have any reason to trust or not trust him. There's a chance he could be good with Jacks."

Jacks looks up at Star and gives her a toothy grin. "Iron Man red," he says, waving his action figure in the air.

"That's right, baby," Star says. "Who else is red?"

"Pider-Man," he says, holding up the Spider-Man action figure.

"That's right! Spider-Man is red too. Good job!" She beams, and Jackson's smile's a little bigger as he turns his attention back to his toys.

When she meets my gaze again, her eyes are sad. "Maybe something made the idiot realize what he's been missing."

"Maybe." I slide off the couch and crawl across the floor to where Jacks is organizing his action figures by color.

"I don't have any answers, V," Star says, "but knowing your dad doesn't want anything to do with you is a nasty kind of scar. I've seen how it's messed with Katie."

"But you've done so well with her. With everything." Star is like me in that she came to Jackson Harbor pregnant and set out to start a new life here without her baby's father. But unlike me, she's built a successful business and isn't drowning in debt.

"That doesn't mean there isn't anything I'd change," she says softly. "Maybe in the long run it'd be better for Jacks if he got to have a relationship with his dad. They want a couple of weekends a month?" She shrugs. "Maybe it could be a good thing for everyone."

I swallow the lump in my throat. "It's the scariest thing anyone's asked me to do," I whisper.

"Hey," Star says. Judging by her expression, I must look tragic. "No one says you have to do it all at once. Maybe you ease in. Start with a short visit where you can be there the whole time and just see how it goes."

"Yeah. Maybe."

She sinks onto the floor beside me and wraps her arms around me.

"Hug!" Jacks squeals, and when he places his little arms around us, the tears I've been holding back find their way down my cheeks.

Chapter Seven

VERONICA

By Monday, I haven't heard from Marcus. Did he really send his new wife to town to ask for visitation rights and then not even follow up with me about it? Or is Kristi-with-a-know-why some *The Hand that Rocks the Cradle* crazy posing as Marcus's wife to get to my child? Or maybe it was all some hangover-induced hallucination?

Unfortunately, I'm sure it's not option three, but I'm not letting myself worry about the next steps until I hear from one of them.

I'm proud of myself for getting to the office in time despite an accident on Lakeview slowing me down, but of course Colton is out for an early meeting, so he can't appreciate my punctuality—not that he would. He only notices when I fuck up. *And you give him plenty of opportunities there,* the familiar voice in my head mocks.

I settle into my work and am halfway through my coffee and most of the way through the inbox when my phone buzzes, and Marcus's name appears on the screen.

Fuckshitdamn.

I unlock my phone and open the message.

> *Marcus: Kristi told me about what happened this weekend. Can I call you?*

Biting my lip, I glance toward Colton's office. He's not here yet, but any minute now he'll be back from his meeting. The last thing I need is to give him ammunition against me by taking a personal call if it's not an emergency.

> *Veronica: I'm at work. Not a good time. But yeah, sending your wife to ask after your son isn't a good look, Marcus. What happened to you not wanting to confuse him?*

There. That'll do until my lunch break, when I can deal with whatever he has to say for himself.

But a few minutes later my phone buzzes again, and I'm dying to know what he said, so I look.

> *Marcus: If roles were reversed and you didn't have any part in his life, wouldn't you want to change that? I didn't want him to feel like I didn't care, and making this work between Alabama and Michigan seemed impossible, but now we're less than an hour apart.*

I read his message three times, making myself really think about it. If our roles were reversed, I wouldn't just want a relationship with Jacks. I'd want *custody*. I know I should be grateful that he's not asking for more, but I've never been so scared.

When I'm reading his message the fourth time, the phone buzzes in my hands again and another text comes through.

> *Marcus: I know we didn't end on great terms, but please don't keep my son from me. He deserves to have a relationship with his father.*
>
> *Veronica: I don't know anything about your wife or your house or your life. And he doesn't know you. You really expect me to pack a bag for him and send him off?*

This time I don't bother putting my phone down. I stare at it, watching those dots bounce again and again until his next text appears.

> *Marcus: Of course not. We want to make this easy for you. We can do it however works best. Kristi thought it might be easier for you if we picked him up, but maybe you'd rather come over here. You could stick around and see the house and get to know Kristi while Jackson gets comfortable with us.*

I close my eyes, imagining spending time at their house. I imagine the perfect Kristi bringing me a drink and handing Jacks a toy intended for an infant. Or worse, something with tiny pieces meant for a much older child. *I need to know I can trust them.*

*Veronica: That doesn't seem a little awkward to you?
The four of us hanging out?*
*Marcus: I think we can all endure a little awkwardness
if it's in the best interest of our son.*

I swallow hard. I can't argue with him there.

*Marcus: Do you have any time off this weekend?
Could you come to our new place? It could be a short
visit so everyone can get acquainted.*

That sounds *horrible*, but I can't think of a single alternative
that sounds more reasonable.

*Veronica: We can come Saturday morning. Text me
your address. And next time? Talk to me yourself
about your son. I'm sure your wife means well, but
she's not his parent.*
Marcus: Roger. Thank you so much for this, Ronnie.

"What happened?"

I snap my head up to find Wes staring at me, worry all over
his face.

"You look like you're gonna be sick," he says.

Taking a deep breath, I place my phone down and put my
hands back on my keyboard. "I'm fine."

"You're not."

"Okay, I'm not."

"Do you want to talk about it?"

I glance at my phone, then back at Wes. I really do work with the nicest people, but I hate bringing my personal problems to the office. "It's just . . . stupid stress. Nothing important."

He cocks his head to the side. "Don't bullshit a bullshitter. What's wrong?"

I draw in a long, shaky breath, but it does nothing to ease the tightness in my chest. "My son's father wants weekend visitation with Jacks."

Wes's brow wrinkles. "I didn't think his dad was in the picture."

"He never has been, but now he has this new wife, and suddenly, they've moved to Grand Rapids so they can be closer to Jacks and are prepared to take me to court if I don't let them see him."

"Well, shit. That's not what I'd call stupid stress. That's heavy." He looks around the office. "Do you even want to be here right now? Is sitting there thinking about this going to make you nuts?"

I hang my head. "I don't want to be that girl who's so fixated on her personal issues that she can't do her job."

"But your job is to help us, right?"

"Yeah . . ."

He beams. "I've got just what the doctor ordered." He pokes his head through the swinging door and into the garage. "Cros, I'm going to steal V for a while. Can you cover the phone?"

"Sure," he calls back. "Give me a minute to clean up."

"Awesome," Wes says. He pulls my chair away from my desk. "Go put on a suit."

"Why?" I'm not sure why laughter is bubbling out of me. Maybe because it's just such a fucking *relief* to have people who care about me. *I need this.* "I can't go to the beach when I'm supposed to be working."

"You're not. You're going to help me scrub the cat."

My laughter grows. "You're going to let me clean the decks of the catamaran as a way to cheer me up?"

"Yep." He grins. "There's not much a little sunshine and hard work can't clear from your mind. Trust me."

COLTON

Monday started rough and hasn't gotten any better.

First, I woke up hard and thinking about a certain honey-haired hellcat I can't get out of my mind. Then as soon as I finished dealing with *that* problem in the least satisfying way imaginable, a text from a buddy down at the courthouse let me know Mike's still off the wagon and spent the night in the drunk tank.

I picked Mike up, drove him home, and told him to go to a meeting today, practically bloodying my tongue to keep myself from lecturing him about how fucking stupid he's being. *He's responsible for his own actions. You can't preach him sober.*

I was already in a bad mood and in my head too much when I ran into Ellie at the gym. It could've been fine. It's not like we're out of each other's lives. She's marrying my best friend, after all, but she was all smiles and laughter with her friends until she spotted me. And then it got awkward. I hate that she pities me more than I ever hated that she gave up on me.

I was ready to brush it off and get on with my day, but then I arrived at work to see that Crosley was covering the phones, and Veronica was out back in a bikini, laughing with Wes as they washed down the decks of our catamaran.

Wes didn't have to say anything on Friday night for me to know he was interested. I see the way he looks at her. And hell, I get it. I bet I look at her the same way. It's the way a man looks at a woman when she's the prettiest damn thing he's ever seen. But Wes is a fucking player. He's not interested in a long-term relationship, and he has no business dating a woman who has a kid.

I just stood there and watched like a fucking lunatic as they worked together. I watched him ogle her. Watched her laugh at his jokes. Watched as she slipped on the soapy haul, and he grabbed her by the hips to keep her from falling. I watched as she stepped out of his grasp, but not before their eyes met and they shared a *moment.*

That was when I made myself *stop* watching. *You called her by another woman's name during sex.*

At least now I understand why she walked away like she did, but hell, could the reason have been a little less mortifying?

My day didn't improve after that. Brady, who handles our corporate sales and gets companies to spend stupid amounts of money spoiling their employees with our services, wanted to meet with us at lunch, and I've had to sit here and pretend I'm not irritated with Wes.

"You okay?" Wes asks as we wrap things up.

Clearly, I was unsuccessful. "I'm fine." It's not his fault I'm all screwed up where Veronica Maddox is concerned. It's not his fault that between the two of us, he's the one who hasn't made a fatal error mid-coitus.

"Not you too." He grins at Crosley. "Think I should give him the same treatment I gave V when she said everything was *fine*? It cheered her up."

I scowl. "What's wrong with Veronica?" A glance at the clock tells me she was due back from her lunch break five minutes ago. "Where is she, anyway?"

"Hey." Wes sticks his pointer finger in my chest, and I scowl at it. "Don't do that grumpy-boss thing. I'm the reason she got all messy this morning, so I told her to take a long lunch and get cleaned up."

I could go the rest of my life without hearing Wes say he's the reason Veronica *got all messy*.

"Desperate housewife number one, incoming," Brady says, and everyone groans.

"Not it!" Crosley and Miles shout in unison, turning toward the garage.

Wes claps me on the shoulder and grins. "Have fun."

I glance toward the front window and fight back a cringe. Addison Wellmont is the pampered, manicured one-percenter housewife her name makes her sound like. Truthfully, I feel for her. She and her husband have a summer home in Jackson Harbor, and he spends his days on the golf course or taking private fishing charters. While there's nothing wrong with those activities, and I appreciate all the business he's thrown our way, he's also a total dick. Addison comes in here to schedule his outings—though I think Brady did a great job setting up online scheduling. It's clear she's lonely, but I've never been interested in married women—not even in my wildest days. I don't care how hot they are or how much they might deserve a little affection. It's just not my bag.

And judging by the fact that I'm standing here alone by the time she pushes through the door, the other guys feel the same way.

"Colton!" She beams at me, her hips swinging in her white tennis skirt as she approaches the counter. "I'm so glad you're the one in here today. Last week, your secretary was being really pushy about me scheduling online or through her."

"Well, that is her job," I say.

Addison laughs brightly. I'm hilarious with crazy truth bombs, I guess. "I *told* her I only do *work* with the Heartbreakers." She winks at me, but if *work* is supposed to be a double entendre, I don't get it.

I'm a little nauseated. "What can I do for you today, Addison?"

"My sister-in-law is coming into town next week, so I need to make some plans."

"Oh." Well, this is something different. "Couple of jet skis? Paddle boards? Sunset cruise? What's her style?"

She shudders delicately. "You misunderstand me. I need to make plans *for me*, so that I don't have to spend time with her." She throws her head back and laughs. The sound is sharp and forced and kind of hurts my ears.

"No judgment here," I say, pulling up next week's calendar on Veronica's computer. "Let's get you scheduled."

She folds her arms on the counter and leans forward. "I was thinking it's time for some private sailing lessons. What do you say?"

I scan the days next week. "You're in luck. Amelia had a cancelation on Thursday and could take you out for either two or four hours."

"Oh." Addison makes a face. "I was hoping you had some availability."

I shake my head. "I'm only a passable sailor. Would be an awful teacher, and unfortunately, I'm booked solid next week, anyway." *Thank the Lord.* "We're getting into busy season."

She shows her bottom lip in a pout. "Fine. I'll take the two-hour with Amelia. I guess I should probably bring along my sister-in-law, since I don't have to worry about her hogging all your attention."

"Completely up to you," I say, tapping the reservation into the system. "Can I do anything else for you?"

The bell over the front door rings, and Addison's mouth pulls into a deeper pout as Veronica strolls inside.

"You're just in time," I say, backing away from the computer. "Addison's going to take Amelia's sailing opening for next Thursday." I turn to face her, ready to dodge into my office while I have the chance, but stop when I see Veronica's face. All the laughter and smiles she had for Wes this morning are gone. She looks . . . solemn.

"Are you okay?" I ask softly.

She nods. "Yeah. Sorry I'm late."

Sorry? No angry retort about how Wes told her to take a long lunch? No sarcastic remark about how I need to learn to use the booking system?

She steps around me and enters the information for Addison's reservation into the computer. "Want me to use the card we have on file?" she asks.

Addison looks back and forth between us, frowning. "Yeah. Thanks." She forces a small smile. "See you around, Colton."

"Bye, Addison."

I wait until the door closes behind her before turning back to Veronica. "Seriously? No snark? Are you sick?"

She cuts her eyes to me before turning her focus back to her computer screen. "You already know everything I have to say about Addison Wellmont. She's petty, she's entitled, and she's trying to get you in bed. Oh, and she's *married*, in case you care."

"There she is," I say, smiling wide for the first time all day. "You had me worried for a minute."

"Sorry to disappoint you. I'm having a bad day and am not in the mood to chitchat."

"You were in the mood to fool around with Wes." The words are out before I can stop them, and if I could physically snatch them back up, I'd be scrambling right now.

She huffs. "I knew you'd think we weren't working, but Wes said the cat needed cleaning and he wanted me to help. I apologize if it appeared I was enjoying said work too much."

I'm a dick. "It's not that. It's . . . I hope you know Wes is a player." *Fuck me. What is my problem today?* Words just keep coming out of my mouth. I told myself I wasn't going to say anything to her about Wes, and I lasted all of, what? Sixty seconds?

"What does that have to do with anything?" she asks, spinning her chair to face me.

I shake my head and turn away. "Never mind."

"Oh, no. You're not gonna get away with that. You brought it up. Now tell me why."

"I got here while you two were outside. I saw the way he was looking at you." *The way he put his hands on you.* "I just don't want you getting any ideas."

"Ideas?"

"About, you know, something happening." Her face pales, and I flinch. I'm not trying to make her feel shitty. "He wouldn't hurt you. At least not on purpose. He's a good guy, but he's too young to understand what a woman like you needs."

"A woman like me?" She stands and narrows her eyes as she saunters toward me, hips swishing with each step. "What exactly is it you think I *need*?"

I shake my head. "I knew I shouldn't have said anything. Forget about it."

I move to step back, but she grabs my arm. "Are you jealous?"

"What?"

"You're jealous." Her eyes widen, as if this is some sort of shocking revelation. "Just like you were at the bar on Friday."

"That guy was a creep. You said so yourself."

"True." She arches a brow. "But Wes is no creep. Therefore, the pattern isn't that you're rescuing me but that you're being jealous and territorial."

I scoff. "There's a big difference between giving it to you straight and being territorial."

She cocks an eyebrow. "Yeah? And if I told you Wes knows I'm just down to fuck?" She inches closer. "If I told you he and I have plans tonight?"

I clench my jaw so hard that I'm surprised my teeth don't crack. "You're not funny."

"No," she says, dragging her eyes down the front of me, "but it's kind of hot when you get possessive."

"I'm not being—"

"No?" Her lips twitch like she's trying not to smile. "You saw Wes flirting with me and decided you needed to give me some speech to scare me off him. You really believe you're not just a *little* territorial?"

"You can do what you want. I just don't want you getting hurt."

"You can't even admit it." She takes another step closer, running two fingers down my chest. My pulse quickens, my heart working double time to rush blood to my dick. "I don't like it when that bitch Addison comes in here and flirts with you. See? It's not so hard to admit."

Her honesty is so unexpected that it nearly leaves me speechless. Maybe I should walk away before I screw up everything by admitting how much I want her. But I feel the dynamic shifting between us, and I'm not willing to let this moment go. I draw in a long breath through my nose, smelling her hair, then dip my head so my mouth is by her ear. "You want to hear me say it?" I whisper. "I hate the idea of you fucking him. I'd hate the idea of you fucking anyone because, despite what may have come out of my idiot mouth, it was *good* between us, and one night wasn't nearly enough for me."

I step back, and she just stares at me. I head to my office, but she doesn't come after me. For once, I've left her speechless.

91

Chapter Eight

VERONICA

*B*less his heart, but Wes pulled out all the stops to distract me from my worries, and it only kind of worked. Who knew that all I needed was Colton to whisper dirty words in my ear? Now, instead of obsessing about the future and a bunch of shit I can't control, I've been thinking about him. About him wanting me. About him actually admitting it.

I was playing with fire, baiting him like that, and now I'm paying the price because I have to go restock the shiny informational brochures we keep out front, and the extras are stored in Colton's office. Oozing sexual confidence is all well and good until someone calls you on it and then you have to keep working in the same building.

I knock twice. "Need to restock brochures," I call.

"Come on in."

I keep my head down as I enter the office. I have to close the door behind me to be able to open the cabinet. Because the fliers are on the bottom shelf, I have to bend over.

When I lift my head, Colton's eyes are on me—or, rather, on my tits. My shirt slipped, and now the swell of one breast and the purple lace edge of my bra are exposed, and he looks . . . *hungry.*

Heat floods me as he drags his gaze back up to meet mine. He might be an uptight asshole, but I can't deny that I like the way he looks at me. *I like his dirty mouth.*

I tug my tank top back into position. "Why don't you take a picture?"

He narrows his eyes. "What?"

So he's going to play dumb? I rise to my feet and walk around to his side of the desk so slowly it would be better described as a saunter. He doesn't bother to stand but turns his chair to face me.

"What was it you said to me on Friday? I'm supposed to make your job *easier*, right? Those were your words?" Shoving a stack of papers to the side, I take a seat on his desk and part my legs until my skirt strains against my thighs. "Maybe you need another view." I run my fingers across the hem of my skirt.

"For what?" His voice is gruff, and no matter how many times he pulls his gaze back up to my face, his eyes drift back down to my thighs. I've never gotten such a power rush from anything in my life.

Heat pools in my belly. *Lower.* I tug at the hem of my skirt enough so I can part my legs another two inches—all I need for him to get a view of my panties. I can't believe I'm doing this. Sure, I'm a coldhearted bitch, but I've never been the vixen who uses her body and sexual confidence to torment men.

But something about Colton has always made me push a little more.

"For when you're alone with your hand tonight. I'm just trying to do my job. Give you what you need to get the work done."

He coughs out a laugh. "How do you know I'll be alone?"

"Because you're too much of a gentleman to fuck another woman when you're thinking about me." I finger the thin strap of my tank top and let it fall down my shoulder. It pulls farther down than I expect, exposing the shell of my bra. His nostrils flare and his eyes are all over me. "There's no one else you want."

"You're wrong."

I'm swamped by a pang of jealousy so intense it hurts, but I do everything I can to keep my face neutral. "You have a date?"

"No." He shoves back his chair, giving me a clear view of his lap and the erection visible through his jeans. He presses the palm of his hand against that impressive length, and my mouth goes dry. He grins as if he knows exactly what he does to me. "You're wrong about me needing a mental picture of you to get off."

My gaze flies up to his. "You're going to pretend you haven't been gawking at me ever since I started working here?"

"I can't keep my eyes off you," he says, cool as hell.

I draw in a long, shaky breath, but it does nothing to ease the erratic beating of my heart. "So you will be thinking about me."

"Why would I settle for a mental picture when I can have the real thing? And why would I settle for my dick in my hand when my hand could be in your hair while I fuck your mouth?"

My breath leaves me in a rush as the image plays out in my

mind. *Yes. Please.* I swear, all this guy has to do is think about sex and it turns me on. When he talks about it, I'm a goner. He hasn't even touched me, and I'm already wetter than I've been with anyone in . . . ever, excluding my night with him. "I hate you."

"Same, beautiful." He palms himself again, his eyes never leaving mine. "And yet here we are. Wanting each other."

"You have no idea what I want."

The cock of his eyebrow says *bullshit*, but he shrugs. "Don't worry. I'll keep my hand and my dick to myself until you ask for them."

"In your dreams."

"You're right about that," he says, eyes all over me and making me so damn hot. "Every fucking night."

I part my legs another inch and slide my hand to my inner thigh, creeping higher. "I bet."

His gaze follows my movements as if his life depends on it. "I've changed my mind. I think I want my dick in my hand after all. You pull that skirt up just another inch and spread your legs for me. I could jack myself off while my mouth is on your pussy."

I shiver. I sat on his desk to play a game, and once again, I've been outplayed. The only way to win now is to call the shots. I meet his eyes. "Take it out."

His tongue skims his bottom lip, and I fucking swear he knows what that does to me. But he obeys, standing first, then unbuttoning his jeans and shoving them down his hips just enough so he can withdraw his cock. He's hard and long, and the tip is glistening. I've never wanted to put my mouth on a guy so badly in my life.

He gives it one long, dirty squeeze, and I bite the inside of my lip to keep from whimpering. "Which will it be? My mouth on you, or yours on me?"

His words make my sex clench hard and leave me aching. I shimmy to the edge of his desk, hooking my thumbs in the sides of my panties before I pull them down my legs and toss them on the floor. His hot eyes follow the movement before quickly returning for a peek between my thighs.

"Pull up the skirt," he says, voice husky, eyes dark. "Let me see you."

Just like that, I don't care who's calling the shots. I want what he's describing more than I want anything. So I obey, tugging the skirt up around my hips. I don't even have a chance to part my legs and expose myself to him before he's there, hands on my knees, doing it for me.

One finger trails across my slit, and he curses low. "You been thinking about this since we talked after lunch?"

"No more than you."

His wicked smile tells me that's still more than I should admit to.

I love the heat in his eyes. Love how his gaze fixes on his fingers as he traces my slit. Love the low, grunting sound of approval he gives me when I part my thighs another inch.

"I've thought about this all fucking day." He turns his hand and cups me in his hot palm as he stands between my legs and looks down at me.

"Why are you all the way up there?" I ask, summoning the best of my sass. "You're supposed to be between my legs."

He slides two fingers inside me so quickly I might call it rough under any other circumstances, but I'm so wet, so ready for him after our verbal foreplay, that it's nothing but pure bliss to have his fingers stretching me. He twists his other hand into my hair and tugs gently, lifting my face. "Is that what you want? My face between your legs? You didn't let me kiss you there long last time." He lowers his head, and my lips part instinctively, needy for a kiss he doesn't give. He touches his forehead to mine as he pumps his fingers inside me. It's good. *So good.* Why is it so good with him?

Our eyes lock, and I shiver, feeling suddenly vulnerable having him watching me so closely when I'm this turned on, when his hand is twisting my insides with pleasure and into need. Self-preservation that has me grabbing a handful of his hair and guiding his mouth to mine. He groans against my lips, sucking lightly before opening over me, drinking me in. His tongue slides against mine, moving in the same rhythm as his hand. Pressure builds. I rock into his touch, raising to the summit of the pleasure building in my core.

He withdraws his hand, and I gasp against his mouth—feel his cocky smile. "Not yet," he murmurs against my lips. Then, in a flash, he drops again, hands on my thighs, face between my legs, his mouth . . .

"Oh God." I'm too close, and when his lips latch on to my clit, my thighs jerk off the desk. His grunt of approval is the next hottest thing to the sight of his head between my legs.

He lied about jerking off. His hands are too busy with me. One between my thighs, the other gripping my ass like he's afraid I might fall if he doesn't hold on.

And I might. His fingers and tongue tease and play, and I stop trying to make sense of what he's doing, stop trying to predict his next move, and just *feel*. I lean back on both hands, trying to keep myself steady, but when he slides those fingers inside me, I fall apart. I'm a glowing star shattering into a million tiny pools of sunshine. I can't move. Can't muster a snarky comment. Can't do anything but let the pleasure wash over me again and again.

I half expect Colton to lift his head and say something cocky, but he doesn't. He doesn't withdraw and he doesn't relent. His tongue laves my clit, his fingers pumping inside me until that first orgasm turns into a second and every muscle in my body trembles.

When he straightens and meets my eyes again, he doesn't move his hand from between my legs. "Fuck, I'd forgotten how sweet you taste."

I want to make some sarcastic remark about how I can't be literally sweet, but I'm still holding on through the aftershocks, and then his mouth is on mine again and I can taste myself. Not sweet, not at all, but on his lips, my taste is the sexiest thing I've ever known.

I reach between our bodies and grip him in my fist. "You have protection?"

"In my wallet," he says. "Take off your shirt. Too much of you is hidden again. Like last time."

"I thought *I* was calling the shots."

"If that's what you want."

Not really. I want him to tell me to get on my knees and then watch as I take his cock in my mouth. I want him to lose himself as much in the pleasure of my mouth on him as I did in his mouth on me. But part of me is back to grappling for control, and we can't have everything.

I reach around him and pull his wallet from his back pocket, then retrieve the condom before smacking it against his chest.

He tears open the package and rolls it on, his eyes always on me. When he grabs my hips roughly, I brace myself, preparing for him to slide in, to fill this ache that's returned despite my orgasm. *I need him.*

"You know how many times I imagined bending you over this desk?" he asks.

I brace myself, waiting for him to spin me around and do just that, but he doesn't. Instead, he hooks his arms under my knees and slides into me, little by little, and then— "Oh."

His lips quirk into a crooked smile. Not charming, bad-boy Colton, but someone softer. More vulnerable, and as much as I crave more of this side of him, seeing any of it scares me.

This is just sex.

I close my eyes and rock into him, searching for the angle that will give me what I need while urging him to go faster, but he drops a hand between our bodies and strokes me. Everything's too much. Too sensitive, too intense, until I let go and then it's . . . *perfect.*

My orgasm hits hard and sudden. He follows, and I have to bite my lip to keep myself quiet.

He gathers me against his chest, his nose in my hair, his hands stroking my back, and I let him. My body is warm and loose, and I'm too spent to object to this closeness. *I don't want to object.*

That's the thought that scares me. The one that has me sidestepping out of his arms and avoiding his gaze.

I straighten my skirt. "I can't believe we just did that."

"Can't believe it, or you have regrets?"

I risk a glance toward him but don't know what to make of the guarded look in his eyes. Does *he* have regrets? Does he think I'm going to turn into super-bitch like I did last time? "I think it was probably a good thing." I swallow. "Get it out of our systems so we can work together without thinking about it so much."

He doesn't reply, and now I wish I'd kept my thoughts to myself and dug for his instead. He studies me for a beat before taking care of the condom and tucking himself back in his pants. And I stand there waiting for . . . *something*.

This guy's a dick. This was just sex. Just a distraction and release we both needed. Why am I overthinking it?

What do I want? Flowers? A declaration of love? I'm being ridiculous.

I don't know if the awkwardness threatening to suffocate me is all mine or if he feels it too. "I'll go."

He doesn't move or say a word until my hand touches the doorknob. "Veronica."

I stop. Turn. I hold my breath, because I'm dying for him to say something right now, and I don't even know what I want.

He bends over and scoops my panties off the floor. "You might want these."

I hate him.

Chapter Nine

COLTON

She hates me.

Veronica has ignored me for four days. She's barely acknowledged my existence and only looked at me when she couldn't avoid it. Now, it's Friday, and I just heard her and Amelia talking in hushed tones about Veronica's "big plans" for tomorrow.

This is a woman who regularly jokes about having no social life. A woman who refuses to join the rest of the staff for drinks after work because she doesn't want to miss out on time with her son. And suddenly she has *big plans*?

It shouldn't matter. It's none of my business. Not by any stretch of the imagination. But knowing she has some big plans tomorrow—with Wes or, hell, *anyone*—is making me lose my mind.

"Veronica," I call when her computer chimes, signaling it's shutting down for the day. I left my office door open all afternoon, hoping to catch some clue about what she's up to. All I accomplished was making myself crazy. "Will you come to my office for a minute before you go?"

She huffs lightly, and her chair squeaks as she rolls it back and comes to stand in my office doorway.

I look her over, admiring the way her blue cotton dress shows off her tan legs. "It's a shame about your voice."

She frowns and props her hands on her hips, her phone in one hand. Is she waiting for a call from someone? Maybe from tomorrow's date? "What?"

I pretend to startle. "Oh, wow. You *can* talk."

She rolls her eyes. "What do you want?"

That's a loaded question. "Shut the door."

The corner of her mouth hitches into a lopsided grin. But she steps forward and kicks the door shut behind her.

I lean back in my chair and study her. "Did it work?"

The other side of her mouth climbs up to meet the first. "Did what work?"

"Monday afternoon. You needed to get me out of your system, right?" I chuckle. "If *I* would've said that, by the way, you'd be talking to your friends about what an asshole I am."

She leans back against the door and crosses her feet at the ankles. "Did you bring me in here to talk sexual politics and double standards?"

I brought you in here because you have plans *on Saturday, and I'll be damned if you're going to be on a date and not spend it wishing you were with me.*

I push out of my chair and walk around my desk to stand in front of her. I step so close that she has to crane her neck to look up at me. "I brought you in here to make sure you're okay." I place a hand on her hip, and her breath catches. "I'm trying to be more attentive to the needs of the staff."

She coughs out a laugh. "*Really.* The whole staff?"

"Nah." I grin. "Fuck everyone else. Your needs are the only ones that get me off." I slide my hand down and around until I'm cupping her ass. I love how she fits in my hands, love how she can't help but press into my touch. Her soft moan is an invitation, and I trail my lips along the side of her neck. "Do you want this?" I ask before dragging her earlobe between my teeth. "Or this?" I slide my free hand up her skirt and let my thumb graze the inside of her thigh.

Her eyes float closed. "You're bad for me."

Her words shock me so much that I nearly stumble back. I've had to bite and claw my way back to a decent life. But I *have*. I've spent the last two and a half years proving I can run with the good guys, that I'm *not* the trouble seeker who will make your life explode around you. To think Veronica sees me as the man I was rather than the one I've fought so hard to become hurts in a way I wasn't expecting. I manage to keep my footing, if not hide my flinch, but I brace myself before I ask, "How do you figure?"

She rocks into my touch, eyes half-mast. I may be bad for her, but that's the face of a woman ready to be seduced. "You either piss me off or make me forget everything I'm supposed to be worrying about."

The knot between my shoulder blades releases. I'm not bad for her because I'm a fuck-up or an addict. I'm bad for her because she doesn't feel stressed when I touch her. *I'll take it.* "You don't look pissed right now."

"Because I'm *turned on.*"

"And that's a bad thing?" I trace the edge of her underwear with my thumb. I'm dying to peel it away and find out if she's wet for me. "Isn't it nice to let go sometimes?"

"Sometimes." Her eyes close all the way, and she sways toward my hand, urging me to touch her exactly where I want to.

"You want this, then? You want me to make you come again?" If she's paying attention at all, she'll hear the desperation in my voice. She'll know just how much that's what *I* want.

I lift a hand to cup her breast and ghost my thumb across her nipple—just enough to tease but not enough to give her what I know she wants. I follow the side seam of her dress down to the hem, balling the material in my fist. "It makes me fucking crazy when you wear a dress. Makes me think of our night together and how I barely had it around your waist before I was inside you and you were moaning my name."

She shivers and closes her eyes, leaning her head back onto my shoulder. "We all make mistakes."

I hum against her neck, and she arches back, searching for more from the hand that's between her legs. "I never forgot how good you felt on my fingers. The sounds you made when you came."

She swallows hard. "Are you going to touch me, or do you just like to hear yourself talk?"

I bite her shoulder lightly. "Ask nicely, and I'll give you anything you want."

I still have her dress in my fist, but I let my knuckles skim the top of her thigh, hinting at more. I need to know she wants this, but I also want her to ask for it. Want to hear her beg me to make her come. Just like she did that night.

The moment our mouths meet, she melts, her shoulders loosening, her hand going to my belt to tug me closer.

Then her phone buzzes, and instead of ignoring it or dropping it so she can use both hands to pull me close, she shifts awkwardly to look at the screen.

Grimacing, I pull my face from her neck and step back.

"I need to go," she says, biting her bottom lip. "*Shit.*"

"What's wrong?"

"Nothing. Just . . . nothing." She flattens a palm against my chest and nudges me back. "Thanks for the distraction, but I have to leave."

VERONICA

Saturday morning, I'm on the interstate while my coffee is trying to gnaw through my stomach lining. Or maybe that's just the worry I've felt since I agreed to do this. Worry that was amplified last night when Marcus texted and said he and Kristi were in town and wanted to swing by and see Jacks before tomorrow's visit. I rushed out of Colton's office thinking I needed to pick up Jacks then get to June's and make the place presentable before they arrived. I was halfway to the daycare before my brain started working and I remembered I didn't have to agree.

I replied and told Marcus we were busy for the evening but we'd see them today, essentially postponing the inevitable.

Despite my many fears and reservations, I buckled Jacks into the car this morning, and we're headed to Grand Rapids and the address Marcus gave me. Jacks has been playing with his toys in the back, and I've been playing some of the upbeat music from the Mommy and Me Kindermusik class we took together last fall. He loved it, and I wanted to keep going, but it was too expensive, and I needed to cut something out when my rent went up.

As much as I tell Marcus I don't want his money, I can't help but think of what Jacks and I could do with it. My student loan and credit card debt keep me drowning in bills from month to month, but if we had extra, we could go back to Kindermusik. Maybe I could get Jacks some swimming lessons. Maybe even an apartment of our own.

Still, I hate the idea of taking money from Marcus. I always have, but now that visitation is on the table, I hate it more. I will never feel right about this if the money is part of my decision. No amount of child support is going to make me give Marcus visitation if I don't think it's the best thing for Jacks.

And then he'll take you to court and get it anyway, the nagging voice in my head says. I don't want it to come to that.

The drive goes far too fast, and before I'm close to ready, I'm pulling into the broad brick-paver driveway just outside of Grand Rapids. The house is a two-story colonial, big enough that my childhood self would've called it a mansion. I know now that it's not, but its size and polish still spark my old insecurities.

"Where are we, Mama?" Jacks asks when I open his door to unbuckle him.

"Remember our friend Kristi we met at the park?" I ask, but the little lines between his brows tell me he doesn't, and I'm not about to say, *Remember that pushy lady who picked you up without asking?* "This is her house," I say as calmly as I'd explain that we were visiting someone from the Jackson clan. "We're going to meet someone very special today."

Jackson's face lights up. "Pider-Man?"

"No, baby. Not Spider-Man." My throat tightens, as if it's trying to constrict enough to keep me from saying the words, but I push them out anyway. "Your daddy. He lives here with Kristi. She's his wife."

The smile falls away, and I can practically see the wheels in his head turning. I told him his father lived in Alabama and his name was Marcus. Jackson's never questioned why his dad doesn't live with us, why he doesn't see him, though I always figured that question would come someday. Right now, he's so young that he assumes our life is normal. That our way is the way it's *supposed to be.*

Today will change that.

The front door flies open, and Kristi jogs out to greet us. Marcus stands in the doorway in softly worn jeans and a dark T-shirt. He's not nearly as handsome as I remember. Maybe spending all that time around the Heartbreakers has ruined me for men I would've otherwise considered attractive.

Or maybe you only have eyes for one tall, dark, and handsome guy these days.

I pull Jacks out of his car seat before turning to Kristi. She's dressed in white jeans and a loose-fitting black shirt, but somehow looks fancy and expensive anyway.

Her smile is radiant, and she clasps her hands in front of her face and bounces on her heels. "We are so excited to have you here, Jackson," she squeals. She opens her arms as if she's going to reach for him, and Jacks buries his face in my chest.

"Kristi," Marcus says from the door, his voice low. "Take it easy."

She drops her arms and smiles wider, but it's clearly forced. This woman's every instinct is to hold Jacks, but at least Marcus is there to remind her to take it slowly. *Who knew I'd ever be grateful for him?*

"It's good to see you, Veronica," Marcus says, giving me that soft smile I used to find so sexy.

I attempt to return it, but I'm sure it looks as obvious as my lie when I say, "You too."

"Let's not linger out here," Kristi says. "It's too hot today. Come inside."

I take a deep breath and follow her into the house. For whatever reason, I imagined them bringing me and Jacks into some fancy sitting room. Maybe I just liked the idea of them being so ill prepared for a three-year-old's needs.

They lead the way past the bright, sunny foyer to a family room off the kitchen at the back of the house, and I have to bat down my disappointment at the sight of this Jacks-proof space. They have some wooden play food and utensils in a basket in the middle of the floor next to a puzzle with big pieces and a pile of books.

Jacks is better off if they aren't incompetent. He deserves time with his father, and you'll only feel okay about that if you know he's safe here.

Shoving down all my conflicting feelings, I lower Jacks to the floor, but he stays glued to my leg. "It's okay," I say, even though I don't believe it.

"Hi, little guy," Marcus says.

Jacks looks up at me, and I muster all of my courage to give him a confident nod. "Go ahead and say hi."

He cautiously makes his way across the room—past the toys and to Marcus, who's taken a seat in a big leather recliner.

Jacks stares at him for a long time, then says, "Hi," and his voice is so small and precious and hopeful that I both hate and love my decision to bring him here today. *Don't you dare break his heart. Don't you dare.*

Marcus smiles his soft, warm smile. "Hi. I'm your daddy."

My eyes burn and my nose tingles, but the last thing I want to do is cry in front of Kristi-with-a-know-why, so I think about the pretty ivory color of the area rug and try not to stare as Jacks grabs a book from the pile. I don't let myself think about it too much when he picks *Guess How Much I Love You*, the same one I've read to him approximately one thousand times since he was born, and I definitely try not to think about it when he takes it back to Marcus instead of me.

"You want to read this?" Marcus asks, taking the book.

Jacks nods, and Marcus pulls him onto his lap.

"Look at that," Kristi whispers.

I'm trying not to.

I wander toward the kitchen, because if I have to sit here and watch my child's absent father read him a book for the first time, I might actually become hysterical. "Your coffee smells amazing," I say when I spot the half-full pot. "Do you mind if I pour myself a cup?"

"Oh my goodness." Kristi throws her hand over her mouth. "Of course not. I'm sorry. I should've offered already."

"Not at all." I yawn and glance toward the family room again, where Marcus is letting Jacks turn the page just like a good daddy should. When I turn back, she's pulling a mug from the cabinet that says *BLESSED* in big block letters. "The drive just made me tired."

Kristi finishes pouring and cuts her eyes to me. "Do you drive overtired a lot?"

I blink at her. "What?"

She passes the mug to me. "I just . . . That's so dangerous, and with Jacks in the back seat . . ."

"No," I say, a little too hard. I'm suddenly the bitchy mom from the playground again. "I don't drive tired, and I've never fallen asleep at the wheel. I wouldn't put Jacks at risk like that."

"Of course you wouldn't. I never meant to imply . . ." She shakes her head. "I'm doing this all wrong. I just know how hard you work and how much you sacrifice for Jackson. We are so happy to be able take some of that burden."

"He's not a burden."

"Oh, look at my bumbling this over and over. Of course not. Never to us, either."

I look down into my coffee. It's black, but I don't want cream or sugar. I want the bitter taste on my tongue to remind me I can't drop my guard too much today. My gut tells me Kristi's one of those girls who'll sweeten you up and share all the good gossip when you're around, but the second you leave the room, she'll share all the dirt she learned about you when you confided in her. And that's fine. I know how to deal with women like her. I don't need her to be my friend. I just need her to be good for and to Jacks.

When I turn back to the living room, Marcus and Jacks are on the floor together, Marcus sprawled on his stomach as Jacks pulls the toys from the basket one by one, examining them. I scan Marcus's face for any sign of annoyance, but he's looking at Jacks with the soft smile he used when he introduced himself to his son. The same smile he once gave me.

We were supposed to be a family. I was supposed to give my boy Saturday afternoons playing on the rug with Daddy, and family walks in the evening, and a dinner table that never felt lonely.

Just remembering that I ever believed in that fairytale is enough to make me feel like a fool. Like I'm still the fifteen-year-old girl who blew Rhett Davis under the bleachers because I believed that he wanted to be my boyfriend. I remember trying to hold his hand on the way into school the next day. The way he yanked it away and laughed before putting his arm around a pretty cheerleader. I stopped believing in fairytales that day, but for a couple of months Marcus tricked me into believing again.

Most days, I'm fine with it being just me and Jacks. Because, in truth, it isn't *just us*. We have Aunt Star and her Katie. We have my sister and all the Jacksons. But most days, I'm not confronted by what the alternative looks like. This big house. How stable and safe it feels.

He deserves this. He deserves more.

"Whoo!" Kristi says, fanning her eyes. "Holy moly." She presses a hand to my arm. "Sorry. I knew I'd get emotional."

Marcus glances over his shoulder and playfully shakes his head at her. "She's a sap."

"I am," Kristi says, grinning at her husband like he just gave her the best compliment, and for a beat I wonder about their relationship. Has Marcus learned to be faithful? Is he honest with her, or is their relationship a series of manipulations?

It's none of my business, and frankly, as long as it doesn't affect Jacks, I don't care. Kristi and Marcus seem to sincerely care about my son.

Kristi turns to me. "I think they're good for a while. Want me to show you the house?"

No. I really, really don't. But I smile, remembering I wouldn't be doing my part as Jackson's mom if I didn't check out the house and make sure there isn't some dungeon where they're torturing children or some such. "Oh, I'd love that," I lie. "It's such a nice home."

I follow her back toward the staircase at the front of the house.

"We really didn't want new construction," she says, leading me up the gleaming wooden staircase. "I always loved the charm of a historical home, but when we saw this house and the neighborhood, it was just too perfect to pass up."

"It's lovely." Good God, this is awkward. I wish I could just do a quick look around on my own and not have to trail after Kristi and feed her compliments. Yes, her home is perfect and tastefully decorated, but I've already run out of ways to say that—and the desire to verbalize it.

"Don't worry about the stairs. We have a contractor coming next week to install baby gates, so we'll be fully baby-proofed before he stays."

Awfully presumptuous of you to think that'll happen anytime soon. But part of me is already processing that it won't be long. I couldn't watch my boy light up like that when he took a book to his daddy and *not* let him come back. It'll kill me a little, but I'll do it.

"Here's the space you're probably most interested in seeing," she says, pushing open the door to a bright, airy bedroom. "We wanted to get to know Jackson before we did a lot of decorating in here, so you'll have to excuse the bare walls. I have no doubt we'll make this place shine with his personality in no time. What really matters for now is he has his own room."

His own room. The only time I was ever able to give Jacks his own room, he was an infant, and we never used it for more than clothes and toy storage. This space is bigger than the room we share at June's, and though it's sparse, it's far lovelier than what we have at home. There's a dresser against one wall with a stack of nighttime diapers on top and a simple toddler bed in the corner. "He's always slept in my room," I warn her, my cheeks heating. "It's just been easier that way. When he stays with my sister, she usually lies down in there until he drifts off. I don't know if he'd be able to fall asleep on his own."

"Oh." She bites her bottom lip and looks around. "Do you . . . co-sleep?"

If I weren't busy trying to hide the fact that I'm in the middle of a total meltdown, I might've laughed at the way she said *co-sleep* the way someone might ask if you have rats. But it's hard to find my laugh when my selfish heart is breaking. "We haven't co-slept in a long time. I just mean he's used to someone else being in the room."

She nods. "Okay. We can work with that."

"Maybe we shouldn't jump right into overnights," I blurt. "Just ease him in, you know?"

"I promise we'll make sure he feels comfortable, Veronica. Even if that means moving his mattress to our bedroom or plopping the guest mattress in here."

I nod so she knows I heard her, but I feel detached as she shows me the rest of the house. A glance inside the lovely owner's suite, a look into the upstairs family room, "Jackson's bathroom," and then back downstairs. By the time she takes me out to the big backyard, where Marcus is pushing Jackson on a swing, the sound of Jackson's laughter doesn't even bring a smile to my face. I'm completely numb.

"He loves it," Kristi says.

"Swinging is his favorite."

"It was my favorite when I was a child too," she says. "We'll be coming to Jackson Harbor on Saturday if that works for your schedule. The weather is supposed to be nice—good for a beach day—and Marcus and I thought you might prefer our first solo visitation to be on your home turf. Then, in two weeks, maybe he could spend the day with us here."

She has it all planned out, but I shake my head. "His birthday party is two weeks from today."

"Oh. We'll just do Sunday that weekend, then."

"Sunday's his actual birthday," I blurt.

"I know." She clasps her hands together and gazes lovingly toward the swing set. "We're gonna make it so special."

I can't change his party now, and in *theory*, a father should be allowed to see his son on his birthday, so I nod. "Okay. I can bring him at lunchtime that day."

"Perfect." She hugs herself, but the arms wrapped around her middle do nothing to contain her sheer joy at having Jackson here and seeing Marcus push him on the swing. As much as I resent the way she swooped in to get Jacks in their lives, I can't blame her for the joy it's clearly bringing. Jacks *is* joy. His smiles, his curiosity, his *love*. I've never minded sharing all that with anyone. Why is this so different?

Because this is the first time you've felt like you could be replaced.

Chapter Ten

COLTON

*V*eronica's late again on Monday morning, and I'm determined to not be a dick about it when she strolls in here. I spent my whole weekend wondering who she was with and what she was doing. I tried to subtly get info out of Amelia, but she just looked at me like I'd grown a second head and reminded me we decided we weren't going to man the front counter on weekends—as if the only reason I could want to know Veronica's plans would be because I wanted her to work.

I ran a bunch of errands, refinished the hardwood floor in my bedroom, and took Mike to an AA meeting in Grand Rapids because he swears he can't face the folks at the Jackson Harbor meeting yet. Bottom line, I stayed busy as hell and still managed to obsess about Veronica's Saturday "plans."

It doesn't matter, though. I'm not going to let those

frustrations turn me into an ass this morning.

It's eight after when she finally pushes through the front door, hands full as always, but my first thought when I see her face is that she's crying. Or, more precisely, that she's crying, and I'm gonna kill the asshole responsible.

And since that's completely irrational, my second thought is that I have no business giving a damn about another guy bringing her to tears. But fuck, the only thing I hate more than the idea of some other guy touching her is the idea of anyone making her sad. Not that I could ever let her know that.

"What happened?" *Smooth. Way to hide your feelings.*

After she sets down her coffee and purse and all her assorted notebooks—*what does she do with all of those?*—she lifts her head and gives me a clear view of her puffy eyes and red nose. She grabs a tissue off the desk. "Wha?"

Not crying. Sick. This does nothing to calm the inner caveman who's been trying to take over since Friday. Switching gears from possessive to overprotective in a flash, I'm striding toward her before I even think about it. "You're sick."

"Just a cold." She doesn't shrink away when I put my hand to her forehead. Not that it would matter if she did. She's burning up so badly that I probably could've felt the heat from my office.

"Not just a cold. You have a fever." I look around the office, the stacks of paper on her desk, and the various sticky notes the guys have left her over the weekend. "Tell me what needs to be done today, and I'll take care of it."

"What? No, I can work."

"You're going home, V. You need meds and at least one day in bed."

She scoffs. "I can handle a cold, Colton."

"Nope. Not here you can't."

She folds her arms. "You're ridiculous. I'll take a DayQuil and be fine."

"You'll take a day off," I say, then, when I realize she's going to keep arguing, I pull my trump card. "I can't have you getting all our clients sick."

VERONICA

I told him I could handle a cold, but the truth is I suck at being sick. I may have been the tough one between me and my twin, but Nic was the caretaker. No matter where we were living growing up, she always took care of me, whether it was in some shitty apartment with Mom, in a foster home, or in the group home later. She'd even come tend to me when I'd get sick in college.

I *hate* being sick. Everyone does, obviously, but it's not just the physical misery that gets me. Anything that makes me feel weak and vulnerable wakes my demons and sets them loose on my thoughts. I practically feel them skittering around in my mind, and I can't handle that.

I can't be like my mom.

But I'm a grown-ass woman now, and Nic has a kid of her own to worry about—two kids, if you count that giant child growing in her belly. I can't ask her to come tend to me. Even if my pride would allow it, I couldn't risk her getting this while she's pregnant.

I remember getting a cold when I was pregnant with Jacks. The doctor told me to take regular-strength Tylenol for the fever and hot showers to ease my cough and congestion. No NyQuil, no prescription cough syrup. It was *miserable.*

So I don't call my sister, but I do call Star and ask her to transfer Jacks from preschool to daycare for me, which I usually do on my lunch break. I must sound awful, because she offers to bring him home at the end of the day too. I thank her profusely, take some meds, and crawl into bed.

COLTON

Veronica isn't answering her phone, and I keep imagining worst-case scenarios. That she was disoriented from a high fever and fell and hit her head. That she fell asleep, and the fever got out of control. Or just . . . *Shit.* Even imagining her feeling bad with no one there to take care of her messes with me.

When I lock up the office, I decide the best thing I can do is to see for myself that she's okay, so I drive to the address listed in her employee file, stopping quickly on the way for a few necessities.

It's a small house in a quiet neighborhood not too far from where the Jacksons and I all grew up. The second I climb out of my car, I feel weird about just showing up like this. She's probably going to laugh in my face. First, I made her go home, and now,

I'm acting like a mother hen. But I grab the bag out of the front seat and make myself knock on the door anyway.

Much to my surprise, it's Star who answers. Her eyes go wide. "Colton! Hi. What are you doing here?"

I clear my throat, as if I needed to make sure she picks up on how awkward I'm feeling right now. "I wanted to check on Veronica. And give her this." I shove the bag at her, ready to get out of here before she asks too many questions.

She glances over her shoulder, then back at me. "Are you in a hurry?"

"What? No. Why?"

She worries her bottom lip between her teeth. "I told Veronica I'd bring Jackson home, but when we got here, she was dead to the world. I didn't want to wake her up, but I couldn't leave Jacks here without someone to watch him, either."

Behind her, the little man in question races toward the door, skidding to a halt at Star's side. He wraps his arms around her leg and peeks out at me. "Hi."

"Hey, bud. Remember me? I work with your mom." I offer him my knuckles, and he frowns at my fist for a beat before tapping it with two fingers.

"I was just about to wake her because Katie has a summer choir concert tonight I don't want to miss. But if you stayed, she could sleep longer."

Well, hell. "Um. I . . ." I look around. Would Veronica even *want* me to stay?

"I think she's sicker than she'll admit, and the sleep would do her a lot of good."

"No. Sure. I get it. Of course I can stay."

Star hands back the bag and pulls open the door. I step into the small foyer while she grabs her purse. "I already fed Jacks dinner, but there are some fruit snacks on the counter if he asks. June's at work until eight, so you can hang in the living room."

I frown. "Are they not welcome in the living room when her roommate's home?"

Star hoists her bag onto her shoulder and shrugs. "Veronica likes to stay out of her way. They spend a lot of time in her room when June's around."

That seems kind of ridiculous, but I keep my mouth shut. I don't know June, and there's probably more to the story.

"There's a tote with toys in it by the couch."

"Um . . . okay." I'm not completely clueless when it comes to kids. I spend quite a bit of time with my sister's toddler, Lauren, but I'm a little intimidated by being in charge of *Veronica's* kid.

Star squeezes my arm. "Relax. He's easy."

I laugh, and the sound exposes just how uncomfortable this whole situation makes me.

Star grins. "So . . . you and Veronica?"

My eyes go wide. "What? No. I'm just . . ." *This is so incredibly awkward.* "I'm just worried about her."

She presses her lips together and looks me over. "Mm-hmm. You seem awfully worried about how this is gonna go."

"Well, there's a good chance she's gonna be pissed when she wakes up and finds me hanging out with her kid."

"You can handle her." She stoops to press a kiss to Jackson's head. "Colton's going to play with you while Mama naps. I'll see you tomorrow morning."

"See you morning," Jacks says.

"Are you watching him tomorrow or something?"

She straightens and arches a brow. "Veronica drops him off at Ooh La La! every morning."

Again, it's not my business, but . . . "Why?"

"His preschool is across the street but doesn't start until nine. I walk him over on my break so she can get to work on time."

"And let me guess," I say, feeling like an ass when the pieces click together, "you hand her a cup of coffee every day when she comes in?"

She shrugs. "If you can't even count on your best friend for coffee, what's the point?" With that, she winks at me and walks out the door.

Jackson leads me into the living room without another word and starts pulling toys from the toy bin. "You like Pider-Man?"

Something tugs in my chest. "Actually, I really do." I put the bag with the soup I brought on the counter that separates the small kitchen from the living room before sinking to my haunches to watch Jacks line up his superheroes.

This kid is freaking adorable, but something about knowing he and Veronica spend most of their time at home holed up in their bedroom is getting to me. I've been such a dick to her because I've been carrying around baggage from our night together at the Jacksons' cabin. The way she walked away—the way she implied I was hung up on Ellie then *dismissed* me— pissed me off so much that I've never given much thought to her stresses outside of work.

I should have.

"Who are *you*?"

I straighten to my full height at the sight of the guy standing in the kitchen. He definitely wasn't there a minute ago. Is Veronica seeing someone? Is this the guy she had plans with last Saturday?

He's built like he lifts weights—or maybe trucks—and is clean-shaven. Something about him makes me want to throw my fist in his face. *Probably jealousy.* "I'm Colton." I lift my chin. "A friend of Veronica's. Who are you?"

He curls his lip. "A friend?" He grunts. "Can't blame you. I've been her *friend* a time or two."

I take a step toward the kitchen. It's impulse. It's possessiveness. It's that inner caveman pounding his chest. "Excuse me?"

"I'm just saying you're not special." He glances toward the living room. "Course, I never watched her kid like some fucking nanny boy."

I glance toward Jacks and find he's splitting his attention between his toys and us. I can't hit this guy in front of Jacks. *Damn shame.* "Why are you here?"

"Just visiting, but since no one interesting is around, I'll be on my way." He smirks and tucks his keys in his pocket. "Have fun with the kid."

He heads down the side hall, and I don't take my eyes off him until he disappears out the door I'm guessing goes to the garage. What a fucking dick. Why is V wasting her time with a piece of shit like that?

"Co-tin? You play?" Jacks calls from the rug.

I take a deep breath, drop my shoulders, and turn my attention back to someone worthwhile. "Absolutely."

Chapter Eleven

VERONICA

I wake up to the sound of Jacks laughing in the living room and groggily roll over to check the clock. It's almost seven thirty. Has Star been here with him all evening? *Shit.*

I push out of bed and try to shake off the cobwebs. I slept like the dead, but I feel a little better now. Good thing, too. I need to get Star out of here and get Jacks a bath.

Following the beautiful sound of my son's laughter, I stroll into the living room, where the late evening sun is slanting in through the blinds.

When the rug between the couch and TV comes into view, I stop in my tracks.

Colton is sprawled on the floor next to Jackson. They're playing with Jackson's favorite toys: his collection of Spider-Man action figures. I have a thousand questions, but the way my son is grinning at Colton punches my heart up into my throat. *Don't get attached, baby boy. Guys like him don't stick around for women like your mama.*

"Mama!" Jacks says, spotting me before Colton. He drops his action figure and runs to me.

I squirt some hand sanitizer into my palm and rub it in before scooping him up. "Hey, buddy. How was your day?"

"Good. Co-tin likes Pider-Man."

I smile at Colton, but look away quickly. My insides feel way too gooey and exposed right now, and I'm afraid he'll see all that in my eyes. "Yeah? How'd Colton end up playing with you?"

"I came by with some soup," the man in question says. "Star needed to run. I stayed so you could sleep." He scoops the toys up and drops them back into the tote before standing and wiping his hands on his jeans.

I stare at the bag on the counter from a downtown deli known to have the best chicken noodle soup in town. It's the sweet and thoughtful kind of thing a boyfriend might do—not that I've ever had the kind of boyfriend who would've gone to the trouble.

I swallow. The cold meds must be making me woozy, because I feel . . . fluttery all over.

"How are you feeling?" he asks.

"Better. A lot better. Thank you. You didn't need to stay."

"I was happy to." Colton tucks his hands in his pockets. "Oh. A guy stopped by while you were napping."

I frown. "A guy?"

"Tall. Dark hair. Clean-shaven. Looks like he could bench-press Crosley?"

"You're sure he was looking for me?"

"He didn't say." Colton shifts awkwardly. "I think he had a key. He let himself in through the garage."

"Oh." The cold medicine is *definitely* messing with me, because Colton seems jealous. That's not new, but with Wes the jealousy was about sex, and this feels different. "That's Landon. He's June's boyfriend."

"Oh. So you two aren't . . ." He clears his throat. "He implied he was involved with you, not her."

I wrinkle my nose, and I'm sure my disgust is all too apparent. "No. God, no. He's a creep."

Colton smiles. "Yeah. I got that vibe. I thought maybe he was the one you had big plans with last Saturday."

I cock my head to the side. *Definitely jealous.* "Why do you think I had big plans on Saturday?"

"I heard you talking to Amelia." His shrug wouldn't fool a soul. "Thought maybe you had a date."

"Wow. Do you always get this possessive after . . ." One glance at Jacks, and I decide not to finish that sentence.

Colton chuckles. "Almost never." His face softens and his gaze drops to my mouth. "This isn't finished between us, and I don't share."

I swallow hard.

"You shared my Pider-Man," Jacks says.

Colton laughs and turns his smile on Jacks. "That's true. We had fun playing Spider-Man, didn't we, buddy?"

Jacks grins. "Pider-Man come to my birthday."

My stomach sinks. "Baby, Mama already told you I don't think Spider-Man can make it to your party."

"No, he come, Mama!"

I grimace but try not to shrink as I explain to Colton. "Jacks went to a friend's birthday party a couple of weeks ago, and Spider-Man surprised them with a special appearance."

Colton looks appropriately impressed. "Wow. That's very cool."

"Yes, but unfortunately now Jackson thinks birthday parties and Spider-Man visits are synonymous. Spider-Man is busy on Jackson's birthday and can't come."

Colton frowns. "Have you called—"

I shake my head, mentally willing him not to finish that sentence. Colton nods. I won't talk about my Spider-Man dilemma in front of Jackson. The Spider-Man at his friend's party is booked up, but I wouldn't have been able to afford him anyway, so calling around to find someone else who can do it isn't an option.

Jacks leans his head on my chest. "Want Pider-Man, Mama," he whines.

I rub his back and force a smile at Colton. "Thanks again for this. I'm sure you need to go, so we won't keep you."

"Co-tin come to my party." He nods at Colton like they've already decided on it.

"Oh, honey, Colton probably has plans." I flash what I hope looks like an apologetic smile. I don't want him to feel cornered into coming.

"I promise to look at my schedule," he says to Jacks before turning his attention on me. "Take tomorrow off. You feel better now, but you won't do yourself any favors if you tire yourself out tomorrow."

"I—"

"All our employees get sick days, V. Just use them and don't worry about it."

I shift Jacks to my other hip. He's getting so big, and I can't hold him for as long as I used to without getting tired. "I'll see how I feel in the morning," I promise. "And I'll let you know."

Colton nods, seemingly satisfied with this concession.

Jacks and I walk Colton to the door, where he turns and studies me for a minute. "Do you need anything?"

"We're good."

"Rest up and feel better." He offers his knuckles to Jacks, who surprises me by giving him the world's cutest fist bump. And, sweet baby Jesus, if I hadn't already been painfully attracted to Colton McKinley, the last ten minutes would've done me in.

Jacks and I watch Colton head out to his truck. When he drives away, I feel like he left the door to my heart wide open, and I don't know how to lock it back up.

*I*t probably doesn't say much for the kind of jobs I end up working, but I don't remember ever getting a *paid* sick day. While I felt a little guilty for leaving my friends at HBA in the lurch, it was a relief to take the day off without having to worry about what it would do to my checking account. Even better, it seemed to help.

On Wednesday, I'm feeling refreshed and hopeful. I'm determined to start the week off right by arriving at the office on time. I'm out of bed before my alarm and get a shower and some work in while Jacks is still asleep in his crib. When I wake him, he's in a good mood and happily dresses without any fits. Getting out of the house should be a piece of cake.

I leave him playing in our room while I swing by the kitchen to grab our lunches. June is leaning against the counter in her robe, arms folded, eyes puffy, and I know my morning just got a little more complicated.

"We need to talk," she says, her voice gruff.

"Oh, June." I shake my head, my heart squeezing for the hurt in her eyes. There's not a doubt in my mind that Landon's to blame. I figured he'd break up with her sooner or later, but I guess she didn't see it coming. "I'm so sorry."

"Sorry?" She barks out a laugh. "You're kidding me, right? How *dare* you?"

I frown. "I might not have thought he was a great catch, but I'm still sorry he hurt you."

"He's not the one who hurt me, Veronica. *You* are. I thought we were friends. Friends don't try to *fuck* their friends' boyfriends." She scoffs. "But I guess I should've seen this coming, seeing as how you're the girl who got pregnant by her sister's fiancé."

My whole body goes cold. It's not that I'm surprised June knows about what happened with Marcus. I never told her, but shit like that gets around. No, this chill in my veins is from the realization that she'd use it against me without ever talking to me about it. "What did Landon tell you?" I ask. Not that it matters. She's decided I'm the bad guy, so I might as well take whatever punishment she's here to dole out.

"The truth." Her cheeks are flushed, like she's getting riled up just thinking about it.

"The truth? So he told you he cornered me right out of the shower one night? He told you he tried to get me to drop my towel? That he propositioned me and promised to *take good care of me*? Like I was something that could be bought?"

"I don't want to hear your bullshit lies. People like you have a hard time for a reason, Veronica. You think just 'cause you've had some rough patches that you get to walk all over anyone you want, but that's not the way this works. You bring on your own troubles. Want a better life for your kid? *Be better.*"

My stomach lurches into my throat. "June, I would *never* try to—"

"I don't want to hear it." She flings a cabinet door open and grabs something from inside before shoving it at me. "Pack your shit and get out."

It isn't the words that set me off.

No. The words I can handle. I've been through worse. But the trash bag she shoves at me brings back old, ugly, twisted memories from a place in my past that I've sworn I'll never go back to.

The words I expected. The trash bag makes me want to scream at the top of my lungs.

I open my mouth to do just that—to tell her what I think of her and her lying, sleazy boyfriend—but Jackson saves me, tugging at my pants with one balled-up fist.

My boy always saves me.

"What wrong, Mama?"

I scoop him off the ground and into my arms. "Nothing, baby. We're just making some plans." I give June one last hard look before morphing my face into the smile my son deserves.

"We're gonna go stay with Auntie Nic for a while. Would you like that?"

Jackson's eyes light up like it's the Fourth of July. My boy *loves* his aunt Nic. Maybe more than he loves me. Who could blame him? She could've thrown me out on my ass when I came to Jackson Harbor. Her fiancé seduced me and knocked me up. A lesser woman wouldn't have wanted anything to do with me after what I did. But not Nic. My twin sister opened her arms for me—albeit coolly at first—and made sure I was safe. That's what she's always done, and I know that's what she'll do now, but I've been trying *so damn hard* to let her live her life without me fucking it up.

To have to admit to my sister that I need help again? That's why I had a roommate to begin with. I was too proud to admit that Jackson Harbor living is too far above my pay grade. Maybe it's not my fault this time, but it feels like it. It always feels like my fault.

"Want a better life for your kid? Be better."

Jacks and I head to our bedroom, but I leave the trash bag behind. More than a decade ago, I promised myself I'd never pack my things in a trash bag again. When I had my baby boy and my life started falling down around my ears, I realized I might end up homeless again. My biggest fear was they'd take him from me. That my boy would become a trash-bag kid like I was. But I won't let that happen. Not so long as there's something I can do to prevent it.

"Why sad, Mama?" Jacks asks when I close the door behind me.

I shake my head, but two rogue tears stream down my cheeks

defiantly. "I'm just so happy we get to spend some time with Aunt Nicky," I whisper, and I drop to my knees and wrap my son into a big hug. "We'll head over there after I pick you up from daycare, okay?"

He's okay. He's safe. He's with you. No one can take him away. He knows he's loved.

He giggles and squirms out of my arms, rushing across the room to the tote with his action figures. "I take Pider-Man?"

Swallowing hard, I wipe my cheeks and stand, preparing to pack our things. "Yeah, baby. You can take Spider-Man."

COLTON

Apparently, I specialize in masochism. Exhibit A? This morning at the gym, I agreed to be Levi's best man.

He didn't expect me to say yes. In fact, when he asked, it was less "Hey, will you be my best man?" and more "I would ask you to be my best man if that didn't make me a dick, but I don't want to do that to you."

Did I take the easy out and avoid the angst-fest that'll be having a front-row seat to my ex-fiancée's wedding to my best friend? No. I insisted—*insisted*—on standing up for them. After all, I know better than anyone how much they deserve to be happy.

Masochism Exhibit B? Veronica is back and seems to feel a lot better, but she's been in a bitchy mood since the minute she walked through the door. But instead of letting her stew about whatever shit she's stepped in today, I've left my office door open and used every opportunity to figure out what's bugging her. *And I've failed.*

When closing time comes, I've pretty much given up on any grand plan to be the guy who breaks through that rough exterior, but I can't help but make one last effort and find myself heading to the reception area and leaning against the counter in front of her desk.

"How are you feeling?"

She finishes jotting something in her planner. "I said I'm fine. Nothing cold meds can't handle."

"You should still take it easy."

I get a hard glare for that piece of advice. "Yes, Mother."

"Why all the notebooks?" I ask, watching her close one only to open another to a page with a long, handwritten list.

She sighs dramatically. "Because they give me a false sense of control over my life."

I'm not sure why I'm out here. She obviously doesn't want to talk to me. *Masochist.*

Straightening, I turn back toward my office.

"What did you say to Landon on Monday?" she asks before I can get far.

I stop. "Who's Landon?"

"The guy you said could bench Crosley?"

"Oh." My scowl settles into place at the memory of the creep. "Nothing. I said I was a friend of yours."

"You're sure you didn't say anything else?"

"I asked why he was there. We really didn't talk for long."

And I don't need to get into the weird silent pissing match that happened between me and her roommate's dickhead boyfriend. Somehow, I don't think she'd appreciate that. "Why? Did he say something to you?"

She meets my gaze for a beat, and I can almost make out the vulnerability in her eyes, but then she looks away and it's gone. "No reason. It's nothing."

"You sure? Because if he's giving you trouble—"

"Nope. It's all good." She turns to shut down her computer. "Guess who canceled her sailing lessons with Amelia?"

I'm pretty sure she's changing the subject on purpose, but I let it slide. "Addison?"

"*Ding, ding, ding.* She said she'll reschedule once *one of the guys* has an opening. Does she think *sailing lessons* is a euphemism?"

I shake my head. "I don't know. Maybe?"

"She's an idiot." She sets her jaw. She's not even looking at me, but anger shines in her eyes. "She has *everything* and she'd throw it all away for a hot fuck."

"Wow. Tell me how you really feel."

She glances my way. "Don't get your panties in a twist. I'm judging Addison, not you."

"Her husband's an ass, V. I'm not saying I'm interested, but after seeing the way he talks to her, I don't find it shocking that she's looking for attention away from home."

"He'll fuck her over if she has an affair," she snaps. She shoves out of her chair and starts stacking her books, arranging her desk like she does at the end of every day. "I guarantee you that guy made her sign a prenup and he'll get out of paying alimony if she screws around. And then what's she going to do? Where's she going to live? Is she just gonna let him take the kids, and if not, what about *their* life? What about their needs? I bet she's never worked a day in their marriage."

I study her, trying to figure her out for the thousandth time since one hot night last summer changed everything between us. "I didn't realize you cared so much." In fact, I thought she hated Addison.

"I *don't* care. I'm offended on principle. I don't understand how someone with so much can be so reckless with their decisions."

But reckless or not, do those decisions really affect Veronica?

It's unlikely, but maybe there's an explanation for why she's so angry right now—one that has to do with the life I know so little about. I feel myself softening. I can't believe I spent all this time assuming she's a bitch for no reason and never bothered to think about her circumstances. "Is this about your roommate situation? Star told me you don't even use the living room when your roommate's home."

Veronica presses her lips into a thin line. "Star should keep her mouth shut. This isn't about me."

Bullshit. "If you say so." I wander toward the front door, throw the lock, and flip the sign in the window. When I turn back around, she's scowling. "You keep glaring at me like that and your face is gonna get stuck that way."

"It's called RBF and it's a serious, uncurable condition," she says, but her lips twitch.

"That's a medical myth." I step closer. "I just so happen to know an effective remedy. Happy to share if you're interested."

She slowly looks me over, her gaze snagging on my crotch. *Jesus Christ. She's fucking shameless, and I love it.* "Why do men always assume their dick's the cure for everything?"

I arch a brow and allow myself another step closer. "I didn't say anything about my dick, but I'm glad to know it's the first thing that came to mind for you."

She licks her lips and bites back a smile. "You're still bad for me."

One more step, and the softness of her breasts against me makes me groan. I lower my mouth to her ear. "That's because you haven't given me a chance to be good." I feel her breaths against my neck as they grow fast and shallow.

"How good can you be with ten minutes?" she asks.

She doesn't wait for an answer before grabbing me by the T-shirt, dragging me into my office, and kicking the door shut behind us.

Chapter Twelve

VERONICA

The second the door closes, Colton's mouth is on mine and his hands are fumbling with the zipper on the back of my dress. I like a man who takes a deadline seriously.

My dress drops to the floor, and he pulls back, nostrils flaring. It takes everything in me to stand tall and all my concentration to keep my hands from covering my stomach. I'm proud of this body in an existential sense—this is the body that grew Jacks, that works hard, that comforts my son when he's sad—but being proud of it in a moment like this? I can't help but wish it were a little better. No man has seen me naked since before I had Jacks, and I know my body isn't what it used to be. There's more softness in my tummy and stretch marks that stripe my skin and make it all wrinkly between my navel and panties.

"You're so fucking perfect," he says, and he sounds almost

angry about it. "Is it any wonder I can't get you out of my head?"

I love that. I don't want to care whether Colton McKinley thinks about me when we're not together, but hearing that he does lights my blood on fire. I grab him by the waistband and tug him back. Our mouths collide as I unbutton his pants and shove them down his hips until his cock springs free. I love that he's already hard. Love how he presses into my hand when I reach for him. Love the tiny grunts of pleasure he makes as I stroke him between our bodies.

"This what you need?" he asks, his fingers finding their way between my legs.

"Hurry. Please." I don't know if I'm rushing him because we're running out of time or because I've spent the entire day feeling like I'm hanging on by a string, and only here and now do I finally feel like I'm in control. Like I'm safe. For these minutes in Colton's office, I don't have to figure out where Jacks and I are going to live or pretend I have it all together. I don't have to be anything but me. Right here, right now, it doesn't matter that I'm a fuck-up, that I've made a mess of my life. I can be selfish. I can be a mess. Right here, I am enough.

"I don't want to be rushed." He growls into my neck, slipping his fingers into my panties. "Fuck, you feel good."

"Hurry," I say again. My thoughts are pressing against my shields, threatening to flood me and ruin this. "Please."

He spins me around until my palms are flat against the door and his chest is against my back. I arch into the hard length of him.

"It's coming, baby. I've got you."

Does he know how I need this? Does he understand why?

How could he when *I* don't really understand?

He kisses my neck and peels off my panties. The condom wrapper rustles, and over my shoulder I watch him roll on the protection.

He finishes then catches my gaze. There's too much tenderness in his eyes when he catches my chin between his forefinger and thumb and presses a hard kiss to my mouth. "We might not be alone. Can you be quiet?" he asks, even as he's grabbing my hips and stroking himself against my entrance.

"Yes," I say, and in the next breath, he's thrusting inside me. Filling me, stretching me. I push my hips back to meet him, and he's so deep I cry out, but he covers my mouth to dampen the sound.

He keeps a firm grip on my hips with one hand and drops the other from my mouth to cup my breast and tease my nipple through my bra. Then his hand's cupping me, sliding to explore where our bodies are joined before settling on my clit.

Oh God.

"Shh," he breathes against my ear, and I don't know if I said the words or screamed them or just moaned, but the pleasure is building so fast and intense that I buck against his hand, making him fuck me harder. Faster. And he's so deep and his cock keeps hitting me just right, and his fingers on my clit, and his mouth on my neck and shoulders . . .

It's so good. So fucking good I'm mindless with it. When I come, pulsing hard around his cock, I don't even care that I moan. The pleasure rolls on and on, and in this moment, that's the only thing that matters.

"Goddamn. Veronica." He says my name again. And again.

Like it's a prayer. Like it's a promise. My name. And I know without a doubt that this time, *I'm* the one he wants.

With a final thrust, he comes, burying his face in my neck as the orgasm tears through him, then we stand there together— him mostly clothed, me mostly nude, pressed against the door and shuddering through the aftershocks of pleasure.

COLTON

I'm not ready to watch her get dressed and walk away from me, but it's happening anyway.

"Someday, I'm gonna fuck you without you rushing off right after," I say, taking care of the condom and zipping up my jeans.

She laughs and gives me her back so I can zip her. "But you can't deny this is more efficient."

I slowly drag the zipper up, letting my fingers skim her back with every inch. "Just the adjective every guy wants to describe his lovemaking. *Efficient.*"

She turns and gives me a once-over. "Sorry. Did you need me to stroke your ego?"

Stepping closer, I wrap her hair around my fist and gently tug until she's looking up at me. "Don't tease me with promises to stroke things when you're about to walk away." I drop my mouth onto hers, and the next thing I know, I'm lost in kissing her again.

She presses her palm to my chest and pushes me away. "You're gonna make me late."

I back off, reluctant, but hell, at least she's smiling as she heads out of my office. *I did that.*

"See you in the morning," I call. "Don't be late."

"But I like pissing you off." Veronica tosses me one last sultry glance over her shoulder before heading out the door, and I don't even pretend I'm not watching. I track her through the window until I can't see her anymore.

"You're such a fucking hypocrite."

I spin around toward the sound of Wes's voice and find him glaring at me, his knuckles white as they clutch some kind of book. *Fuck.* How much of that did he just see? *And what did he hear?*

"What do you mean?" I sound guilty.

"I heard you warn her off me—heard you tell her I'm a fucking player—and then *you* swooped in. And what about you, Colt? Are you looking for the long game? Looking to put a ring on it? To play *daddy*?"

My jaw works, but I have no defense. I'm no player. Not anymore. And, hell, I don't know what this thing with Veronica is all about, but I don't have any illusions that she's looking to play house with a guy like me. Even if that idea is starting to hold some appeal.

"That's what I thought." Wes shakes his head and stares out the front window. "I'm *interested* in her. Like, for real."

"Why do you assume I'm *not* interested?" I shoot back. "Maybe I'm into her."

"Oh, I noticed you were *into* her about the time I realized you were fucking her in your office as if she's some sort of cheap secretary cliché."

My jaw clenches. "Back off, Wes. I'm not the guy I used to be. I care about her."

He huffs out a dry laugh. "Sure you do. So, I'm sure you know why she was upset today. Or what had her so down last week I dragged her out of here to cheer her up. I mean, *I* know, but if it's not just sex—if you care about her so fucking much—I'm sure you can tell me what she's going through."

A sick feeling settles in my stomach. Veronica hasn't told me shit, and he knows it. "None of this is your business."

"You made it your business when I was interested in pursuing her. Such a fucking hypocrite." He hurls a book across the room, and it smacks against the front window before falling to the floor. Then he turns on his heel and storms through the swinging door into the garage.

I screwed this up. There's no getting around it. But I let him go, and I pick up the book. *A Lot from a Little: Money-Saving Hacks That Will Change Your Life.*

Was Wes going to give this to Veronica? I glance toward the garage and then out toward the front lot, as if either he or Veronica will appear and explain. But I'm afraid I already know. Wes got this book for Veronica because she's confided more in him than she ever has in me.

I rub my chest and wish the ache away.

Chapter thirteen

VERONICA

I've lost count of the number of times I've had to swallow my pride and ask my sister to come to my rescue. It's not my favorite pastime, but we've been here so many times before, she can see it coming a mile away. I texted her to let her know we were coming over and that I needed to talk with her. I think she already knows what I'm going to ask.

When Jacks and I climb onto the porch Wednesday evening, she's standing in the doorway, disappointment on her face before I can even explain what happened. Suddenly, I feel like we're sixteen again. Me screwing up everything, Nic trying to fix it. A familiar angry defensiveness rears its head.

"Hey, buddy," she says, smiling at my son. "Lilly's in the living room. Why don't you head in and find her?"

"'Kay!" Jacks bounds into the house in search of his favorite cousin, and Nic watches him for a few beats before stepping onto the porch and closing the door behind herself.

"Did you lose your job?" she asks.

I flinch. It's so easy for her to assume the worst. "No. I still have a job, but June kicked us out." I wave toward the car, where my scant possessions are piled in the passenger seat and filling the hatchback. "I'll need some help getting the furniture, but June wanted us out right away, so . . ." I snap my jaw shut and look at my feet. I hate this. Hate feeling like a child in trouble. Hate knowing that Nic would never find herself in a position like this.

"What'd you do?"

"Nothing."

She huffs out a breath. "She kicked you out with no notice for no reason."

"I didn't say that."

She folds her arms and rests them on her rounded belly as she sets her jaw in a way I know matches mine. "I'm listening."

"You're judging. I haven't explained anything yet, and you've already decided this is all my fault."

She closes her eyes for a beat. "There's a pattern, Ronnie. You can't deny that."

Of course there is. This is me. I swallow, but the lump of pride in my throat refuses to go down. "I have never asked you to take me in. Not once. And if you don't want to do it now, Jacks and I can go stay at the motel down on I-45 until I can find a place."

She scoffs. "Can you even afford that?"

Not without missing another student loan payment, but if she doesn't want us here, I'll figure out something. "I wouldn't want to inconvenience you," I snap. *What ever happened to*

Ronnie and Nicky against the world?

Nic looks out toward the quiet street. "I can be willing to give you a place to stay for a while and still ask questions."

I swallow hard. I'm screwing this up. Just like I screw up everything. "June's boyfriend made a pass at me, and I turned him down. He must've taken offense, because he told June that I propositioned him. I suspected this could happen, but I'm not quite ready to give some asshole access to my body in exchange for an overpriced room." And just like that, the dam breaks and all my stubborn anger melts away into tears. I'm crying too much lately. Coming apart at the seams.

Nic drops her hands to her sides and steps toward me. "Ronnie." She wraps her arms around me and strokes my hair. "I'm sorry. I'm so sorry this happened. I don't ever want you to feel like I'd expect you to . . ." She sighs into my hair. "I'm just sorry. I want things to be easier for you."

I take three shaky breaths before stepping back. "I don't want to interrupt your life."

"You can sleep in the guest bedroom upstairs."

"Thank you. I'll start looking for a place to stay tomorrow." Another deep breath. Another stitch to pull myself together, to hide these ugly insides.

My sister worries her bottom lip between her teeth. "Can we talk about this? I know you don't make much money, but I don't understand why you struggle as much as you do. You work full-time, and I know you have side jobs too. Where's it all going?"

The worry and suspicion in her eyes would break my heart if I didn't have such a thick wall around it. "I have student loans," I say, and it's true. "And credit card debt." Also true. Just not the whole story.

"If you want, I could sit with you and make a budget," she says tentatively. "Maybe with some better planning—"

"Please spare me. You married a rich doctor and haven't had to work or pay your own bills in years. I don't think I need money management advice from you." Hurt passes over her face, and I immediately regret my words, but I don't take them back. I can't let her take a closer look at my finances. It'll only upset her. "I'm doing my best."

I can't sleep.

Jacks is out like a light on the crib mattress in the corner. Since he's stayed overnight here a few times, I know he'll be okay if he wakes up and I'm not in the room, so I roll out of bed and pad down to the kitchen for a glass of water.

When I hit the bottom of the stairs, I hear voices down the hall—from Ethan and Nic's room. I don't mean to listen, but I hear my name, and when I step into the kitchen, they grow louder.

"You're my wife, and you're seven months pregnant. Of course I worry about you."

"Letting Veronica stay here for a few days isn't going to add any stress to my life."

He scoffs. "I can't say your sister's *name* without adding stress to your life. You're going to lose your mind having her under the same roof. And do you really think it'll only be a few days? Do you forget who this is?"

My stomach cramps and I want to run away before I hear more, but my feet won't listen.

"We have the room, and I'd feel terrible turning her away."

"I'm just saying you have a lot on your plate with the contractors and Lilly and preparing for the baby. I don't want to see you taking on Veronica's problems too."

"But shouldn't I? Ethan, we have *so much*. We don't have debt, and we're building our dream home. We never have to worry about what happens if the car breaks down or we end up with an unexpected medical bill. Maybe it's time we shared our good fortune a little more."

"I'm not opposed to that, baby. I *know* we're lucky, but I don't want to give her money if it's only going to perpetuate these patterns—not when it means stressing you out and bringing you down. I seriously have to question why your sister doesn't have it together a little more than she does. She's driving a car we gave her, was living with a friend for the last year—"

"I think she paid her some rent."

"But still. Jacks' preschool is government subsidized, and I know Juliette helps her so she can get the part-time rate at the daycare. What's she spending all her money on?"

Nic whispers something I can't make out.

"I didn't say that," Ethan says. "I just know you, and I know your sister, and I don't like you feeling like it's your responsibility to fix everything."

I hang my head and turn back to the stairs, abandoning my quest for water. Why is it that the people who think they could do better living on a shoestring budget than everyone else are the ones who've never had to? I've made mistakes. It's true. But I'm paying for those with interest—literally. Hearing how Ethan feels about me *hurts*. I admire this family so damn much, but I'll never be one of them. I'm the screwup. The stray they'll let stay for a couple of days to appease their own consciences.

When I return to the bedroom, Jacks is making happy little sleep sounds, and my chest squeezes painfully with how desperately I love him.

I want better for him than what I have, and I'm going to work my ass off to get it.

COLTON

"I want it to be a surprise, so make sure everyone who's working on this can keep it a secret," Easton Connor tells me on the phone on Thursday.

Easton's a retired football player engaged to Shayleigh Jackson. He proposed at the hospital last November, the day Shayleigh gave birth to her little boy, and now he's planning a surprise engagement party. He's planning to take her out on the lake so the rest of the family can get everything ready for the party without her catching on. Since he has more money than God, he wants the whole enchilada—sunset cruise, dinner, champagne, private yacht. It's part of the high-end services we started offering when we bought the business two years ago, and one of the most lucrative parts of what we do.

"I'll make sure they know," I say, squeezing my temples and

trying to chase away the headache that's been building there all day.

Wes isn't talking to me, and I can't stop thinking about everything he said and insinuated last night. The truth is, I have no idea how to make Veronica open up to me. The only times we've ever gotten along for more than a few minutes, our hands and mouths have been involved. While I'd like her to confide in me the way she confides in Wes and Amelia, I can't assume that's what *she* wants.

I'm jotting down details about Easton's plans when Veronica saunters into my office with her notebook, her expression making it crystal-clear how she feels about finding me on the phone rather than ready to answer whatever questions she has.

My gaze instantly drifts to the hem of her dress and the skin exposed there, all the way down to the heels on her wedge sandals.

She grins at me, propping a hand on her hip, and kicks the door closed behind her.

"What do you think?" Easton asks, and I wince because I have no idea what he said.

"Sorry. You'll have to repeat that. One of my staff members just walked in." I narrow my eyes to make sure my message is clear: *This is a business call.*

Veronica's chuckle is low and sultry. I swear, she knows she frazzles me and fucking loves it.

"I'm thinking around five thirty? Could you do that?" Easton asks.

"Could you?" Veronica whispers in a breathy voice.

"Of course. I can make that work." I write five-three-oh on

the paper in front of me in case Veronica's mind-rattling presence makes me forget. How am I supposed to think straight when she's leaning on the door I fucked her against less than twenty-four hours ago? "Whatever you want. Just say the word."

"I'm so looking forward this. I just want it to be perfect."

"We'll do everything we can. We'll write a contingency plan in case it rains."

"Perfect. Can't wait."

Veronica's smirking when I hang up the phone. "Anything you want, man. Just say the word, man. I'm there for ya, bro," she mocks.

"I don't sound like that."

She chuckles again. "You sound *exactly* like that. You're like a little puppy when it comes to the Jacksons. Chasing them around, desperate to please them, to be one of them."

"First of all, that was Easton. He's not a Jackson."

She huffs. "Barely."

I push back from my desk and turn in my chair. "Second of all, you don't know what you're talking about."

"Actually, I do. I've lived this before. You're their foster brother."

I flash her a confused look. I know she doesn't know much about my past, but I thought she knew the basics.

She rolls her eyes. "Not *literally*. But they were your family when your family was no good."

My chest feels too tight at this way-too-accurate summation. How many times did I run over to the Jacksons' house when my dad was in one of his moods? How many times did I pretend Frank Jackson was my real dad because I hated mine so much? "I guess you could say that."

"Nic was just like you, you know. She'd do anything to make our new families like us. Clean the kitchen, put away the laundry—do whatever the other kids in the house demanded of her."

"That doesn't surprise me. She's good people."

"She was a *doormat*." Veronica clenches her fists. "You can't be like that. People will stomp all over you."

"This isn't just *people*." Why does she make me want to pull my freaking hair out? "It's the Jacksons, and you, of all people, should be grateful for them."

"I *am* grateful. But you can be grateful without being pathetic."

Fucking seriously? "You're doing it again."

"Doing what? I'm just saying it how I see it."

"You're trying to piss me off," I say. I don't say, *You're trying to push me away.* Because I'm not sure she even realizes she's let me close enough for that. Because I'm realizing she doesn't *want* me close enough for that, and that truth burns.

"I'm making an *observation*," she says.

I push out of my chair and walk around my desk, stalking toward her. "Why don't you tell me what's really going on?" I cup her face in my hand and stroke her cheek with my thumb. "We both know my friendship with Easton Connor isn't what's bothering you right now."

She drops her gaze to my mouth and sighs. "I don't want to get into it."

"Why not?"

She bites her lip as if she's not sure about what she's about to say. "Because that's not what this is."

"Then what is it?"

"It's casual. It's exactly what it needs to be." She slides her hand down my chest and over my abs until her fingertips fan across the waistband of my jeans, and arousal pumps through me. "No strings. No expectations. You can stop worrying. I'm not going to turn into that girl who expects you to transform into Prince Charming and ride to the rescue when things are rough. That's not who I am, and that's not who you are."

How can words that are meant to reassure me feel like a punch in the chest?

Maybe I should admit I want more. Or maybe I should just face the fact that she's right. I'll never be that guy. Maybe I've changed, but my past will never go away. If I want her, I'll have to take what I can get.

I slide my hand into her hair, making a mess of her ponytail, and lower my mouth to her ear as I cup her breast. At least Wes isn't here today, so I don't have to worry about him overhearing us again, but the truth is I don't just want her in this office. I want her in my bed. In my shower. Bent over my couch.

"I can do casual," I say, relishing the way she arches into my touch. "But I told you before, I won't share." Maybe this makes me a dick, but I need this at least. I need to know the little she's offering me is mine alone.

"That's not very enlightened of you."

"I can be enlightened or I can make you come." With one hand under her skirt, I cup her sex, feeling her slick heat through the cotton. "Your choice."

"You know what I want."

I kiss her hard, but my touch between her legs is whisper-light. Teasing. Promising. When I break away, her eyes are hazy. "I won't touch anyone else as long as we're doing this. I want that to go both ways."

"Already done." She tosses her notebook to the floor before fumbling for the button on my jeans. "I'm not sleeping around. It's just you."

"Good." I swat her hands away and drop to my knees, where I shove her skirt up around her waist and nuzzle my face between her legs. She threads her fingers through my hair, and when I look up at her, her eyes are closed. She's so beautiful. Even as I peel away her panties, even as I hook one knee over my shoulder and explore her with my tongue, I already want more.

Chapter Fourteen

VERONICA

There are certain words mothers use to cut each other down. Words men and childless people would probably see as harmless. Words struggling moms everywhere have to pretend don't cut them deep. And at the top of the list?

"I could never do that."

These words are used in reference to so many choices we make as mothers but usually the ones we're supposed to feel guilty for. Did you hear your child wake up crying from his nap and finish your shower, hoping he'd calm himself and go back to sleep? *"I could never do that."* Did you stick to a tight budget at Christmas, knowing the toys you could've overspent on will be donations within a year anyway? *"I could never do that."* Does your child spend nine hours at daycare every day so you can work? *"I could never do that."*

For three years, I've endured these subtle attacks from well-meaning mothers. Little cut after little, they sliced into my confidence as a mother and, together, they start to feel like one massive wound.

Today, standing in the middle of Ooh La La!, Kristi's the one holding the blade. I suppose it's my fault for explaining our weekly schedule when she asked about seeing him next Wednesday.

"I just couldn't," she says. "You must feel like you don't get any time with him."

I almost point out that she's not helping me get more time with Jackson by taking him for visitation, but I don't. I'm enough of a mess about letting her and Marcus walk away with Jacks. The last thing I need is him seeing me argue with them.

Luckily, Marcus comes to the rescue before I have to force out a polite response. "Do you want us to bring him to your place tonight or meet you here?"

I haven't told Marcus and Kristi that I've been kicked out or that I'm living with my sister. If I have my way, I never will. *I can fix this. I just need time.* "I'm going to be hanging out doing some work today, so just bring him here."

"We'll have him back by three," Marcus says, smiling at Jacks, who's in his own little world pretending his fork is a spaceship.

Kristi frowns. "Why three? We could go to dinner after we're done at the beach."

Marcus shoots her a look. "We said we'd ease in, remember?"

Her eyes get all teary. "I know. It's just hard when we don't get to see him for another week."

It's all I can do to stomp down my irritation. I know my kid's amazing, but she doesn't even know him yet.

155

Be glad Jackson has more people who love him. Definitely don't punch her in the face.

"It'll be okay." Marcus squeezes her shoulder before turning to Jacks. "Ready to go to the beach, buddy?"

Jacks beams, then looks at me. "Build sandcastle?"

"I'm staying here with Aunt Star," I tell him. "But I bet your daddy will build a sandcastle with you."

The little furrow in his brow tells me he's thinking about this, but Marcus must've made a good impression last weekend, because Jackson stands on his bench and opens his arms so Marcus can pick him up.

"Call if you need anything at all," I say as they head toward the door. I feel the fissures spread through me—the glass before it shatters. "Bye, baby."

"Bye-bye, Mama," Jacks calls, waving at me over Marcus's shoulder.

My eyes burn with tears, but I hold them back, waving goodbye until Jacks is out of sight.

"Come on, V," Star says, appearing at my side. She squeezes my shoulder. "Let's get you upstairs so you can have a good cry. Then we'll go put your furniture in storage and check out those apartments."

"I'm gonna have to beg Nic to let me stay with her until I get a real job, aren't I?" I groan as I collapse into Star's couch three hours later. The apartment hunt is a bust. Barely anything's available, and if the choices I saw today are any indication, Jacks and I would probably be better off mooching off Nic and Ethan for a while. But *God*, that sucks.

"First of all, you have a real job," she says. "No one who works as hard as you do should feel like their work doesn't count."

I grab her hand and squeeze it. "You're my favorite."

"Thank you, and it's true. Secondly, you need to start taking child support from Marcus."

I grimace. "It feels so dirty. 'Here, have some time with my kid in exchange for some cash.'"

"That's not why you're doing it and you know it." She sighs. "You need this money, V. Anyone in your position would."

"You manage without it," I argue.

She shakes her head. "I didn't have a choice. You do. Just take it."

I nod. "It would certainly help, though I doubt it will make a decent apartment suddenly become available."

"You know you and Jacks can crash here for a while if you need to."

I arch a brow at her. As much as I love her cozy two-bedroom unit over the bakery, there's not enough room for four of us to live here without being all over each other. "Yeah, right. I can't take over your living room."

"I could sleep out here for a couple of weeks, and you and Jacks could have the bedroom."

I frown. "Thank you for the offer, but I'm not taking your room away from you." I pull my phone from my purse, checking the clock for the fifth time in the last thirty minutes.

"One more hour," Star says. "Hang in there."

Kristi sent me a picture of Marcus and Jacks playing in the sand about an hour ago, and I was so grateful to see evidence that the day was going well, but now I'm ready for them to bring him back to me.

"I hate this," I mutter, dropping my phone in my lap and leaning back and staring at the ceiling.

"I know."

"And I hate that I hate it."

"I know." She frowns and strokes my hair. I've always loved this about Star—how she can just let me be sad or upset and not feel compelled to jump right in to fix-it mode. "When do they see him again?"

I swallow. Every time I think about our visitation schedule, I'm filled with dread. "They want to see him next Sunday, and I'm trying to stay cool about it."

Because she's my best friend, she puts it together fast. "You don't even get to spend his birthday with him? Who do they think they are?"

"I know. It's crappy, but I planned his party for Saturday, and since I'm *really* not ready for them to be a part of that, Sunday's my only choice." I blow out a breath. "But once he starts doing overnights with them, it'll only be every other weekend."

"Will that be better or worse?"

I take a deep breath, doing my best to overwrite the dread. "I can't decide. Less frequent, but *overnight*?" I shudder. "You may have to sedate me."

"Get you drunk? Bitch, do you doubt me?"

I laugh. "I don't want to talk about this anymore. Tell me about your guy. He still around?"

She grins. "Yeah. He's around."

"And . . ."

She shrugs, but she can't stop smiling. "And I like him."

"That's it? You're not going to give me a name or an occupation? Nothing?"

"Sorry." Her grin tells me she's not sorry, but before I can dig for more, my phone buzzes, and I comically scramble to pick it up, desperate for another proof-of-life text from Kristi.

It's a text with a picture, but not from either of the people who are currently caring for my son.

> Colton: Look what I found while I was cleaning out my storage unit today.

The picture shows two action figures—Spider-Man and Venom—next to each other in Colton's big palm.

I type out a quick response.

> Veronica: I knew you were a closet nerd.

Next to me, Star clears her throat loudly. "I've gotta be real with you. If you'd told me Colton McKinley was sending you pictures of his *toys*, I would've pictured something way hotter."

I giggle-snort and tap my shoulder against hers. "Dirty."

"Do you want to explain?"

"Explain why Colton is sending me pictures of Spider-Man toys? You really have to ask when you're the woman who left my Spider-Man-obsessed son in his care when I was sleeping?"

She turn up her palms. "I had to go."

"You could've woken me up."

The corner of her mouth twitches. "Yeah, but he was acting like an awkward teenager coming to visit his crush, and I wanted to draw that goodness out for as long as possible."

I roll my eyes. "He was not."

"Oh, yes he was. Colton's hot, but until Monday night, I had no idea he could be adorable too."

I glance at my phone again, at the picture of the toys that mean he was thinking about my kid, and remember the little fist bump he gave Jacks. My chest feels warm and too full. "Yeah, he can be kind of cute."

Star squeals. "I knew it. Was he like this when you two hooked up, or was he all hot alpha, pulling out the seduction tricks?"

"The first time, it was my idea."

Star's spine goes ramrod straight, and I realize what I said as she points an accusatory finger at me. "You said the *first time* it happened. When was the *last* time?"

I hold a hand over my eyes, part my fingers, and mumble, "Yesterday."

She literally bounces in her seat. "*Yesterday?*"

"And the day before that."

"Yeah, you did!"

I drop my hand so I can glare. "Why are you like this?"

"I'm happy for you. That's all." She rubs her hands together. "And did he call you by someone else's name this time?"

"Jesus. No. I would've kicked him in the balls."

"But you didn't. You played with them instead, am I right?"

"I hate you."

"You love me. What happened? What made you go from *he's such a dick* to *I want his dick*?"

"I'd gone too long without an orgasm, and it caused me to make bad decisions." I bite back a smile and add, "Repeatedly."

She *howls*. "Oh my God, I knew this was coming."

"You did not."

"Well, maybe I *hoped*. And listen to you, blaming it on orgasm deprivation when you two have always had sizzling chemistry."

I narrow my eyes. "When we're *starving*, we lower our standards about what we're willing to eat. For example, I hate buffets, but if I haven't eaten for a week, I'll line up to eat some of that hovered-over grub and conveniently forget I might as well be licking a petri dish of bacteria."

She presses her lips together, but her chest shakes with laughter. "You poor baby," she finally says. "And how was the buffet? It must've been awful if you went back *repeatedly.*"

I slouch then rest my head on the back of the couch. "It was so good. Steak dinner with fine wine. The perfectly tender filet and then dessert when you don't expect either."

Star doesn't even try to contain her laughter this time. The bitch full-out belly laughs. It's the most fun I've had all week.

Chapter Fifteen

VERONICA

This is the first time I've done a big party of any sort for Jackson's birthday. We got together at Nic's for his first and second birthday, but parties at that age are more for the parents than they are for the kids. I knew he wouldn't remember it anyway, so I didn't let myself spend the money.

This year is different. This year, he has friends from his new preschool and ideas about what "birthday" means. Six months ago, I rented the coveted playground-adjacent shelter at the Jackson Harbor city park. The plan was to have pizza and cake and let him play with his cousins and friends. Up until a couple of weeks ago, I was so excited about this party. Up until a couple of weeks ago, I was sure he'd have an amazing time. But then we went to his friend Cooper's party, and Spider-Man made an appearance. Since then, Jackson's obsession with seeing "the real-life Pider-Man" hasn't wavered.

I've been honest with my kid—or as honest as you can be with a three-year-old who believes Spider-Man is real. He knows Spider-Man isn't coming today, but I still feel like I'm disappointing him.

"Girl, quit stressing," Star says. She's taping plastic tablecloths on the picnic tables in the shelter. "We might not have an actual Spider-Man appearance planned, but we have the *coolest* Spidey decorations in town, and the balloons are awesome. Jacks is gonna love it."

I blow out a breath. "I know. I just can't help but want to give him everything, even though I know not having it all will be good for him in the long run."

"You're a responsible mama making responsible decisions. Would you rather hire Spider-Man or be three hundred dollars closer to getting your own place?"

I force a smile. I wish this sacrifice meant I was closer to us getting our own place. Instead, it just means three hundred dollars of credit card debt I won't have to juggle on top of everything else next month. "I'm over it. Almost, at least."

"Atta girl," Star says. Reason number 53,273 that I love my best friend: she understands why I don't want to ask my sister for money, and she never pushes me to take help when it's offered. Star understands what it's like to desperately want to make it on your own. "Oh, God, I remember when Katie was six. She was invited to this little girl's birthday party, and we didn't realize the party had a theme. This little girl had a cake designed to look like a Tiffany box with pearls spilling out of it, and she and all her little friends were dressed in fancy blue dresses, except not my

Katie, because we'd missed the memo."

"God, that's the worst," I mutter, tying balloons to a pole.

"Yeah. But get this—when I asked the little shit if blue was her favorite color, you know what she said to me?"

"What?"

Star flips her red curls over her shoulder in an obvious impression of a prissy child and says, *"Um, Tiffany blue, duh!* Like she was insulted I didn't understand it wasn't just any blue but *Tiffany blue.*"

"Dear Lord. Maybe our kids are better off because we're poor."

Star unfolds another plastic tablecloth and nods. "With any luck, they won't grow up to be entitled assholes."

"That's all a mom can hope for," I say, laughing.

"Birthday boy, incoming!" someone calls.

I turn toward the parking space right in front of us, where my sister and her family are climbing out of their SUV. Ethan and Lilly take in the scene while Nic opens the back door to unbuckle Jackson.

Jackson climbs out, and his eyes go big at the sight of the decorated pavilion. "Whoa!" he shouts, then he rushes toward us. "Pider-Man everywhere!"

Warmth fills my chest. "You like it, buddy?"

He nods enthusiastically and turns in a slow circle between the tables. And *hell,* I understand why people with money give their kids so much. I can't imagine resisting the impulse to go bigger and better if I had the means.

Nic waddles toward us, her hand on her belly. "Need any help?"

"You helped by keeping Jacks while we decorated. Everything's ready." I look at my watch. "The pizza will be delivered any minute, and the guests should start to arrive shortly after that."

"Pizza sounds *amazing*," she says, rubbing her stomach.

"You had leftover pizza for breakfast," Lilly says, following her.

"Like I said," Nic says, "it sounds amazing."

"I don't think she's having a baby," Lilly tells me. "She's having a pizza."

Everyone laughs, and Nic blushes.

"That's all she ever wants to eat," my niece continues, smiling, "and they say you are what you eat, so that baby's gotta be at least ninety-percent pizza by now."

"Leave Mom alone," Ethan says, ruffling Lilly's dark hair.

My heart feels so full at those words and the reminder that while I might always feel like I'm on the outside of the Jackson family, Nic has become one of them. Even her stepdaughter is her daughter now.

Is that how it'll be for Jackson and Kristi? Will she just be Mom *someday?*

I shove the thought down. Everything is going smoothly with Kristi and Marcus. I need to reroute my thoughts from the doom and gloom they keep wanting to jump to. Jacks seemed to have fun on Saturday and is looking forward to seeing them again. On Monday morning, I gathered all my courage and texted Marcus to tell him I was ready to have a conversation about child support. We're going to talk when I bring Jacks to their house tomorrow, but today I want to focus on my son. Not on visitation schedules or child support or where we might live. Just Jacks and his birthday party and the fact that we have so many people to celebrate with.

Soon enough, the pizza arrives, and the guests a few minutes after. Ava and Jake bring little Lauren, Brayden and Molly come with seven-year-old Noah in tow, and even Shay and Easton show up with the new baby. Star's daughter, Katie, surprises me by walking over from their place in town, and a couple of Jackson's favorite friends from school come with their moms.

Life is good.

The big kids help get the littler ones settled and pass out plates and juice boxes while Star and I distribute the pizza, breadsticks, and apple slices. I'm so busy that I only wonder a couple of times whether Colton will show. So busy that I almost don't notice when the kids are running off to play on the playground and he's still not there. *Almost.*

Despite him sneaking a few kisses this week and being sweeter than usual, there was no frantic office fucking—unless you count Wednesday night. He was working out in the garage, I went out there to give him a message before I left, and he pushed me into a dark corner, kissed me until I was breathless, and used his hand between my legs until I had to bite his shoulder to keep from screaming. I tried to return the favor when he pointed to the time, reminded me I needed to pick up Jackson, and smacked my ass on the way out the door.

I suspect that Wednesday's fun might've had something to do with the fact that Wes was hosting a full-day expedition, but it's not like either of us had time for more than that anyway. We've been swamped and short-handed, and Colton's been out of the office most of the day running ATV tours and helping on the boats.

"What's that look for?" Star asks between bites of cheese pizza. We're trying to eat while the kids are distracted. Any minute now, they'll remember we have cake and come rushing back.

"What look?"

"That sad puppy face." She glances around the pavilion and the barely touched food on all the kids' plates. "This is a sign of a successful party, girl. Stop stressing."

"I'm not stressing." Not at all. Why *should* Colton come? It's not like we're close. We're fuck buddies. That's it. Sure, Jackson would love to see him, but while bonding over Spider-Man might mean everything to Jacks, Colton was just killing time until he could pass him off to me.

"Sure you're not. You carry stress in your face."

"RBF strikes again."

She laughs then her jaw goes slack. "Was that you?" she asks, nodding toward the parking lot.

I turn to see a big man dressed in a . . .

"That's Spider-Man," Katie says, arching a brow.

It *is* Spider-Man. He gives us a wave and strolls past the pavilion to the playground.

Nic leans toward me and whispers, "Who's the hottie in the costume?"

I shake my head, still trying to process what I'm seeing. "I didn't reserve anyone."

Lilly grins. "I bet it's Uncle Jake."

Ava shakes her head. "No, honey. Uncle Jake is at the swings with Lauren."

"Levi?" Nic asks.

"He and Ellie are at an art show in Chicago today," Ava says.

167

We scan each other's faces, but all the Jacksons are accounted for. Did someone find another Spider-Man and book him for the party after all? Maybe Jacks told Kristi this was what he wanted and she made the arrangements? Somehow, I'm having trouble imagining her doing that when she isn't here to take the credit, but maybe I've underestimated her.

All the adults leave their pizza behind in the shelter and follow Spidey to the playground. For one, stranger danger, but also because whoever this guy is, there's not a soul here who'd be willing to miss Jackson's reaction.

Jackson's eyes lock on the masked stranger. "*Pider-Man!*" he shouts. And *ohmygod, my heart.* My little guy looks so freaking happy. His big brown eyes are wide in wonder, and I've never seen his smile stretch so big across his face.

"I've got the pictures," Star says next to me, already putting her phone camera to work. And this is why everyone needs a best friend like her.

"Thank you," I say without taking my eyes off Jacks.

Spider-Man stoops to his haunches and offer Jacks his fist. Jacks taps his hero's knuckles with his own, and that's when I realize what should've been obvious the moment I noticed Colton hadn't shown up for the party. "Oh, shit," I breathe.

"What?" Star asks, her attention on her phone and capturing Jacks as he drags Spider-Man by the hand around the playground. If I hadn't already figured it out, I would know after seeing the way he walks. I've never met a man who has a walk as cocky as Colton's.

"I think I've got a thing for Peter Parker," I whisper, because my freaking heart is doing some gymnastics in my chest. Damn,

I'm in trouble.

She chuckles. "I thought that might be him." She pulls her attention off picture duty for a beat to study my face. "You catching feelings, V?"

"He found a Spider-Man costume and surprised my son for his birthday. What do you think?" There's an edge of panic to my voice.

"Not just the swoony gesture," Star says. "He makes the outfit look *good*."

"For real," Shay says, coming to stand beside me with her baby cradled in her arms. "I had no idea anyone could look that hot in spandex."

"It's the muscles," Star says. Spider-Man lifts Jacks up in the air, and Star does an eyebrow waggle and motions toward her crotch. "And *that*. Mazel tov, girl."

"You're into the superhero thing?" Easton asks Shay, scooping the baby from his fiancée's arms. "Because that can be arranged." He dips his head down and whispers something in her ear that makes her blush.

Within a few minutes, all the other adults have lost interest, and it's just me and Star standing in the middle of the playground while Jacks lives his best life with Spider-Man in tow and his friends following along like he's the best thing since fruit snacks.

"You need to take a deep breath," Star says. "You look like a starving woman waiting for her steak dinner, *if you know what I'm saying*."

I bite back a smile. "Shut it."

"Girl, the pheromones are rolling off you. I'm afraid what the contact high might do to the animals in this park. Think of the children."

I laugh. "I can't help it. I didn't get any"—I look around to make sure no one is listening—"*steak* this week."

She drops her phone to her side and gapes at me. "For real? The hot and heavy cooled off that fast?"

"We've been busy."

She turns to where Spider-Man is teaching Jacks and Noah some defensive maneuvers in the grassy area beside the playground. Spider-Man does a surprisingly graceful somersault and jumps immediately to his feet. I can't decide if I'm turned on or falling, and the second option is terrifying. "Obviously, you can't let that stand."

"I can't exactly complain that my kind-of-boss-slash-fuck-buddy isn't ravishing me frequently enough for my tastes."

"There's not an HR form for that?"

"Not last I checked."

Star chuckles and nudges me with her shoulder before returning to her picture-taking duties.

And me? I just soak it all in.

COLTON

Today was risky. I debated talking it over with Veronica before I rented the Spider-Man costume, but if the last two months of working with her have taught me anything, it's that she doesn't like to take help from me—from anyone—so this was definitely an "ask forgiveness, not permission" situation.

As ridiculous as I felt when I first put on this costume, it was super fun. And even if it had been miserable, the look on Jackson's face would've made it worth it.

As for Veronica? I'm not sure if she knows who the man under this mask is, but she's been grinning so damn much that I hope she at least *suspects* it's me.

When she calls all the kids back for cake and ice cream, I tell Jacks I have to leave, and he gives me a massive hug. "Best day ever," he says before running toward his mom. I only let myself watch him for a beat before I head to the parking lot on the other side of the park, where I left my truck.

"Spider-Man?" Veronica calls, running after me.

I stop, and when she catches up, she grabs me by the wrist and yanks me behind a tree. "Everything okay?" I ask.

She takes my mask and peels it up halfway so only my lips and nose are exposed. "Thank you," she whispers, and then she kisses me.

This isn't an angry kiss or a fuck-me-now kiss or a make-me-forget-everything-but-pleasure kiss. This is the kiss of a woman who's finally starting to like me. And the best part? When she breaks the kiss, she's grinning. I would do backflips to make her smile like that every day.

"Thank you," she says again, sliding my mask back into place.

"Best day ever," I say, echoing Jackson's words.

Chapter Sixteen

COLTON

When I visit Mike Sunday morning, he's in the best mood I've seen him in since I picked him up from a night in the drunk tank, but most importantly, he's sober and planning to stay that way. Seeing him like this is an eye-opener. He's alone and struggling. Apparently this all started with a new girlfriend who's a drinker. One of those "one drink won't hurt" types. But that's the thing about alcoholics. In meetings, we say, "One drink is too many, and a thousand is never enough," but most people don't really understand. His girlfriend sure didn't, and when he made it clear he couldn't play the "just one drink" game with her again, she left him.

I can't imagine sobering up all alone a block and a half away from a liquor store that would happily take my money and give zero shits about the consequences. Both times I sobered up, I did it in rehab with a huge support network. This last time, I thought I was alone, that I'd lost it all, but I wasn't really. The Jacksons all rallied around me. Even Ellie was there to support me, despite the fact that it was my father's mistakes that almost got her killed. They all wanted me sober. I had it better than I ever realized.

I keep my visit short and show myself out, but when I'm closing his apartment door behind me, I'm surprised to see Veronica standing at the door across the hall, Jackson on her hip.

"Co-tin!" Jackson says, smiling at me.

"Hey, it's the birthday boy!"

Veronica spins around, her eyes wide like she's been caught doing something she shouldn't.

I look around, trying to figure out what could've brought her to this part of town. "What are you doing here?"

"I'm supposed to meet the landlord to look at this apartment."

There aren't really bad neighborhoods in Jackson Harbor, but there are some buildings on the edge of town where the less fortunate rent. Thanks to all the summer homes in the area, Jackson Harbor is an expensive place to live. A lot of my own employees commute in for work from Lincoln Grove, a less expensive area about twenty-five minutes away. Those who want to stay close and not blow their entire check on rent are forced to live in places like this, where landlords don't do shit to keep up the properties and are still able to charge outrageous rates for undesirable living conditions. I would hate the idea of Veronica living here regardless, but I hate the idea of her living here alone with a kid even more. "Why?"

She sets her jaw. "Because we need a place."

Jacks turns shy. He buries his smile in his mom's shoulder

while still peeking at me out of the corner of his eye.

"Who's that on your shirt?" I ask him, spotting the telltale webbing across the back.

"Pi-Man," Jacks whispers.

"I love it," I say. "I want one just like it."

"Can you say *thank you*, Jacks?" Veronica asks, and I almost stumble back. Does she have any idea how much her face lights up when she looks at her son? I've always thought she was pretty, but seeing the way she looks at her kid is enough to knock me over.

Jackson straightens and looks at his mom, then at me. "Thank you." Then he buries his face in her shoulder again.

"Listen . . ." I look around to make sure the landlord hasn't appeared while I was distracted by the beautiful woman in front of me. "This isn't a very nice place to live."

Her smile is tight. "There aren't a lot of affordable options in Jackson Harbor, so I can't exactly be choosy."

"What's wrong with the place you're staying now?"

She looks away from me. "I got kicked out."

My hackles go up. I've never met her roommate, but the little I know about her tells me this situation was screwed up from the start. And now she's kicked V out? "What for?"

She huffs and adjusts Jackson on her hip. "Looks like he made it," she says, nodding to the shaggy-haired guy coming up the stairs at the end of the hall. "Not that this game of Twenty Questions isn't super fun."

I glance toward the guy strolling toward us and my gut pinches. Maybe he's just a greedy bastard when it comes to his tenants and otherwise a trustworthy human, but I don't want to leave Veronica alone with him. "Just let me do the walk-through with you," I say softly. "To make sure this guy doesn't try to take advantage."

She hesitates. The guy is closer now, so she can't exactly argue without making things awkward. But this is Veronica, and I can count on one hand the number of times she's passed up an opportunity to argue with me, so I'm surprised when she gives me a sharp nod before turning to the guy. "Are you Ken?"

"Yup. Ms. Maddox?"

"That's me."

He looks back and forth between me and Veronica. "Thought it was just you and your kid who'd be moving in?"

"For now," she says sweetly. "But my boyfriend wanted to check the place out with us. In case he moves in when his lease is up."

Ken frowns at me. "You look familiar."

I give him a wide, toothy grin and point a thumb behind me to Mike's apartment door. "I'm Mike's buddy. I'm the one who called about getting the shower fixed." And called and called again. I threatened to bring my lawyer into it before Ken finally got off his ass and gave my friend a place to bathe.

He narrows his eyes. "Yeah, I remember you now."

With that look, I know Veronica isn't going to get this apartment. This guy already has one tenant he can't fuck over because of me. He's probably not looking to add another.

I should feel bad about that—Veronica wouldn't be here if she didn't want to potentially sign a lease—but I can't bring myself to muster up even a little smidge of regret. There's no freaking way I'd be comfortable with her and Jacks living in this building.

Nevertheless, the guy unlocks the door and pushes inside, going through the motions. The place doesn't look so bad at first glance. It's been freshly painted. The smell of bleach still hangs in the air, and though the thin carpet has seen better days, it's clearly been shampooed recently.

Jacks buries his nose in his mom's shirt. "Smell bad," he whispers.

Veronica pats his back and shushes him. "Does the building have any security?" she asks Ken.

He grunts. "Yeah. Lock on the door and a chain above it if you got reason to be nervous about that stuff. This ain't the Ritz. We don't have a guard at the entrance or anything."

Veronica's eye twitches.

"I think she's asking about general surveillance for the complex," I say, then frown as I look around. This living space is twice the size of Mike's, but where is the bedroom? "Is this a studio?" I'd think she'd at least want a one-bedroom with a toddler, and a two-bedroom would be even better.

"Jacks and I don't need much," she says, dodging my gaze. Her posture says it all: this is all she can afford. A studio apartment in a run-down building.

Hell, we don't pay her a fortune, but we pay decent. She can do better than this.

I remember that book Wes threw at me the other day. Something about living on a tight budget. Obviously, Veronica's struggling.

I glance at the bored-looking landlord and remind myself it doesn't matter. She's not going to get this place anyway. But what if I hadn't run into her? And if she doesn't end up here, is she going to live somewhere worse? I'm not sure there is worse in Jackson Harbor, but if she decides to consider options in Lincoln Grove, this place starts to look nice. *Shit.*

Veronica strolls slowly through the apartment, opening drawers in the kitchen (one gets stuck a quarter inch opened, and another won't close completely), turning on and off the faucet (it drips), testing the lock on the window (it's flimsy). She doesn't bother going into the bathroom, and I'm hoping it's because she's already decided it's worth spending more on rent to live somewhere that's a little better cared for.

She doesn't say much as we leave, and I stay by her side all the way out to the parking lot in case Ken is watching. When we get to her car, she finally meets my gaze. Her eyes are tired. Her posture defeated. "That was the most depressing thing I've seen in a while," she says with a sigh. "I think I'd conveniently repressed memories from my last apartment hunt and forgotten why we ended up moving in with June to begin with."

I grimace, glancing toward the building. "Jackson Harbor real estate is brutal, but can't you—"

"Don't." She holds up a hand and shakes her head. "Okay? Don't ask why I can't afford a nicer place. I have student loans and more credit card debt than God ever intended, and those bills aren't going anywhere, so I don't want to have to explain all the bad decisions that got me here."

I blow out a breath. "Okay. I get it." *But I want to help. I want you to confide in me.*

She flashes me a weak smile and opens the back door. I'd like to say I'm a good enough man that when she leans over to put Jacks in his car seat I don't stare at her ass, but then I'd just be a liar too. I'm pretty sure those jean shorts—or at least the thighs in them—came straight from my dreams.

When she straightens and turns back to me, I see a flash of that vulnerable woman who confided in me at the lake. I kiss her before she can hide behind a smirk or a smart remark. It's not a long kiss or an exceptionally deep one, but it's firm and strong. It's a kiss that wants more.

"What was that for?" she asks.

I shrug. "You looked sad, and I . . ." *I wanted to be the one to make it better.* "I wanted to."

She glances at Jacks, who's studying the book she gave him, then back at me. "We should go."

"Let me take you to breakfast," I blurt. "Or lunch, or . . ." I'm a mess. "I'd like to hang with you and Jacks today."

She swallows. "I wish we could, but we have plans out of town."

What are they? Where are you going? What happened with your roommate? But hell, *I wish we could* is progress. "Okay. Drive safely and text when you get home."

For whatever reason, this earns me a smile. "Seriously?"

"Yeah. I worry." I shrug.

"You surprise me." She nods. "Okay. I'll text, then."

I press another quick kiss to her lips and make myself back away. "I wouldn't object to pics, either."

She gapes. "Oh my God, you didn't just say that."

"I wouldn't want to be completely unpredictable." I wink at her and go to my car. I don't think I've ever been this happy that a woman has agreed to text me.

VERONICA

Veronica: We're home.
Colton: Good to know. I was about to send out a
search party.

In the dark in my sister's guest bedroom, I stare at the winkie face at the end of Colton's text and my chest fills with warmth. In some ways, it's hard to believe this is the same guy who would growl at me when I was late for work. In other ways, I think I knew this side of Colton was there the whole time.

Veronica: Sorry I didn't text sooner. We got stuck in
traffic and home later than I expected, so I had to rush
right to bath and bedtime.
Colton: Did you have a good day?

I roll to my side and study Jacks. Kristi and Marcus ran him around so much that he was out as soon as his head hit the pillow. It's bittersweet, knowing how much fun he has with them. I couldn't do this if he didn't love it, but it's hard to give part of his childhood to people who've been absent up until now.

Veronica: My day was okay. You?
Colton: Don't reveal too much there, V. I'll write an
exposé with all the sordid details of your life.

I grin down at my phone. He has no idea how much I'm fighting the instinct to share *everything*, to turn this casual fling into something deeper. I'm not sure what scares me more— letting him see me or knowing he might not want that.

> *Veronica: See, I'm just trying to protect you from the worst.*
> *Colton: One detail from your day. Just give me one. I'll start—I planned Levi's bachelor party.*
> *Veronica: Let me guess. Strippers? Booze?*

I wince as soon as I send the text. Colton doesn't drink, and I didn't mean to suggest he'd fall off the wagon during Levi's party.

> *Colton: We're taking the Sunseeker out for the day. Fishing (and yeah, I'm sure drinking for most of the other guys) and then docking in Traverse City, hitting dinner and the dance club there, and coming back the next day.*
> *Veronica: Wow! That sounds amazing. I wonder what Ava has planned for us. Probably something incredibly classy.*
> *Colton: Don't change the subject. Your turn.*

I don't know if there's a single detail I could share that wouldn't raise a whole bunch of other questions about Marcus and the custody situation. If we were in person, I might open that can of worms, but it's too much for some silly text messages. *Casual. Keep it casual.*

But what can I say? My day turned out okay, but it was stressful as hell. In theory, I should be *less* stressed. Marcus and Kristi plan to give me child support, and the number they tossed out would be truly life-altering, but then Kristi started in on Jackson's speech and how they're going to search for a good speech therapist for him. *"I have a friend who's an SLP, and she agrees he's delayed and needs professional intervention."* She wasn't telling me anything I didn't know.

Jacks has a speech therapist through the Early On program—or he did, but he aged out when he turned three. Twice a week for the last six months, the therapist came to his daycare to work with him. When she wrote up his progress report, she suggested I get him reevaluated at the beginning of next school year, but said she was really happy with the progress he made with her and thought he'd catch up on his own.

Having Kristi talk to me about my son's speech like I'm an oblivious parent burned. I tried to stay calm while I explained there isn't an exact metrics for kids' speech. I told her about the therapy he's had and the suggestions of the therapist, but my frustration must've been apparent in my tone, because Marcus and Kristi gave each other a long look.

Marcus sighed and said, "We're just trying to help," and Kristi said, "This will all be easier and better for Jacks if you stop thinking of us as the enemy."

If that conversation wasn't bad enough, there was the absolute deluge of gifts Marcus and Kristi gave him. He was so freaking excited to show them all to me when I got back to the house to pick him up. They must've bought every age-appropriate toy on the shelf. His bedroom was bursting at the seams with superhero toys and plushies, a new tiny desk, a chalkboard with colorful chalk, and so much more *stuff* I couldn't process. Meanwhile, he gets a single two-foot tote when he's with me that holds all his toys.

One thing from my day? I'm on the verge of being able to afford a decent apartment for the first time in my life, and, ironically, simultaneously being thrown into a crisis of faith in my ability to provide for my child.

But I'll have to save that little meltdown to share with Star, because I'm pretty sure it would make Colton run screaming. Or it should.

> Colton: *Just one thing, V.*
> Veronica: *How about the color of my underwear?*
> Colton: *Nope. That's something I like to see for myself, not be told about. You can do this. One thing.*

I smile as I realize something I can share.

> Veronica: *Jacks and I got stuck in traffic—like, dead stop, cars in park, people getting out and chatting while they waited. He needed to pee, and he was so worried about having an accident, so I taught him he could pee in an old water bottle. He couldn't stop giggling. It was pretty much the cutest thing ever.*

I nearly laugh just remembering it. It was such a silly little moment, but it was exactly what I needed. Maybe he spent his day making memories with his other family, but he can still giggle with Mama.

Colton: Big weekend. Birthday party, Spider-Man, and learning to pee in a bottle.

Veronica: No kidding. Thank you again for the Spider-Man magic, BTW.

Colton: You're welcome. It was pretty freaking awesome.

Veronica: Well, I owe you. Pick your poison—French maid costume? Naughty teacher? Catwoman?

Colton: BRB. You just made my brain explode. (Can I choose all of the above?)

Veronica: I'm having trouble picturing Catwoman teaching in a French maid costume, but I'm sure we can figure out something.

Colton: I'll think on it and let you know. Anyway, you have enough going on right now with looking for a new place. What happened there? Have you had enough of hiding out in your bedroom at June's?

How dumb is it that I don't want to explain because I don't want Colton to know what a mess I am? I *like* his attention. I like him looking at me like more than a coworker he can't stand but wants to fuck. This morning he said he wanted to hang with me and Jacks, and I about melted right there. Other than Marcus, there's no one else I've ever wanted to let close like this. Given how it turned out with Marcus, my absolute terror doesn't come as any surprise.

Veronica: I'm going to make some changes. Jacks deserves better than what I've been settling for, and that means doing what I need to for more money and finding a place of our own. No worries—I am upping my budget after today.

Colton: Good to hear it. Have you told Ellie you're looking? She can help. I'm sure you noticed places go fast around here, and she usually knows what will be available before it lists.

Ellie's a real estate agent, and since I'm not buying a home, it hadn't occurred to me to ask. Honestly, asking people around me to help makes me feel a little slimy. Mom was always getting handouts and sweet-talking her way into anything we needed, and I try so freaking hard to be different than her. But Colton's right, and if I'm going to find anywhere decent in this market, I'm going to need help.

Veronica: I'll call her in the morning.

Colton: Good. Now, about your underwear . . .

A laugh bursts from my lips. I glance toward Jacks, but he's doesn't stir.

Veronica: I thought you said you preferred to see over being told.

Colton: And isn't this one of the reasons modern technology is so amazing? There's a camera right there on your phone.

Veronica: No way. Not happening. If you want to see my panties, you're gonna have to do it the old-

fashioned way.

Colton: Promise?

Veronica: Goodnight, Colton.

Colton: Goodnight, Veronica. I'll see you tomorrow.

Veronica: Will you? Because I saw your schedule for the week, and I'm beginning to think you'll never fuck me against your office door again.

Colton: Then I guess you'll have to find some time to see me outside of work. I have all sorts of doors in my apartment I think you'd enjoy.

The butterflies in my stomach are out of control. But of course, I'm a single mom who's sharing a room with her kid. Alone time outside of work hours isn't exactly easy to come by.

Or it didn't used to be.

The butterflies in my stomach fall dormant the moment I remember I have next Saturday free. And why. It's Jackson's first overnight with Marcus and Kristi. I'll have two days and one night completely child-free, and the thought makes me slightly nauseated.

Veronica: I might be available Saturday.

Colton: Then I might be counting down the days. Enjoy those dreams about me.

Veronica: You don't think too much of yourself, do you?

He sends another winkie face in reply, and I put down my phone and hug my pillow against my chest.

Chapter Seventeen

COLTON

On Sunday night, I was on Cloud Nine. By Friday, I'm seriously questioning whether I'm setting myself up for heartbreak by pursuing Veronica.

Something's been off all week. I thought I'd be living for the weekend—so eager to get time alone with Veronica. Instead, I'm wondering if she and I are even on the same page. Sunday night we were trading texts like a real couple. Joking, flirting, sharing. But Monday, she was back to her old self. Except worse. Instead of being contrary, she's been *quiet*. And distracted.

She might be a hot mess when it comes to personal organization and getting her ass to work on time, but she's never been a mess when it comes to the way she does her job. Until this week, when she's dropped balls right and left and stonewalled me when I've tried to ask what's going on. Did I really think she'd open up to me after one decent conversation over text?

And then there's the woman in front of me who's sending up all the red flags.

"I'm looking for Ronnie," she says. She's already said that, but she didn't like my answer. Too fucking bad.

I've known enough drug users that I can recognize the eyes of someone who's strung out. I can see it in other ways, too. The track marks. The glassy eyes. The shitty coordination. As someone who's escaped the iron grip of addiction but who also knows how it can destroy everyone and everything in its path, I feel pity and disgust simultaneously and in equal measure.

"What can I do for you?" I ask, and because I was once the addict people shouldn't have trusted, my gaze goes to the cash box to make sure it's locked before lifting my gaze again.

"Just need to talk to Ronnie."

I shake my head. "No one by that name here. Sorry." Guilt dogs me for it, but I want this woman out of my shop. I don't want to see any reflection of what I once was.

"Yeah, she is. My friend looked it up on his computer. Veronica Maddox. She works here. She's my daughter."

I probably wouldn't have seen it if the woman hadn't said so, but now I can spot the resemblance in the shape of her face and the color of her hair. "She's not in. I'm sorry."

I'm not sorry. Veronica's out for lunch, and I want nothing more than for this woman to leave before she has an excuse to stay.

The woman gives me a sad sort of smile—the kind that says she's down on her luck and could be just fine if someone like me would help out.

I know that smile. I used to be a pro at giving it.

"I have something for her." She puts a brown-paper-wrapped package on the counter with a shaky hand. "I can trust you to get that to her, can't I?"

I eye the package, bile rising in my throat. Is this why Veronica suddenly has a bigger budget for apartments? Because she's handling packages for her drug-using mother? She wouldn't risk it. Would she? Not when she could lose Jacks.

I fold my arms, refusing to touch it. "You can't leave that here."

"Why not? It's for my daughter. It's important."

"Too bad."

She returns the package to the dirty tote on her shoulder. "Okay. I'll come back."

"You can come back when you're sober," I say, widening my stance. "Until then, keep your distance."

The woman sniffles and nods a few times before turning around and slowly making her way out the door. I hold my breath until she's out of sight, but even then, I'm shaky.

I glance down at Veronica's desk and spot a stack of printed-out apartment listings. I frown as I flip through them. She said she was upping her budget, but a lot of these places are more than twice what the slum on the east side of town was going to cost her. How can she suddenly afford so much more?

Jacks deserves better than what I've been settling for, and that means doing what I need to for more money and finding a place of our own.

What exactly did she mean when she said doing *what she needs to* for more money?

188

She wouldn't do something stupid. She wouldn't risk Jacks.

I'm almost sure of it, but it's the *almost* that's leaving me unsteady. But if we're going to do this—if we're going to try for something bigger and better—I need to know for sure.

Twenty minutes later, she's back at her desk, and I'm determined to get some answers.

"Lunch go okay?" I ask.

Her hand goes to her stomach. "Yeah."

That's the other thing. Whatever's been bothering her this week is making her sick. She's been sipping ginger ale at her desk every day.

With a sigh, I lean on my doorjamb and study her. Worry pulls on her features, and she's paler than usual. "The apartments in those listings look nice," I say, nodding to her desk.

She glances at the stack then swallows. "Much better than what I was looking at before."

"How are you . . ." *Fuck.* It seems really shitty to come right out and ask how her money situation has changed. I certainly don't want to imply she's doing shady shit with her mom to improve her cash flow. Instead, I say, "We could probably give you a raise in a month or so. If that would help."

She frowns at her phone.

"Veronica?"

She shakes her head. "Sorry. What?"

"I was saying we might be able to give you a raise. If it would help."

She taps on her screen for a few seconds before shoving the phone in her purse.

"I just don't want you to do anything you might regret for

money." I stare at her a long time. "I know you'd do anything for Jacks, but easy money isn't always worth it."

Her eyes fill with tears, and she shoves back from her desk. "Excuse me." She disappears down the hall toward the bathroom.

I almost follow her, but the bell over the door rings, and Addison Wellmont strolls in.

"Hey, it's just the man I want to see," she says, grinning as she saunters to the front counter. "Martin wants me to get all the details you can give me about your corporate events. I think he's considering bringing the team out here in August."

"That's great." I force a smile and pull out the brochures she needs. My attention is half on her and half down the hall as I go through the details of several popular packages.

"You know how Martin is," Addison says, her hand on my wrist. "He wants what he wants."

Jesus. I was distracted and put down my guard, and now she's too close to me, her breasts practically pressed against my chest, that hand she had at my wrist sliding up my arm.

I step away just in time to catch Veronica coming back from the bathroom, still drying her hands on a paper towel. She catches one glimpse of me and Addison, and instead of coming to the counter and rescuing me, she turns around and pushes into the stairwell.

My unease creeps up another notch.

"Don't you think?" Addison asks, and I have no idea what she's talking about.

I can't focus. "Sorry," I say, stepping back again. "Excuse me. I need to check on something."

I walk to the stairwell, but the minute the door swings shut behind me, I start into a jog up to the roof, hoping that's where she is. Six flights of stairs later, I force myself to slow my steps and open the door as quietly as I can.

Veronica is standing at the far corner of the terrace, her elbows propped up on the railing, her gaze on the beach below. Her long hair lifts off her neck in the breeze, and I wish I had my phone with me so I could capture her like this. One picture to look at whenever I want. She's stunning.

"Skipping out on work to catch the view?" I ask. I'm trying to make a joke of it, but it comes out crisp with hard edges.

She jerks to attention but doesn't look at me. "Sneak up on people much?" She swipes at her cheeks.

Protectiveness surges in my chest. "Are you crying?" I cross the terrace to stand next to her, but I don't see any sign of what could've upset her.

"No."

There's a wedding on the dock below—a small group of maybe a dozen people in attendance, watching the bride and groom hold hands in front of the officiant. Finding no answers down there, I study her—her smudged mascara and the streaks on her cheeks. "You are." Protectiveness surges in my chest. "Who made you cry? Is this about your mom?"

She recoils like I've slapped her. "What about my mom?"

Fuck. "She was in here looking for you. She tried to—"

"She was? *Here?*"

"Yes." And there goes my ridiculously paranoid theory that Veronica is getting extra cash by doing something unsavory for her mother. Guilt gnaws at me. "She had a package for you, but I told her not to leave it. I thought . . . I told her not to come back until she was sober."

She flinches and mutters something I think might be "The last thing I need to deal with right now."

I glance at the wedding and then back to her. Is the wedding what has her so upset? Is she torturing herself by watching her ex say his vows or something? Is that why she's been off all week? And fuck, why does it piss me off, thinking she could care enough about some other asshole that seeing him get married would make her cry? "Do you know them?"

Some of the belligerence falls away as she shakes her head. "No."

"Then what's wrong?"

She drags her gaze off the wedding and steps away from the railing, turning for the stairs. "Nothing."

I scoff. I should've known better than to expect honesty. "Why are you so determined to shut me out?"

She freezes, her back to me. "Why do you even care? What does it matter to you?"

"Because I . . ." I don't have a good answer to that. She makes me fucking crazy, and if I were reasonable, I'd back off and quit pursuing this. But there's nothing reasonable about how I feel about her. "Do you really need an explanation any time someone gives a shit about you?"

Apparently, that's enough, because she sighs and slowly turns back to me. "Weddings make me cry." She shrugs as if that explains everything.

I glance toward the wedding on the dock again in time to see the bride and groom walking up between their guests, hand in hand. "So you *do* know them?"

"Not even a little."

I'm not a complete idiot. I know some girls cry at everything—weddings, Hallmark commercials, public proposals. But Veronica is tough. She's the kind of girl who can look our worst asshole customers in the eye while they curse her up and down and not bat a lash. Petty nonsense doesn't get to her. Except this week it has. She's been *off* and her stomach's always bothering her too. It's almost as if . . .

Almost as if I'm a complete idiot who totally missed the most obvious signs. The ginger ale. The easy tears. The way she's been so distracted. I mentally do some math then squeeze my eyes shut. "Shit."

"What?" She worries her bottom lip between her teeth in a gesture that's so uncharacteristically vulnerable that my suspicions ramp up a notch.

Fuck. Fuck. Fuck. My gaze drops to her stomach. "Are you pregnant?"

Her eyes go wide. "What?"

I wave toward the wedding. "You don't even know them but you're crying. *You*, ball-buster Veronica Maddox, are ruining your makeup over a stranger's wedding, and I'm not supposed to think anything of it? You've been sick all week and volatile, irrational, and overdramatic." I swallow hard and then shove out the other question—the one I need to ask before I can lose my nerve. "Is it mine?"

Her jaw drops, and before I can decipher that reaction, she spins on her heel and stomps back to the stairs, slamming the door closed behind her.

I chase after her and catch her on the landing between the

fourth and fifth floor. I loop my arm beneath her breasts and pull her back against my front. We're both breathing hard, and this position reminds me way too much of how it felt to take her against my office door. My dick is getting the same kind of ideas that got us into this trouble to begin with.

"Let me go," she snarls.

"Not until you answer me," I say, my lips against her ear. And because I can't fucking resist touching her when she's in my arms, I splay my hand against her stomach, rubbing my thumb along the underside of her breast. "I deserve to know." I trail my mouth down her neck to the strap of her tank top and back up.

She surrenders for a single beat before tearing herself from my arms and spinning around to face me. "Is that what you think of me?"

"I don't think anything. That's why I'm *asking*."

"You think I'm just some enterprising trash who gets knocked up by every guy she messes around with? Is that why you offered me a raise?"

"No, I—"

"You think I'm going to have your baby so I can trap you into a relationship you don't want—"

"I didn't—"

"You think I'm just in this for the money. I want you to swoop in and save me. As if I want someone to take care of me for the rest of my life." She shoves a palm against my shoulder. "I'm not that girl."

"Veronica . . ." I don't know what to say, and I don't have a chance to figure it out before she disappears down the stairs. "Veronica!" I call, chasing behind her. She pushes through the door on the main floor enough ahead of me that it's closed again when I reach it. "Just wait a minute."

I plow into reception and run into something solid. Or someone.

"Let her go," Wes says.

I glance toward the front of the building, where Veronica's already climbing into her car. "Shit." I lunge to move around him, and he drives his forearm into my chest to throw me against the wall.

"What the fuck did you say to her?"

I glare. Wes is a strong guy, but he doesn't have half the fighting experience I do. "I don't want to hurt you. Just get out of my way."

"Not until you tell me what's going on with you two."

I use my shoulder to shove him back, and he retreats a step, though probably only because her car's already pulled out. "I don't know, okay? I like her. I . . ." I drag a hand over my face. "I care about her, but I don't know if she even wants me to."

Wes's face softens. It's so subtle I wouldn't notice if I didn't know him so well, but it's there, and it makes me feel like a fool. "If I ask you something, will you answer me honestly?"

I blow out a breath. "I'll try."

"Is she pregnant?"

There is no humor in my laugh. "Funny. I just asked her the same thing, and you saw how well she took it."

"I mean, she's been off, right? My sister was like that when she was pregnant—kind of spacey and constantly feeling sick."

"Yeah. I know. That's why I asked."

He shakes his head. "If she's having your kid and you don't

step up . . ." He must see the anger in the set of my jaw, because he holds up his hands. "Okay, okay. I know you aren't going to leave her to raise it alone, but this is the last thing she needs right now. She's struggling, man."

"I know, but I offered her a raise, and that didn't go over well."

"But it's not about money. Not really."

I glance toward the parking lot and the empty spot where her car used to be. "Then what is it? What's going on with her?"

Wes studies me, and for a minute, I think he's not going to answer. "You really don't know?"

"No." My voice is gravelly, giving Wes all the proof he needs of how much that upsets me. "It's fine. You don't have to—"

"Her kid's dad showed up out of the blue a few weeks ago, and he and his wife suddenly want to be in the picture. Nothing before this, but now they're all about visitation, and she's living with her sister because her roommate kicked her out."

My stomach sinks. First of all, that's a fucking lot for anyone to deal with on their own. But then there's also the fact that she didn't tell me any of it. *Maybe she just doesn't want to get close to a guy like you.*

"I gotta go talk to her." I sidestep him and walk to the door and push outside.

"Colt?"

I turn. "Yeah?"

"You really care about her?"

I nod, because I'm feeling too many things to trust my voice.

"Then be good to her. That's all I want."

That may be all he wants. It's all I want too. "I'll be good to her," I say. "If she'll have me."

Chapter Eighteen

VERONICA

I feel sick to my stomach, and there's a one hundred percent chance that the two shots of tequila in front of me are going to make it worse, but fuck it. *Fuck Colton and his assumptions. Fuck Marcus and Kristi with their high-and-mighty "interventions."*

All week long I've been trying to be okay, trying to get through the days without obsessing about the fact that this weekend Jacks will be doing his first overnight visit with his father, and all week long, all I've wanted to do was get my boy and run away.

Mom tried that once. We lived in her friend's garage for five days before CPS found us.

"You okay?" Jake Jackson asks, wiping down the taps behind the bar.

"I'm fine." Or I was. Until he asked. But now my eyes are burning, because it still takes me by surprise when someone other than Nic gives a shit about me.

Except Colton. You were starting to expect only the best from Colton. Starting to think he saw something in you that you didn't even see in yourself.

It's so ridiculous. I've been a mess all week. Emotional, quick to tears, and with a stomach so torn up from stress I should probably buy my antacids in bulk. He had every right to ask, and I had no right to flip out the way I did. So why did it hurt so much to have him think I'm knocked up?

For the same reason weddings make you cry, the little voice in my head whispers. She sounds a lot like the therapist my college advisor made me see. I will drink *all* the motherfucking tequila if that's what it takes to drown her out.

I might drink it either way. It's not like I have a kid to go home to tonight.

Marcus and Kristi got a last-minute consult with some high-profile SLP, so instead of getting him tomorrow morning, they're picking Jacks up from daycare this afternoon and he'll spend two nights with them instead of the one we initially planned.

I already feel like I'm losing him, and I hate myself for every instinct that tells me to keep him from them. I know he's safe. I know he's having fun. I know they can provide amazing things for him. *The only reason I hate this is because I'm selfish. Just like my mother. My mother, who's apparently tracked me down and is no doubt looking for money.*

I plan to drown my sorrows until this terrible knot at the pit of my stomach goes away. I'm not going to dig into emotions better left alone just because Colton McKinley makes dumbass assumptions about me.

"Hey, Colton," Jake says, and I stiffen.

"Hi, Jake. Do you have any of the new NA stout left?" His voice is as smooth as velvet, and so deep I just want to close my eyes and listen.

Instead, I spin on my barstool and glare at the tall, bearded, fine-ass motherfucker standing behind me. "What are you doing here?"

Jake clears his throat. "I'll go get that beer."

"Hey." Colton shoves his hands into his pockets and slowly looks me over. It's not the I-wanna-fuck appraisal I've become accustomed to. I wish it were. That would be easier to handle than the tenderness in his eyes. "Can I buy you a drink or something?"

Turning back to face the bar, I grab my untouched shot of tequila and roll it between both hands. "I'm covered. Thanks, though."

I'm grateful for the crowded bar and the fact that the stools on either side of me are occupied, but then the guy next to me glances over his shoulder at Colton. I don't look to know what or how Colton silently communicates with him, but the guy nods, and less than a minute later, Colton's taking his stool.

I throw back the shot, wincing as it burns a path down my throat. "Why are you here?"

Jake appears and drops a coaster and a pint of beer in front of Colton before disappearing again.

"I need to apologize," Colton says.

I huff out a breath. "Do you? For which part? Calling me volatile and irrational, and overdramatic? Or for low-key implying I'm involved in shady drug shit with my mom for the extra cash?"

"V . . ." He blows out a breath and taps my empty shot glass. "I guess this answers my question."

"You think? You aren't going to accuse me of being irresponsible enough to drink when I'm pregnant?" I regret the words even before they're all out of my mouth, but when he pales, I regret them even more. He's trying to have a real conversation, and I'm doing what I do best and being a bitch about everything. I sigh. "Sorry. You don't deserve that."

"Maybe I do. Just a little."

I hold his gaze for a beat before turning away.

"The possibility occurred to me, and I panicked," he says. "It was never intended to be a judgment of you, and it's no reflection of how much I trust you."

I grunt. "Not that you do." This softer, careful side of Colton scares the shit out of me. It feels like if I let him look at me too long, he'll see right inside my soul. And I'm afraid he won't like what he finds there at all. "I'm not pregnant." This is probably a terrible place to have this conversation. Who knows who is listening and what kind of rumors will fly tomorrow? But fuck 'em. "We've been careful, and there's no cause for concern. Even if one of the condoms had failed, I have an IUD."

From my peripheral vision, I can see him nodding. "Listen, I came here to say I'm sorry and to let you know I don't *expect* anything from you. When this started, we agreed casual, and I'm not trying to change the rules. I know I have a past, and I completely understand if that means you can't trust me."

He thinks *his* past is the problem? I draw in a ragged breath. "I trust you."

"Want to tell me why you were crying, then? Tell me what's

been bothering you all week?"

No, but *Jesus*, my reluctance to share is to blame for this misunderstanding anyway, so maybe it's time to come clean. I take a deep breath. "Like I said, weddings make me cry. Even strangers' weddings." I blow out a breath. "And I've been extra sensitive because Jacks and I got kicked out of June's for bullshit reasons, and this weekend, Jackson is staying overnight with his dad and stepmom for the first time."

"Why didn't you just say that?" he asks.

My lips twitch. "And ruin my street cred?"

He coughs out a laugh then props an elbow on the bar and rests his chin on his fist as he studies me. "You're ridiculous."

"Me? You're the one who chased me down to talk because I shed a couple of tears. Did you even find someone to watch the front at HBA, or did you just leave us to be robbed?"

He grunts. "Wes has it covered. He's worried about you too."

My eyes fill with more tears. Dammit, I *am* acting like a hormonal pregnant lady. "I hate this."

"What? Letting me see your ooey-gooey insides? You ever consider what it'd be like to stop wasting so much energy pretending you're a hard-ass?"

It's the only way I can protect myself.

Dozens of memories flood my mind. The social workers and teachers who "just wanted to help," the foster homes who found me "too difficult," the pleas from my mother who made me believe we could go home if we made it hard enough on our foster families. I spent my entire adolescence being forced to play one part or another and believing no one would love me if I let them see me for myself—knowing that if they did love me, it didn't matter, because I could be taken away from them too. "Do you remember when you asked me what happened to that vulnerable woman you talked to at the Jacksons' cabin?"

He nods, studying me. It feels so good and so terrifying to have his full attention like this. To know he's soaking up every word.

"You wanted to know what happened to her, but she's still here."

He takes my hand from my lap and squeezes it in his. "I never doubted that. I was just hoping you'd trust me with her."

I swallow the lump in my throat. "When you grow up in the system, you learn that very few people want to be bothered with the real you. You learn that you're better off wearing a mask, to hide yourself."

"I can't imagine what that must've been like."

I stare at my shot glass so I don't have to meet the tenderness in his eyes. "They took us away from our mom and told us we had to be *good*. We thought that meant perfection. Nic did everything she could to give it to them, but not me. I hated them for taking us and resented the role they expected me to play." I dare a look at the man next to me. "It's been over a decade since I walked out of the group home we ended up in, and most days, I'd still rather have everyone around me think I'm a bitch than let them know how much it hurts that I'll never measure up." I hold my breath, waiting for the awkward platitudes.

Instead, he says, "You were right. We are so much alike."

I swallow. "I never should've said that crap about the Jacksons. I was pissed at Ethan because he wasn't exactly thrilled when I showed up on his doorstep looking for a place to stay.

He doesn't trust me—and while I know I haven't done anything to earn his trust, it hurts. But that's *my* baggage, and you didn't deserve to have it projected onto you."

He shrugs. "You saw the truth and called me on it." He finally pulls his gaze off me, and I expect it to feel like a relief. Instead, I miss the warmth from his eyes. "My dad was an abusive ass. Not physically—at least, never in a way he couldn't justify—but mentally, emotionally. You were right about my relationship with the Jacksons. It wasn't just that Levi was like a brother to me. His whole family was there for me in a way mine never was. Don't get me wrong, Mom's great, but she had her own coping mechanisms to get through those years with Dad. She was withdrawn, lost in her shows and her books. I don't blame her for it, but . . . yeah, the Jacksons were the only real family I had. But you were wrong about me trying to be perfect for them. I never doubted they'd be there for me, no matter what. Then I self-destructed in a big way, and they didn't turn their backs on me. Even when they should have. Now I want to make up for those mistakes, and I think you understand that more than you want to admit."

I shrug. "But they aren't my family. They're Nic's family. I'm just . . ." Memories from a Christmas long ago flip through my mind. *I'm the little girl hiding in the bushes.* "I'm on my own, and I've had to learn to be okay with that."

Neither of us speaks for several long moments, and neither of us rushes to look away as the happy bar sounds around us take over. This is a happy place—where people celebrate and play, where they meet and reconnect—and it feels all wrong for this moment with Colton.

Finally, I swallow and offer a soft apology. "I'm sorry you had to deal with my mother."

"It's not your fault."

"What do you think was in the package?"

He drags a hand through his hair. "Honestly, I thought the worst, but now I have no idea. You think Nic knows she's in town?"

"No. She still hasn't forgiven Nic for . . ." My chest tightens and the shot of tequila tries to lurch into my throat. "It's a long story, and I don't want to get into it here."

"Not here or not with me?"

"Not here."

He blows out a breath then lifts his hand to my face and tucks a lock of hair behind my ear. "Jackson's with his dad this weekend?"

"Yeah." The word comes out as raw as the reality makes me feel.

"Then come home with me?" he asks softly.

"Why?"

"Because I'm sick of pretending I don't want more from you. Because touching you at the office was never enough." He grazes his thumb over my bottom lip. "Because I saw you cry today, and it shook me. I need you in my bed and in my arms."

He leans forward and brings his mouth to mine. Here. In the middle of Jackson Brews where anyone could see. I'm so shocked that I don't even kiss him back at first.

I've spent most of my life being the girl with the hard shell around her heart, but somehow, this guy can make it fall away. It's terrifying, but it's also wonderful. It's so lonely behind that wall of bitchiness I throw between myself and every potentially meaningful relationship I've ever had. I'll never be the kind of person who can be open and vulnerable with each person she meets, but I want to be with Colton.

When he pulls away and studies my face, I dare to hope that with time, he could see through the facade of the tough girl to the scared foster kid behind it; see all the hope and fear I have for the future and everything I'd be willing to sacrifice to give Jacks a good life; see all my many faults but also the good pieces of me; and see how much I love my kid and how hard I'm willing to work. For once, I've found someone I could trust with my heart.

Chapter Nineteen

COLTON

The second Veronica walks into my small apartment, I say a little prayer of thanks to whatever had me cleaning this morning. This is the first place of my own I've had since Ellie and I broke up. Back in my wilder days I never gave a second thought to bringing a woman home with me. It was a chance to fuck. A chance to have some privacy. It never *meant* anything. But I've never brought a woman here, so somehow, the decision to break that pattern with Veronica feels weightier.

She runs her gaze over every corner of my living space, taking in the PlayStation controller on the coffee table and the coffee cup on the small island that separates the kitchen from the living room. It's as if she's cataloguing every detail and comparing it to what she thinks she knows about me.

"It's not much," I say. Suddenly, I wish I had something to

offer her. A home. The kind of comfort and security she deserves. Things she probably wants for herself and her child. I'm acutely aware of how poorly I fit that mold. Financially, I'm all tied up in Heartbreak Bay Adventures, and my past speaks for itself. I couldn't blame her if that was enough to make her want to stay away.

She stills in the middle of the living room and studies a framed picture on the console table. It's from a few summers ago. Levi and I are in swim trunks at the beach, and Ellie stands between us. We each have an arm thrown around her shoulders, and we're all smiling like goons.

When I look at that picture, I see myself with two of the best friends I've ever had, but I realize Veronica probably sees it as a framed picture of the woman I was supposed to marry. "It was a good day," I say roughly. I want her to understand. I want to go back in time and fix the mistake I made at the Jacksons' cabin last year. I have no memory of calling out Ellie's name, but that weekend, I was so lovesick watching her and Levi together, so lost in my own thoughts of *what if* that I don't doubt it happened. "I'm so sorry about that night. Ellie and I have a lot of memories there, but I never meant . . ." I sigh. "I regret that I hurt you."

Veronica turns and studies me. "Ellie's really awesome," she says softly. "I can't blame you for being hung up on her."

I shake my head. "I'm not, though. I loved her, and there was a time in my life when I thought I needed her to save me. I thought she was my only chance of getting clean." I step closer, taking Veronica's hands in mine. "It's better that I had to do it without her. No one should have to be responsible for someone else's sobriety. That's an impossible weight to ask anyone to carry."

She lifts her hand and traces my cheekbone before grazing her fingertips over my beard and the line of my jaw. "You're amazing."

I scoff. God, I want to gobble those words up, but they're so far from the truth that I can't even pretend. "There's not a single thing that's amazing about me. You're the one raising a kid on your own—and he's a freaking *amazing* kid. You're the one who's overcome so much." I grab her by the wrist and press a kiss to the center of her palm before releasing her. "Want something to drink? I don't have any booze, but I have a wide selection of sparkling water and a couple of NA beers."

"I'm not thirsty."

I swallow, suddenly self-conscious about how unprepared I am for guests. "Or . . . dinner? We could order something or . . . I think I might have some chicken in the fridge?"

"I'm not hungry." She steps closer and slides both hands into my hair. "And you didn't bring me here to feed me."

"That's true, but I'm trying not to be selfish." My heart squeezes as I look down into her eyes. She's the most beautiful thing I've ever seen, and she wants me. It was easy enough to believe she wanted me for a quick fuck last summer, or for the fiery sex in my office. But that she came home with me tonight because she might want something more than that? With me? It's hard to wrap my head around. I'm not the guy who gets the happy ending.

Maybe that's why Wes's crush on her bothered me so much. Because even though he's been a bit of a player, I could easily see him becoming that kind of guy. He doesn't have the sordid past or addictions that'll be a factor for the rest of his life. Veronica would be better off with a guy like him.

"What are you thinking?" she asks.

"That I can't believe you're here. I can't believe I get to spend the night with you. I get to *be* with you."

The corner of her mouth quirks into a lopsided grin. "Um, we *have* done this before. Am I that forgettable?"

"No, we haven't." I dip my head and run my lips down the side of her neck. "I've fucked you and licked you and made you come, but I've never gotten to savor you. And that's exactly what I plan to do tonight."

She moans softly and tips her head the other way to give me better access. "I stand corrected."

Her hands find my chest, her nails scraping down my T-shirt. When she grabs the hem, I take half a step back so she can pull it off over my head. She tosses it onto the couch, and I bend to kiss her neck again.

"I fucking love the way you smell." I bite her gently at the juncture of her neck and shoulder. "I always knew when you'd been in my office because your perfume lingered there."

"Body oil." She releases the button on my jeans and unzips me. "I don't wear perfume."

"Whatever it is, I love it."

She grins up at me, sliding her hand into my boxer briefs and stroking my dick. "I know."

Shit, that feels good. It takes a feat of inhuman strength to keep from thrusting into her grip, but *damn*. "You know?" I can't think straight.

"One day I was in your office filing something, and Amelia walked by and caught you sniffing my hair." She bites her bottom lip. "After that, I couldn't bring myself to wear any other scent."

"So you're saying you made me crazy on purpose."

"How could I resist when you made it so fun?"

I tug down one strap of her lacy tank and kiss her shoulder, even as I guide her hand away from my cock. "I'm planning to kiss every inch of this soft skin and won't let your hand rush me."

"You're sure about that?"

I chuckle, peeling the tank down farther to reveal the swell of her breast and the top of her lacy bra. "Oh yeah."

Then she drops to her knees before me and . . . holy fucking shit, her mouth.

"Veronica," I say.

She swirls her tongue around the head of my cock before looking up at me through her lashes and taking me deeper, moaning.

"Fuck." It's good. Good, good, so fucking good. I can't remember why I was trying to slow things down or why I wanted anything else, because right now, my entire world, my entire existence, revolves around her warm lips sliding up and down my shaft. The soft stroke of her tongue, the subtle vibration of her moans, the sight of her breasts nearly spilling from her bra.

I slide my fingers into her silky hair, and she hums in approval, taking me deeper. I don't need to guide her mouth—wouldn't want to regardless, not when every stroke of her tongue is so damn perfect—but I need to touch her, to be closer in any way possible, so I keep my hand in her hair and plunge the other in to join it.

Blood pumps into my shaft, and my balls draw up tight with pleasure. She pulls me so deep that her eyes water. I try to withdraw, but she grabs my hips and holds me in place, her nails biting into my skin as she swallows around me and— *Fuck*.

My hips buck as pleasure shoots down my spine and my orgasm hits, hard and relentless. I shudder as I let go, and she slides her hands up and down my thighs, carrying me through the aftershocks.

When she finally releases me from her mouth, she looks up at me with a satisfied smile, and I can only shake my head at how much I crave her. Even now.

I scoop her off the floor, and she shrieks. I toss her over my shoulder and carry her to the bedroom, her laughter bouncing off the walls until I gently lower her to the bed.

She's still grinning as I crawl onto the mattress and over her. "I would've happily walked my own ass into the bedroom if you'd just asked," she says, her chest still shaking with laughter.

I dip my head down to taste her grin, and she nips my bottom lip. "What fun would that be?"

"Caveman."

I kiss the tip of her nose. "Would you prefer a gentleman?" I trail kisses down her neck and over her collarbone. "A slow seduction?" I peel away the shell of her bra with my teeth, exposing the swell of her breast to my greedy lips. It's not enough for either of us, and she wiggles out of her top and bra to give me access to her soft skin.

She arches into my mouth. "Guys are all talk about going slow. When it's game time, none of them have the patience."

"Be careful," I say, licking the areola around one perfect nipple. "That sounds like a challenge." I lick and tease, and she holds her breath until I finally pull it between my lips.

Her laughter's long gone, melted away into happy sighs that gather into hungry whimpers as I work my way down her body, tasting every inch. The valley between her breasts. The sensitive patch beneath her navel. I find the button on her shorts and toss them aside with her panties.

Spreading her thighs, I settle between her legs and slowly lower my head, prepared to show her just how much patience I can have when it comes to her pleasure.

VERONICA

I've had a lot of orgasms in my life—quite a few of them with this very man—but I've never had one like that. Colton was both relentless and torturously unhurried. He used his hands and mouth—tongue and lips and teeth and dirty words whispered against my inner thighs—to wind me tight and bring me to the edge, only to pull back just before I came and start all over again. I didn't know an orgasm could leave bone and muscle ineffectual and obliterate worries so completely. But here I am, a veritable puddle of satisfaction in the middle of his bed.

I don't know how many minutes or hours have passed, but I secretly hope time's stopped so I can spend forever here in his arms, where I feel so safe.

"Tell me about Marcus," he says, his voice low, his fingertips stroking small circles on my stomach.

I stiffen at the name but only for a moment before letting out a sigh and all my tension. There's no use trying to hide what I did or trying to pretend I'm better than I am. I got pregnant with my sister's fiancé's baby, and I can't take that back.

"You know, I wanna say he's the biggest mistake I ever made, because part of me will always feel rotten for doing that to my sister. But I can't." I put my hand on top of Colton's and guide it up to rest between my breasts. "If I hadn't fucked up and slept with Marcus, I wouldn't have Jackson now. I can't regret that."

Colton presses a soft kiss to my bare shoulder. "How did it happen?"

I release a dry laugh. "You mean to tell me you don't already know?"

"How would I know?" he asks. And his voice is so gentle that I'm glad he's behind me and I can't see his face. The tenderness in his eyes might make me fall apart, and just talking about this makes me feel frayed at the edges.

"Everyone thinks they know. Everyone assumes I'm some skanky slut who seduced her sister's fiancé. Everyone thinks I couldn't handle her having something I didn't. For a long time, that's even what Nic thought."

"Is that what happened?" he asks, and there's no judgment in his voice. He just wants to know.

"No. I never cared that she had something I didn't. I always knew she deserved better than me."

His lips are warm as they brush across my shoulder. "I want to know the real story."

"Marcus . . ." I swallow hard. "He's real charming, ya know? One of those guys who's so fucking smooth. I knew he was a charmer, that everywhere he went, girls would fall over themselves trying to get his attention. He makes you feel so good when you have it. But he knows exactly what he's doing. You see, after he and Nic got engaged, he'd come by all the time. I should've known it wasn't right, but he was just this nice guy—my future brother-in-law. I never had a brother, and for a while, I imagined this was what brothers do. He always wanted to help me out. At the time, I was grateful to have someone who knew how to fix the front door when it suddenly didn't latch right. Someone who knew how to fix the leak in my kitchen sink and then the one in my roof, and who dropped everything to help when my tires were slashed."

"That's a lot of bad luck," Colton says, clearly already thinking what it took me months away from Marcus to suspect. "Was this over years, or . . ."

"All those things happened in a three-week timespan. I can't prove he did any of it, but I wonder. Anyway, he'd come by to help with all these little disasters, and while he was there, he'd feed me bits and pieces and make me question my own sister's love for me."

"Like what?"

I squeeze his hand, pressing it harder against my breastbone, as if his closeness can protect me from my own shame. "Small stuff at first. And he'd act like he'd slipped and didn't mean to tell me. Things like how she'd always roll her eyes when I called, and he didn't understand what the big deal was because I'd never keep her on the phone for long. Or that she didn't understand why I was wasting money on a master's degree when I already had so much student loan debt. Then he mentioned she'd confessed to wanting to move away so she wouldn't have to deal with me. He said he talked her into staying in Jeffe, that he'd reminded her I was the only family she had left."

"Do you think Nic really said any of that?"

I shake my head. "No, but I know all of it fed into *my* insecurities. And at the same time, he was feeding me bullshit about his own struggles with happiness and guilt over wanting what he couldn't have. He wasn't specific at first, and I listened because he was a nice guy and he deserved someone to listen to his troubles. He claimed Nic would take it personally if he tried to talk to her about it." My eyes burn. I've never explained the details of what really happened to anyone. I did a terrible thing, and I've never believed my side of the story was relevant.

"You thought you were being the friend he needed."

I nod, and a tear slips out and rolls down to the pillow. "He seemed so lost, and little by little, he let it out that he wasn't sure if he was going to go through with marrying Nic. I already knew they'd decided to wait until after they were married to have sex, but he told me it was because he was having second thoughts. He made me swear I wouldn't tell her, and I didn't want to hurt her— especially if they ended up married—so I didn't say anything. He fed me so many pretty words, and he did it so subtly that I didn't even realize what was happening. By the time he told me he had feelings for me, that he was all twisted up because he was falling for me and didn't want to hurt Nic, I'd already swallowed a hundred of his lies. He took my face in his hands and said, 'You're the person I so desperately wanted her to be.' I never thought anyone could think those things about me. *Nic* was the good one, but I believed him. I believed that this guy—this horny bastard who really just wanted to get in my pants—was going to leave my sister so he could be with me. I believed everyone would be better off if he did and it was just a matter of time. He was trying to do it without hurting her."

"You can't blame yourself for his lies," Colton says, kissing my shoulder again.

"I have to, though," I whisper. "I let myself believe what I *wanted* to believe, but deep down, I knew the truth. I didn't want to see it, so I let myself believe this guy somehow knew me better than anyone else. I bought into everything. All the shit he told me Nic said about me, all the shit he claimed to be questioning about his relationship with her." It's been almost four years, but my stomach still churns when I think about what I did. "When he kissed me, I let him. When he touched me, I let him. There's no excuse. *No* excuse. And though I can't regret decisions that gave me Jacks, I will always regret doubting my sister's goodness. Doubting her heart when it's bigger than anyone else's I've ever met."

Colton rolls me to my back as he moves over me. He rests his weight on his elbows and stares down at me. "Your heart's pretty big too."

"He says to his bitchiest employee."

He grins. "You can't fool me anymore, V. Not after letting me peek inside. I *see* you." He dips his head and kisses my breastbone, right over my heart. "You think you're gonna scare me away, but every inch you expose just makes me want to see more."

Warmth floods my chest. "I knew there was a reason I was crushing on you."

He arches a brow. "You have a crush on me? Do tell. And don't leave out any details."

I laugh. "Do you think I would've dragged just anyone into that garage last summer? I'd been crushing hard on you for months before then."

"And then I ruined it." His face goes solemn. "I hate that I ruined it."

I shrug. "You were where you were. And maybe it doesn't matter. We're here now."

He kisses me hard on the mouth. "And I'm so grateful for that."

Chapter Twenty

VERONICA

I wake to a dim, lamplit room and Colton's lips on my shoulder, his hands stroking down my sides. The windows are dark, and water's running in the bathroom. The room smells like lavender.

"Hi," I whisper, smiling into my pillow. "I didn't mean to fall asleep."

"You can go back to sleep if you want," he says, skimming his lips down my arm. "But if you want to get out of bed, there's a bath in it for you."

"Is that what I smell?" I roll over and grin at him. He's the same sexy Colton I've always known, and yet today, he's different. His eyes are different. Softer somehow. "Why do you have smell-good bath stuff? Not that I'm complaining."

He smirks. "You smell lavender Epsom salts. I ordered them

from a grocery pickup once, and they subbed out the regular ones with the smell-good kind."

"I wouldn't judge if you liked bubble baths, you know."

He nips at the tender skin on top of my breast. "I'm man enough to admit that I enjoy a good soak. I work out hard, and sometimes my muscles need it. I'd prefer a hot tub, but until I have a place for it, baths will have to do."

"Mmm, a hot tub sounds nice. Let's save our pennies." As soon as I hear my own words, I wince. Colton McKinley takes me home once, and I immediately talk about our long-term future and a major joint purchase. I may have resisted letting this relationship happen, but clearly now that I'm in it, I have zero chill. "Can we forget I just said that?"

He climbs over me, rolling me to my back beneath him and pinning my hands above my head. "No can do."

I wince. "I swear I'm not going to turn into a stage-five clinger just because you brought me home and said nice things to me."

He arches a dark brow. "No?" He shifts his grip to hold both my hands in one of his then uses his free hand to stroke down my side. Shivering, I arch beneath him. "We'll just see about that."

"You *want* me to cling?" I spread my legs wider, letting him settle between my thighs before hooking my feet behind his back.

He smiles, but there's not much amusement in his eyes as he looks down at me. It's more like . . . *wonder.* "I just want you to come back. I just want . . ." He swallows hard. "I know I'm an asshole and nearly impossible to work with. I'm also fully aware you have a lot going on personally and professionally, but I want a chance."

"A chance? At something with *me*?" I chuckle softly. "I can't believe those words are coming from your mouth. A few weeks ago, I was convinced I was the worst thing that ever happened to you."

He frowns, and I feel guilty for my teasing. "You made me want things. Seeing you at work day after day . . ." He releases my hands. "There are a lot of things I've had to accept I can't have despite getting sober, but I resented adding you to that list. I'm sorry if I was an asshole who took that out on you."

There's so much vulnerability in his eyes that it cuts something deep inside me, leaving me raw and exposed. I slide my hands into his hair and guide his face down to mine, kissing him deeply.

I kiss him long enough to say I feel the same. Long enough to show him my scars. Long enough that the bathtub overflow drain starts guzzling.

Colton pulls back, chuckling softly. "I think your bath's ready." He stands and scoops me off the bed and against his chest. Squeaking, I throw my arms behind his neck and hold on. He carries me to the bath, turns off the tap, and gently lowers me into the water.

I look around the steamy room in wonder as my muscles melt into in the fragrant water. Steam fills the air, and a hodgepodge of candles flicker from the vanity and the ledge. Music I couldn't make out from the bedroom plays softly in the background, and there's a steaming mug of tea on the rim of the tub. "If I didn't know better, I'd think you were trying to seduce me."

Colton lowers himself onto a stool by the tub and swishes a hand in the water, checking the temperature. "Maybe I am."

"Psst," I say, waiting until he lifts his eyes to mine to finish, "I'm a sure thing. And anyway, I've made your life difficult enough this summer. I'm pretty sure I don't deserve any of this."

"You haven't, you know. You haven't made my life harder at all."

I sigh dramatically. "I'm gonna miss our fights."

He flicks his hand at the surface of the tub, splashing water in my face. "Better?"

Leaning out of the tub, I wipe my wet face on his chest before sinking into the warm water again. "That's more familiar."

We're quiet for a long time. He swishes his hand in the water, and I close my eyes and let myself relax. When he finally speaks again, there's a nervousness to his voice I'm unfamiliar with. "If we're going to do this, I want to do it all the way. I don't want to sneak around and pretend we're not together. I want to take you out and buy you things. When Jacks is with his dad, I want you in my bed."

My heart swells at his words, but at the same time, they make me nervous. "That's a plan I could get behind, but Colton . . ." I take a deep breath. I wasn't prepared to have these conversations this weekend, but everything with Colton is always leveled up in intensity, so it shouldn't surprise me. Somehow, we're here already. I feel it too. "I might not be as available as other girls you've dated. Jacks comes first, and sometimes that means disappointing the other people in my life."

"Of course. I love that about you. I love . . ." He swallows. "I love what a good mom you are. And when you're ready, I want to spend time with both of you. I know he's part of your life, and I hope you'll eventually trust me enough to let me be part of his. You can set the pace on that. I know you'll do what's best for Jacks."

My eyes fill with hot, unexpected tears. *This man.* "I wish I were as confident as you."

"Hey." He kicks the stool to the side and kneels on the floor by the tub, taking my face in his hands. "Hey, there's absolutely no rush on this. I mean that. What I feel for you doesn't have an expiration date."

I swallow back another wave of emotion, but a warm stream of tears rolls down my cheeks anyway, and he wipes them away with his thumbs. "That's not why I'm crying."

"Then tell me."

"I don't get happy endings, Colton," I whisper, and the confession feels like ripping out stitches from a fresh wound. "I always fuck them up."

He climbs into the tub and pulls me into his arms as water sloshes over the sides. "Same here," he whispers into my hair. "But I'm thinking we can probably figure it out together."

VERONICA

Saturday night, we're at Jackson Brews, and I feel lighter and happier than I have in weeks. It's been hard to be away from Jacks, but Colton's made it better.

We spent the night talking and slept in this morning before going out to breakfast. Around lunch, we met up with Ellie to look at different rental possibilities, and all of them were a thousand percent better than the place on the other side of town, but I felt sick every time I thought of signing a lease for an apartment I can't afford if Marcus stops paying child support. Ultimately, I didn't move forward on any of them. I'll have a chat with Nic tomorrow about waiting until I know one way or another about the teaching job. I can't bring myself to rely that much on my child's father.

At lunch, I took a FaceTime call with Jacks, which left me both relieved (he's happy!) and more depressed than before. I keep telling myself this'll be an adjustment, but trusting anyone other than Star and Nic with him is the scariest thing I've ever done.

"You're awfully smiley tonight," I tell Colton after our waitress takes our order.

He chuckles. "I'm spending my weekend with the beautiful woman who's been on my mind for a year. I have a lot to smile about."

I kick him under the table, and he flinches.

"Ouch. What was that for?"

"Stop being so freaking sweet."

"I had no idea being sweet was a punishable offense."

I bite back a smile of my own. "You're going to make me fall for you, and then I'll be heartbroken when you realize you're not that into bitches."

He grunts. "I don't think you need to worry about that."

"So you are into bitches?"

The corner of his mouth twitches like he's trying to repress a smile. "I plead the fifth."

"What?" I laugh. "Colton, I *embrace* the title of bitch. You know what *bitch* stands for? Being In Total Control of Herself.

That's me, and I'm not sorry."

"I wasn't going to say anything about you being a bitch."

"So what were you going to say?"

He shakes his head. "You'll kick me again."

"But now I need to know."

"You promise no violence?"

I bite my bottom lip. "I feel like that's a promise I'll end up breaking."

"No doubt."

"Tell me," I growl.

With a sigh, he climbs out of his side of the booth and scoots in next to me. He scoops one arm under my thighs and settles me onto his lap. My body instantly wakes up, sending alerts to the pertinent areas about things I'm pretty sure Jake wouldn't appreciate us doing in a booth at his bar.

"What are you doing?" I ask.

"Protecting myself," he says, nuzzling my neck. The rough slide of his beard brings memories from last night flooding back, and I'm so distracted that I barely notice he's pinned my legs to the seat with one arm.

"So you'll tell me now."

"Maybe." He skims my ear with his lips, making me shiver. "Or maybe I just like the excuse to have you up against me."

"You were going to tell me why you're into bitches."

His chest shakes. "I was going to tell you why I'm into *you*."

I rest my head on his shoulder. He's solid and warm, and something about being in his arms makes me forget that my life is raveling out of control. I wish I could stay here all night. "Don't do that," I say, sighing. "I'm already working at a disadvantage here."

"How do you figure?"

I pull back far enough to meet his gaze, then arch a brow. "You do own a mirror, right?"

He pokes my ticklish side, making me laugh so hard that I have to bury my face in his chest to keep from screeching.

"Oh my God. Look at you two."

My head snaps up at the sound of Amelia's voice. She's standing at the foot of the booth, shaking her head with wonder. Behind her, Star turns up her palms as if to say, *"No use hiding it now."*

I make to move off Colton's lap, but he holds me fast, so I awkwardly say, "Hey. What's up?"

Amelia claps like a giddy toddler. "Freaking finally." She turns to Star, but when she sees Star's expression, she scowls. "Why don't you look surprised or excited? Did you know about this?"

Star shrugs. "I mean, I didn't know they were doing it in *public.*"

I roll my eyes.

"Well, I love it," Amelia says.

I move to shimmy off Colton's lap to sit beside him. This time, he doesn't stop me.

"Don't stop the public groping on our account," Star says.

I subtly scratch my neck with my middle finger, and she laughs.

Amelia points a thumb toward the bar. "We were just gonna grab a drink, but this place is packed and there's nowhere to sit. Do you think we could—"

"Nope." Star grabs her by the wrist and drags her away from our booth. "We'll be fine. Leave them alone."

Amelia waves goodbye, and Star winks at me as they head to the bar, where they'll no doubt charm some unsuspecting guys into giving up their seats.

"So, you told Star about me?" Colton asks when they're gone, a cocky tilt to his grin.

"Of course. She's my best friend." I frown at him. "You didn't tell anyone about me?"

He shrugs. "I didn't want to tell Levi."

Right. Because he's a Jackson, and my sister's brother-in-law, and things could start to get complicated. "I get that."

"But Crosley's suspected for a while."

"I thought *I* was a loner, but even I need someone to talk to about this stuff."

His lips twitch. "I didn't say I didn't talk to *anyone*."

"Who?"

Right then, our waitress shows up with our drinks and lets us know the kitchen's running behind.

"You could've gotten an actual drink," Colton says, nodding to my diet soda. "It doesn't bother me."

I shrug. "I didn't need one. Now I want to know who you told about me."

He ducks his head bashfully. "My mom."

I cough on my drink. "You told your mom about the girl you were fucking in your office?"

He pinches my side. "My mom called last weekend, and I told her about the pretty girl I was seeing." His face softens. "I told her what a good mom you are and how incredible Jacks is."

God. *My heart.* I'm a goner. If he'd told Levi we were fooling around, it wouldn't have meant shit to me, but he told his *mom* about me and my kid. "You really did?"

"She wants me to bring you down to Florida so she can meet you," he says, and my eyes must go as wide as saucers at that, because he chuckles. "No rush, V. She's a mom. Of course she wants to meet the woman who makes her son happy."

"She doesn't come home much?" I ask.

He clears his throat and swipes a thumb through the condensation on his bottle of NA beer. "Nah. Too many bad memories here." Before I can figure out what to say to that, he frowns at my soda again. "I don't want you to feel like you can't have a drink around me. I'm not tempted, if that's what worries you."

"I'm not worried." I study him and ponder his complexities. Such a bossy ass, but so tender inside. "Can I ask you a personal question?"

He nods. "Anything."

"Keep in mind that I'm pretty ignorant about this stuff. The only addict I've known personally is my mother, and she never really got clean, so . . ." I draw in a breath and make myself slow down. "I thought you went to rehab for pills."

He nods carefully. "Yeah. The second time was opioid abuse. I got a back injury racing motocross, and needing them for the pain turned into needing them to feed my addiction." He pauses for a beat. "The first time was recreational stuff. After that, I should've known better than to touch those fucking pain pills, but I was in denial. I didn't think of myself as an addict. I didn't want to." He shrugs, but his expression betrays him. His choices and his mistakes weigh heavily on him.

"So that's why you don't drink, even though alcohol was

never your issue? And I've heard you talk about AA meetings. I thought people with drug problems went to NA."

He nods. "Yeah. And while I was never drunk day in and day out, it'd be really naïve to say I never had an issue with alcohol. I have a handful of drunk-and-disorderlies on my record that prove addiction doesn't stop with pills and blow." He sighs and shrugs. "As for AA, honestly, I just like it better than NA. The crowd is older—at least in Jackson Harbor—and it seems like the people stick around longer. When I'm having a bad week, I need to see that. I need to see the guy who's been sober for forty years, and the mother of four who got sober when her youngest started kindergarten—and to know that same mother is now picking her grandkids up from kindergarten every day."

I know what it's like to need to see people who fixed their own messes. Isn't that what drew me to Colton in the first place? "That makes sense. I never wanted to ask, but I've wondered."

"You can ask me anything. About who I am now or about the things I did. You just need to be prepared to not always like the answer." He meets my gaze and holds it for a long time. "I'll never be able to have just one drink, V. I'll always be an addict. That doesn't go away. So when I say you should feel like you can have a drink when we go out, it's because I don't want you waiting for some elusive day when we can drink together. I can't. I won't."

"I don't care about your past, and I don't care about alcohol. I don't *need* it." I slide one hand behind his neck and press my mouth to his, thinking, *But I just might need you.* I brush my lips against his until his jaw softens and he kisses me back.

Across the bar, someone whistles—I'd put money on Amelia—but I ignore it and revel in this kiss in this moment with this man.

COLTON

"I had fun tonight," Veronica says, slipping her arm through mine as we make our way to the HBA building.

"Me too." Making Veronica laugh and smile has been the highlight of my year. Right next to the way I plan to make her moan and beg when we get back to my apartment. "When we get upstairs, we should—"

"Ronnie?"

Veronica freezes as a woman rises from the shadows in front of the building. I recognize her mother immediately.

"Ronnie, I've been looking for you." She stumbles toward us, that brown package in her hand again.

Veronica backs up a step, and I instinctively place my body in front of hers. "I don't have anything to say to you," Veronica says.

"I wanted to give you this." Her mother's hand is shaking as she extends the package.

"I don't want it. I don't want anything from you until you can prove you've changed."

She takes another stumbling step closer. "But—"

"Get *away* from me." Veronica steps around me and rushes toward the door while her mother looks on helplessly.

I move to follow then stop and turn to the woman. "If you ever want to get clean—and I mean completely stop using—you can come find me here, and I'll help you. But until then, you need to leave." With that, I head into the building and follow Veronica upstairs.

When we get into my apartment, she goes straight to the window that overlooks the street. From here, we can see her mother walking away.

"Has she always been . . .?"

She nods. "She used to be so good at hiding it. I didn't understand why they'd take us away when she seemed like all the other moms."

"Really?"

She huffs. "No. In retrospect, the signs were there. I just didn't want to see them. She'd sober up from time to time, but it never lasted. I didn't want to believe she had a real problem, though, so I told myself the story a lot of enablers do. That she had it under control, that she just used to unwind but could stop if she wanted. I told myself she'd had a hard life and couldn't cope."

"You were a kid."

She tosses her purse on the counter and pulls open the fridge. "I believed that shit well into college."

"When did things change?"

"When I was pregnant." She grabs a sparkling water and cracks it open. "I haven't seen or talked to her since before Jacks was born."

"What happened?"

"It started during the short weeks Marcus and I were actually together. She asked me for money." She sighs, and the weight of the world is in that sound. "I took out a cash advance on my credit card to help her get these guys off her back. I figured Marcus had all this money, so I could afford to help for once. But then the guys came for me because she'd told them I was going to help her. It was the scariest night of my life. One grabbed me from behind. The other held a knife to my throat. I knew they wouldn't leave until I got them their money, so I did. Another cash advance on a different credit card. More debt at a ridiculous interest rate."

Useless, protective rage fills me as I imagine it. "She owed them more money?"

"She *still* owed them money. I don't know what happened to what I gave her, but I have a pretty good guess."

"With drugs, it's just like booze—when you're an addict, there's never enough."

"The next day I tracked her down in one of her favorite haunts and told her I didn't want to see her face until she'd cleaned up."

"And you hadn't heard from her since?"

"She only called when she needed money, and since I didn't want to be stupid enough to help her again, I blocked her on my phone after I moved here. I couldn't risk leading her to Nic."

"I thought you said your mom wouldn't track her down. That your mom hadn't forgiven Nic?"

"She always held a grudge against Nicky for not fighting harder to get out of our foster homes—as if it were up to us." She puts down her drink and looks out the window again. "But it's my fault my mom hates my sister. When I realized in my twenties that Mom had gotten mixed up with a dangerous crew, I told her she'd better stay away from Nic because Nic was buddies with the guys at the police department and wanted to turn Mom in. Mom hates cops. Hates any threat of the authorities. I knew she'd keep her distance."

"Did you tell Nic what you'd done?"

231

"No." Her voice is raw. "I know it's awful, but Nic will do anything to protect her family, and I knew, even before they'd held that blade to my throat, that I had to protect her. I couldn't let her risk herself for Mom. I always planned to tell her someday. The whole thing. But I don't know if it'd be worth the hurt it would cause her."

"She can handle it. She's like you."

She screws up her face. "How do you figure—other than appearance?"

I study her for a long beat, marveling at how she could be so blind to her own qualities. "She's strong."

Chapter Twenty-One

COLTON

"Guess who just got an interview to teach second grade at Jackson Harbor Schools!" Veronica says, racing into my office. She bounces on her heels, squealing.

I grin. Not just because I'm really enjoying the view of her bouncing in front of me in my favorite little white dress, but because I know she's been waiting for this and because she deserves it. But I lean back in my chair and pretend to think. "Crosley?" I ask. "No—Brady?"

She rolls her eyes. "You're such a pest."

"I'm *your* pest." I roll my chair forward, wrap my arms around her waist, and grin up at her. "Congratulations," I whisper. "I know you've worked hard for this."

Her eyes fill with tears, which she makes a valiant effort to blink away. "I'm so nervous."

I slide my hands down to cup her ass and squeeze. "No need for that." With one tug, I pull her forward and into my lap so she's straddling my chair—and me. "You're going to be amazing."

"Could you tell me that, like, twenty more times between now and the interview?"

"I could tell you twenty more times today if you want. You're amazing and you deserve this."

Her expression softens. "Thank you."

"I had nothing to do with it. You scored this interview all on your own."

"No, I mean thank you for . . ." She shrugs her shoulders and drops them dramatically. "Everything. For believing in me."

"It's easy." I sweep my lips across hers. "What's *not* easy is waiting to have you in my bed again."

She laughs and threads her fingers through my hair. "It's only been four nights."

"I think you mean *it's been four nights,*" I say with a dramatic flair.

"Poor baby."

"You and Jacks could come stay this weekend," I offer. I've kept myself from saying it at least a dozen times this week, but I'm giving up on self-restraint. At least when it comes to Veronica. "We could play Spider-Man in the living room and take him out on the cat, and then after he goes to bed, you and I could have a little sleepover of our own." I know before she looks away that she's going to say no, so I squeeze her hip. "Hey, no pressure."

"It's not that I don't want to." She drops her gaze to my chest, avoiding my eyes. "That sounds amazing, but maybe we should skip the sleepover part. I don't want to confuse him."

I want to plead my case and tell her all the reasons staying at my place this weekend instead of his aunt Nic's would be fun and exciting and not at all confusing. But what the hell do I know? Only that I need to be patient. "No worries." I cup her face and tilt it up so she meets my eyes. "You control the accelerator on this, okay?"

She nods. "It's just that my mom used to drag us to one boyfriend's house after another, and . . ."

And they were as bad for her as the drugs.

She scans my face again and again. "I need to do better for Jacks than she did for us."

"You are. And you will." I bury my hands in her hair and kiss her. I mean to reassure her, but I realize quickly enough that I'm trying to reassure myself. Things are good. We're in this together, and we'll get there. Eventually.

VERONICA

The last two weeks have been the best of the whole summer. It's been a long time since I've opened up to anyone like I've opened up to Colton. In truth, I've probably never been this transparent, but Colton makes it easy.

Weekends without my son, on the other hand, may never be easy. I know, intellectually, that I should enjoy the freedom I get from his visits with his dad, but it's hard to enjoy something when a piece of you is missing. Nevertheless, I'm trying to be optimistic. I decided to use his weekends away to get a few extra hours at HBA and catch up on laundry and errands. I'm telling myself this will mean I can be a better mom when we're together. I can't deny I've also been looking forward to another weekend with Colton.

On the Saturday morning of Jackson's second weekend away, I'm hanging out in the reception area of HBA when Kristi walks in.

I jump out of my chair. "What happened? Is Jacks okay?"

She waves away my panic. "He's *fine*. He and Marcus are at the zoo today."

"Okay." I glance around the office as if I might see some hint as to why she's here. I always tell them where they can find me, but that was in case Jacks needs me.

Her smile wavers. "I wanted to talk." She glances toward the street. "Could we go for a walk?"

I don't want to assume anything, but knowing Marcus as I do, my mind spins with the possibilities. Trying not to jump to conclusions, I flip the sign in the window to indicate I'll be back in an hour, grab my purse, and lead Kristi out of the office.

We're both quiet as we make our way to the walking path that snakes along the bay, the only sound the distant traffic and our shoes on the pavement.

"What's going on?" I finally ask. I try to keep my voice gentle. I might not be Kristi's biggest fan, but when a woman reaches out to you for help, you listen. It says a lot about my faith in Marcus, that I was just waiting for him to let her down.

Kristi studies her feet as we shuffle forward. "I've been doing a lot of thinking, and I want to make you a deal."

I frown. "What?"

"I know you struggle, and Marcus explained you got into some trouble a while back trying to help your mom. I could help with that. My parents worked hard and were very successful, so I have a sizable trust. I want to share that good fortune with you."

I stop walking, and, despite the hot day, the hair on the back of my neck stands up. "I don't need anything from you."

She folds her arms and looks me over. The pity in her eyes makes me want to rage. "But you do. You have a seasonal job, your car isn't reliable, you got kicked out of your house—"

"Who told you that?"

"—and Marcus tells me you were drowning in student loan debt even before the credit cards became an issue. I could fix all that and make sure you're very comfortable."

"Listen, if this is about Jackson, I assure you he has everything he—"

"I want to give him a better life," she blurts, her voice loud enough that the walkers and runners on the path around us look our way.

I take a step back. "His life is fine." I don't want this woman's pity money. Jackson and I get by, and if I land this teaching job, we'll be a little more comfortable. "I don't need you putting us up in some fancy apartment."

She cringes. "That's not what I'm suggesting. *I* want to give him a better life. With me and Marcus."

I stare at her, the sounds of the nearby traffic humming in my ears. Is this a nightmare?

"He deserves to be raised in a *family*, not a broken home."

"Just because we don't have a house doesn't mean we aren't a family."

"I'm prepared to pay you for all you've endured and the burden you've absorbed the last few years. I'm sure we could come up with a number that—"

"You cannot *buy* my son."

She gasps. "Of course not. I wasn't suggesting I could. I was saying I'd like to *help you*. We can give Jacks a better life, and of course we'd want his mother to have a better life too. We're not looking to cut you out of the picture—just to be the ones who provide his daily needs."

"You want him to live with you. Full time." I feel empty at the mere thought, but then rage boils over and fills all those crevices. "No. Absolutely not. I won't do that to him."

Tears spill from her eyes and stream down her cheeks. "God gave you what *I* so desperately wanted. A baby with Marcus's eyes. His sweet little grin."

A baby with Marcus's eyes. No wonder she's been so clingy and obsessive about Jackson. The woman wants a child of her own. I don't know if she can't have a child or if Marcus won't. It doesn't matter the reason she hasn't gotten the child she wants—she can't have mine.

She sniffles. "I know we can work something out. Make it easier on you. You could still see him whenever you wanted. We'd split holidays. He could stay with you a couple of times a month. But you need to think about what's best for your son—about what kind of life you want him to have."

This *is* a nightmare. This is *my* nightmare come to life. "No. I've let you swoop in out of *nowhere* and have a relationship with him, but you've crossed a line."

She holds out her palms. "Before you decide, I want you to

see where he'd go to school. We have it picked out—it's a private pre-K academy where he can *thrive*. Plus, I have a list of all the other activities he could be involved in throughout the year—activities a single mom wouldn't have the time to run him around for."

"I always make time for my son." My voice trembles. I knew this was coming. I *knew* it, but I disregarded my gut because I bought into their bullshit about wanting to help. They don't want to help us. They want to take him.

"Come visit, sit down with us and look at all we could do for him if we had primary custody, and *then* make your decision."

"My decision's already made." I turn and walk away, praying she can't see how badly my hands are shaking.

COLTON

When I get back to the office after my Saturday morning excursion, Amelia is behind the counter and Veronica's nowhere in sight. "Where is she?"

Amelia nods to my office. The door's closed. "Jackson's stepmom showed up and they went on a walk. When V got back, she wouldn't talk to me. She's been in there since."

When I enter my office, Veronica is sitting sideways in my chair, her knees drawn up under her chin as she stares blankly out the window. My chest aches to see her like this.

"Hey, baby. You okay?"

"No," she says, her voice dull and even. She doesn't look at me.

I close the door softly. "Tell me what happened."

She doesn't answer. Doesn't move.

I walk around my desk, perch on the edge, and stroke her cheek. "Talk to me."

She swallows and her eyes fill with tears. "Kristi and Marcus want full-time custody of Jacks." The words send those tears spilling down her cheeks. "Kristi offered me *money* if I'd agree. A new car, a place to live. She even offered to pay off my debt."

"The fuck?" I roll my neck and force myself to take a breath, but it barely tempers the anger bubbling in my blood. "What'd she do when you told her to fuck off?"

Finally, she turns to me. "Thank you," she whispers, and the pain in her eyes feels like a blade through my gut.

God, I want to hold her. "For what, babe?"

"For not asking what I said." She gulps in a breath and more tears spill over. "For knowing I wouldn't be tempted to trade my child for a bunch of cash."

"Babe." I shake my head. I can't handle it anymore, so I slide off the desk and guide her out of the chair.

"I think they have someone watching me. Or a PI or something. She knew I'd been kicked out of June's, and I never told them that. Does that make me sound paranoid?"

"No." I swallow my rage. "It doesn't."

She buries her face in my chest. "I'm so afraid I made a mistake letting them in his life. I'm so afraid they're going to take my boy."

"The hell they will. Where's Marcus been the last three years?

Where does he get off thinking he can take over now?"

"They think I'm failing Jacks," she whispers against my chest. And the next words come out so softly, I almost can't hear. "And I'm terrified they're right."

I smooth down her hair and press a kiss to the top of her head. "We'll get the rest of the crew to take care of wrapping up the day."

She blinks up at me. "Why?"

"I'm gonna take you home and take care of you."

Chapter Twenty-Two

VERONICA

I'm vaguely aware of Colton leading me out of his office and up the stairs. Vaguely aware of him leading me inside his apartment and to the couch. I can hear him in the kitchen, and the sound of the kettle registers shortly before he cups my hands around a warm mug.

I'm shutting down. Just like I used to. Just like my mom did. Am I going to turn into her? Would Jacks be better off with Marcus and Kristi?

"Why is this happening?" I ask. "Why does everything have to be such a battle?"

Colton sinks onto the couch beside me and pulls me against his chest. He strokes my hair, but his words register like I'm underwater. *"Shh. We'll take care of it. I'm here. I've got you."*

I risk a glance at his face, and the fierce compassion in his eyes is like a rock against a pane of glass. I shatter, shaking, sobbing, and he keeps holding me, rocking us back and forth until my body calms and my tears subside.

Once my hiccupping inhales are the only remaining evidence of my breakdown, he shifts our positions so he's leaning against the arm of the couch and I'm cuddled against his chest. I breathe him in—his goodness and his strength. His steadiness. He doesn't rush me to talk or to stop crying. He just gives me time and a safe space to purge these emotions.

"I don't want to let him go," I whisper finally.

"Of course you don't. And you don't need to. You're his mother. You're the one he's been with from the beginning. They're crazy to suggest changing that now."

I close my eyes, relishing how steadfast his belief in me is. "Are they, though? They have money. They have this amazing house with this killer backyard. They want to send him to this fancy preschool and have a speech therapist for him. I'm over here on the government charity plan, and I know too much to pretend it's the same as what the expensive, private programs can provide."

"Does all that really matter, though?" He kisses the top of my head. "You're his mother, and you love him so much. You're a fucking amazing mom, Veronica, and that's not me trying to make you feel better. It's true. Is money a substitute for love?"

"Of course it isn't, but . . ." I close my eyes. "My mother loved me and Nic. You have no idea how madly she loved us, and I have never doubted that love. But as an adult, I also know we probably would've been better off if she'd let us go. She fought so hard to keep us, and as a result, we were in and out of the system.

We could never get comfortable with a new family or in a new home—because she loved us too much to let us go. She loved me so much that if I behaved in foster care, it was a betrayal to her. '*Show them who they're dealing with, Ronnie,*' she'd say. '*Give 'em hell until they bring you home.*' And that's exactly what I did."

"I remember you mentioning getting kicked out of a good place—the one you watched through the window at Christmas."

"Nic was always so pissed at me for ruining our chances with those families."

"Did you ever consider that maybe it wasn't your fault? That maybe you just felt that way?" Colton asks, big hands splaying across my back.

I scoff. "It was absolutely my fault. And it was intentional. I did everything to make life hell for our foster parents, and I did it because I thought it proved I loved Mom. I thought the fact that Mom wanted us back so badly proved she loved us." I close my eyes, mentally holding up my adolescent beliefs against the way I see the world now. "The first time I held Jacks in my arms, I saw my whole childhood differently. I looked at his beautiful face and knew I could ruin everything for him if I wasn't careful. I promised myself something that day. If my life ever came to a point where I believed he'd be better off without me, I would let him go. I would do for my son what my mother couldn't do for us." The tears threaten to return, so I close my eyes and take a deep, steadying breath.

"I have no doubt that's true," he says softly.

It's easier, somehow, finding my footing with Colton holding me. I spend so much of my life feeling like I'm floating with no tether. No one to keep me grounded—no one to catch me if daring to reach for the sky means I fall. It's scary how much I need this. How much I need *him*. Maybe I'm asking for trouble by leaning on him, but for the moment, I let myself.

"After I walked away from Kristi, I kept thinking . . ." I shiver and struggle to find the words, but Colton waits patiently. "I thought of everything Jacks would have in his life if I let them have custody. I thought of my mom and my childhood and all the times I needed her to let us go. I thought of all the homes we could've called ours, and I had to wonder if I'm any better than her."

"Veronica." He takes my chin in his big hand and tilts my face up so I meet his eyes. "Your mother's an addict, and you were taken away from her because she was using. She couldn't provide you with the very basic things you needed—a safe place to call home at the top of that list."

His words sting even though I know he doesn't mean them to. "I can't even provide him with that right now."

"But haven't you? He's always had somewhere safe to sleep. Always had his mom. No question."

"But is that enough? The fact that I don't use drugs? Will I look back on this time and hate myself for keeping him from all these opportunities?" My voice cracks. "Will *he* hate me?"

"You're a single mom who works her ass off to provide for her kid. You make the best of bad situation after bad situation, and when you and Jacks get home at night, you're devoted to him. Not drugs. Not some fantasy of what it means to be a mother. I know you want more for Jackson than you can afford right now, but Kristi has made it abundantly clear that she and Marcus are in a position to provide those things for him. That's true no matter where he lives. You're not keeping him from his father. You're not keeping him from school or from having a full belly. You're not teaching him that he needs to be a social delinquent to prove his love. You're just being the best mom you can be. Giving him love and safety. He truly has everything he *needs*. The rest is just for bragging rights."

He's saying exactly what I need to hear, and I know he's right. But now that I've let my fears slip into the light, I need to get the rest out. "What scares me is I think my mom believed she was doing right by us by fighting for us too."

Colton's quiet for so long I think he might not reply, but then he finally says, "I don't think so. I think she knew you'd be better off without her, but it didn't matter. In AA, they say alcoholics don't have relationships; they take hostages. That's true about addicts when they're using, too—we're slaves to the drugs, and we become selfish. Don't let decisions driven by addiction make you question your value as a mother."

"I know you're right, but I have to question my own impulses. There's nothing that matters more."

He combs his fingers through my hair, and I settle against him again, letting some of the fear and tension go—if only for this moment. "My parents had all kinds of money when I was growing up, V, and I'll tell you now that it caused more problems than it solved. And my father? Hell, you want to talk about being better off without a parent? He's the shining example."

My breathing evens out as his argument really sinks in. "I don't want to let him go," I say again, but this time, guilt doesn't hang heavy on the words. "I want to keep doing everything I can to give him a good life."

"Of course you want to. And you will. I'll be here to help. If you need me."

I curl my fingers into his shirt, balling it in my fists as if that might keep him close. "I do."

"Good. Because I want to help," he says. "We're gonna get through this."

We. I didn't realize how badly I needed to be part of a *we*, how badly I need to know there's someone in my corner. Finally, I find the strength to push off his chest.

He holds my face between his hands and presses a firm kiss to my lips. "You're not alone," he whispers, and there are no words I want to hear more.

VERONICA

I'm honestly surprised to see Kristi again on Sunday. After yesterday, I expected her to send Marcus to bring Jacks back to me, but I have to give her credit. She might've shown her ass by offering me money for my child, but she's not going to hide from me after what she should see as an embarrassing mistake.

"Thanks for bringing him," I say as Jacks run right past me and into the house.

Kristi cranes her head to the side, looking around me and beyond the door. "Whose place is this?"

"My sister Nic's." I don't mention that Jacks and I are staying here for the time being, but I can't help but wonder if she already knows. Can't help but wonder if she knows a lot about me and my life that I never told her. Nevertheless, I won't give her any potential ammunition to use against me.

"The sister who was engaged to Marcus when you got pregnant?" She presses her lips into a thin, judgmental line. "I don't think I would've forgiven *my* sister so easily."

A thousand retorts spring to mind. I could throw shade on her relationship with her sister or point out that Marcus was just as much at fault for what happened as I was, but I don't have the energy for either path. Once, Kristi said this would be easier if I didn't constantly assume she and Marcus were the enemy, and she's probably right. Not that she makes it easy. So I say, "Nic is the most amazing person I know."

"Clearly." She folds her arms and takes a breath. In no way is her demeanor that of someone who's about to climb her ass back into her car and drive home.

"So, everything went okay this weekend?"

She beams. "Better than okay. The boys had so much fun at the zoo yesterday, and then last night, Jacks and I went to this Mommy and Me music class. It was incredible. He loved every minute of it."

Mommy and Me. The words are like nails on a chalkboard, but I started my day determined to be the bigger person, and I'm not going to take the bait. "Thank you," I say, and I hope my words sound sincere. "Thank you for giving him such incredible experiences. It means a lot to me."

"Of course. All we want is what's best for Jacks." Sincerity shines in her eyes.

"Well, I appreciate it." I take a step back, moving toward the door, but she doesn't change position. "I'll see you in a couple of weeks, then." *Please leave.*

"Have you given it any more thought?" she asks, and this time there's nothing gentle about her expression. Kristi's a bulldog under that sweet Southern exterior. "Adjusting the custody arrangement?"

"The answer is still no." I stare back, matching the stubborn will in her eyes twice over. "And it will still be no tomorrow and next week."

She rolls her eyes. *Rolls her eyes.* As if I'm being unreasonable and not reacting the way any mother in my situation would. "Veronica, I understand why that would be your first reaction, but I want you to take your own needs out of the equation. Make the choice that's best for Jackson."

"I am." I lift my chin. "I'm his mother, and I've been the constant in his life since the day he was born. I may not have a lot of money, and I may not have access to some prestigious preschool, but none of that changes the facts. When he's with me, he is loved, cared for, and provided for. If you and Marcus want him to have access to more material things or expensive schools, then we can talk about how you can help, but I will remain Jackson's custodial parent. End of conversation."

She shakes her head slowly. "I wish you could see how selfish you're being. We don't want to have to bring lawyers into this."

My blood boils in my veins and my neck heats. "I am *not* being selfish. Maybe *you* are. Did you ever consider that?" *So much for keeping a cool head.*

"Is that what you told yourself when you were sleeping with your sister's fiancé?" she asks, a smile quirking her lips as she cocks her head to the side. "Or what you told yourself when your behavior got you both kicked out of so many foster homes that they wouldn't risk putting you with another family? I bet your mom told herself she wasn't being selfish when she fought to get you back over and over. And when you were a teenager and she'd pick you up from the group home so the two of you could—"

I don't even realize I'm moving. One second, I hear a screeching in my ears and feel like I'd do anything to keep her from finishing that sentence. The next, my first is flying toward Kristi's face. It lands with a *crunch*.

Kristi stumbles back and falls backward, screaming. She curls onto the ground at the bottom of the steps. Blood streams down her face, and she clutches her arm.

I can only stare in horror. I haven't lost my temper like that since I was a teenager.

"What happened?" Ethan asks behind me. He rushes down the stairs and crouches on the sidewalk next to Kristi. "What's your name? Are you okay?"

"I'm Jackson's stepmom. She punched me," Kristi says, her voice garbled. "I think she broke my nose."

Ethan throws a disdainful glance toward me over his shoulder, and my shock ebbs enough for me to shrink. I feel four inches tall under Ethan's angry gaze. "Veronica, run inside and get ice, and ask Nic to find the sterile gauze pads from the medicine closet."

I only stare, convinced this is all some bad dream.

"Now!" Ethan snaps. His face changes as he turns his attention back to Kristi. "It's gonna be okay. I'm a doctor, and I'll take a look at it, but if it's really broken, we might need to take you to the emergency room."

"You see why I don't think you should raise Jackson?" she asks between sobs. "Do you see?"

I run into the house—run from the blood that's *my fault*, and run from her words, but they've already penetrated my defenses, and the truth in them is a poison that has me rushing to the toilet and losing my dinner.

Chapter Twenty-Three

COLTON

Veronica hasn't said a word since I arrived at Nic and Ethan's place. Apparently, Mrs. Jackson distracted the kids until Ethan loaded Kristi in the car for the hospital, and then she took them over to Shay and Easton's "to visit the baby." Translation: Get the kids out of the house before everything exploded.

Nic called me not long after Ethan left and asked me to come over. "Veronica needs to feel like there's someone here who's on her side," she said.

I didn't hesitate, and I was pulling into their driveway ten minutes later. She filled me in on Kristi's potentially broken nose, and I filled her in on the identity of the woman her sister punched and the contentious custody situation. Nic softened after her shock ebbed.

That was an hour ago, and Veronica still hasn't spoken or

moved from where she's curled on the end of the couch. I haven't pushed her. No one knows what was said between them before V threw that punch, but I don't see any benefit in rushing the information out of her.

A slamming door has Nic and I snapping our heads toward the garage. Heavy feet stomp toward the family room. When Ethan enters the room, he's glaring daggers at Veronica. "You're fucking lucky her nose isn't broken," Ethan says, "and even luckier that when they asked if they should call the police to file a report, Kristi said no."

Veronica lifts her head at that and exhales, some of the tension leaving her shoulders.

I squeeze Veronica's hand, and for the first time all night, she squeezes back.

Nic's eyes fill with tears. "Press charges? Ronnie lost her temper, but she didn't mean to hurt her."

Ethan squeezes his eyes shut for a beat before pulling a deep breath and turning his attention on his wife. "Baby, I know she's your sister, and I know you want to protect her, but she's a grown woman, and tonight she assaulted another grown woman on *our* property while our daughter was in the house. I'm not just gonna let this go."

"We can talk about it later," Nic says, a feisty spark in her eyes. "Right now, I'm less worried about your unhappiness and more worried about my sister's." She turns to Veronica. "What did she say to you?"

She blinks, and tears roll from her eyes and down her nose. "She said I'm no better than Mom, and that's why I should give them custody of Jacks."

"That's bullshit." Ethan blanches. "Custody? They haven't even been in his life until a few weeks ago."

Nic nods. "Exactly."

Ethan drags a hand over his face. "That's insane, but Veronica, you've gotta know we wouldn't let that happen."

"Could you really stop her?" Veronica asks, voice hollow.

"Maybe. Instead you decided, what? To give her a fighting chance at this by losing your temper?"

Nic swats his leg, and Ethan grunts and backs away from his wife.

Veronica sits up. "I know," she says. "You're right. Don't worry. I'll find somewhere else to stay."

"Of course not," Nic says at the same time as Ethan says, "Thank you."

Nic glares at her husband again, and he holds up both hands. "Fine. You two figure it out, but you know damn well that if it'd been *my* sister who'd just busted up a woman's face on our front porch, I would've kicked her out on her ass too."

"Well, it wasn't Shay," Nic says. "It was Ronnie, and I'm the only family she has, so you're going to have to handle this differently."

"Babe," he says softly, but she gives him one more pointed glare, and he sighs and backs out of the room. "I'll be in the basement if anyone wants my opinion on any of this."

"I appreciate it," Nic says, her smile tight. She rubs her belly and turns her attention back to her sister. "You and Jacks are welcome to stay here as long as you need, but please, no more fistfights on my front porch."

Veronica swallows hard and nods. "I'm so sorry."

Nic waves away her apology. "If I'd been standing there when she said that shit, I probably would've beat you to it."

Veronica doesn't crack a smile—only bows her head.

Nic's eyes are filled with pity as she stares at her sister. "How could they ask for primary custody of Jackson when they've only recently been in his life?"

I pull V's hand into my lap, holding it between both of mine. "That's what I said."

"It's madness," Nic says, "and anything she said to get under your skin, she said because she *knows* they don't have a chance."

"They have a lawyer," Veronica says, her voice rough. "They aren't going to let this go."

"Do you have a lawyer?" I ask, then realize immediately that it's a stupid question. "Of course you don't. They know you can't afford a lawyer, but they don't know my dad worked with some of the best lawyers in the state. A couple of them owe me favors. I'll make some calls. I'll get you in to see someone this week."

Nic gives me a grateful smile. "Thank you."

Veronica just stares at her hands. "I'm gonna get packed."

Nic rubs her belly. "Veronica, you don't have to go. I'll talk to Ethan."

"It's fine." She heads toward the stairs.

"She and Jacks can stay with me," I say.

Veronica stops, and I can see her profile just enough to catch her cringe. "We're going to stay with Star. We'll leave as soon as Jacks gets back."

It's a punch to the gut, but I keep my face impassive. "Want me to help you pack?"

"I've got it." Veronica disappears up the stairs.

Her twin turns to me, biting her bottom lip. "So you two . . ."

"Yeah." My voice sounds rough, sounds like I'm not so sure.

"She didn't tell me." Nic's eyes fill with tears. "She didn't tell me about any of it."

"She doesn't want to be a burden."

She wipes at her cheeks, but the tears keep coming. "I'm her *sister*." She drags in a shaky breath. "You'll be good to her?"

"Of course."

"I've messed up. When she and Jacks needed a place to stay, I shouldn't have pushed back so much. I shouldn't have . . ." She shakes her head. "Will you just . . . try to take care of her?"

I swallow, feeling as unsteady as Nic looks. "In any way she'll let me."

At Star's place, Jacks runs to Katie's room to show her his new book. Star wraps Veronica up in a tight embrace, but Veronica withdraws without returning the hug. *It's not just me.*

"I hate Kristi-with-a-know-why," Star says, folding her arms. "And fuck Dr. Jackson."

Veronica shakes her head. "Don't say that. He's just trying to protect his family, and right now, that means keeping them away from me." Her voice cracks, and it's a relief. She's been stony and silent since we left Nic's.

"He's overreacting," Star says, and while I kept my opinion to myself, I agree heartily. "I hope Nic withholds blow jobs as punishment."

Veronica cracks a smile. "Please don't make me picture my very pregnant sister giving a blow job. This day has been traumatizing enough."

Star glances at me and backs toward the hall. "I'll give you two a minute."

When she's gone, I half expect Veronica to freeze up again, but she buries her face in my chest, wrapping her arms around my waist. "I'm so sorry."

"Hey." I stroke her hair. She's shaking against me. "What are you apologizing for?"

"I don't want you to be pulled into the middle of this. I don't want you to feel like I'm something you have to fix. I wouldn't blame you if you wanted a way out of this relationship."

"Listen"—I cup her jaw and lift her face until her eyes meet mine—"I *don't* feel like that. There's nothing about you that needs fixing, baby. You're just having a really hard time right now, and I want to be here to help you through it. I don't need to find a way out because I don't want one."

"But why? Why would you take this on?"

Her question makes me feel like my heart is being squeezed in her fist. It kills me that she has to ask, and I hate that I can't say the words. It's too soon, and I refuse to do anything that will scare her away. So instead of saying the three words that'll terrify her, the ones that just might scare her away for good, I say, "Because I want to. And I'm an asshole who does whatever he wants, remember?"

Her frown cracks, and she huffs out a laugh.

"There's my girl."

She leans her head on my chest again, and we stand there

for a few minutes, her clinging to me like I'm her lifeline and me breathing her in like she's fresh air.

When she pulls away, she squeezes my hand. "Thank you."

"For what?"

"You're kind of my rock right now. Thank you."

I've never been someone's rock before. I was always the one flying high—literally and metaphorically—and I wasn't sure I'd ever be a symbol of stability for anyone. I want so badly to be that for her. "Anything you need, just say the word."

She blinks up at me. "I need you to tell me you see me, because I keep feeling so scared that you're going to walk away when you realize I'm not Ellie. I don't have it together like her, and maybe I never will."

I frown. "You really think I still want *Ellie*?"

"No. No, I just . . ." She swallows. "Someone more like her, maybe."

"Hey, V?"

"Yeah?"

"You're a hot fucking mess." She snorts, and I keep going. "Your life is super complicated right now; you have more baggage than a 747. You have no respect for punctuality, and sometimes when you get emotional, you get bitchy, and worse, you try to push me away."

I cup her cheek, lower my head, and touch my nose to hers. "You're also smart and beautiful and sexy. You love with an intensity and purpose I admire so much. You're real and you're complex. I *see you* and all your bumps and scars. You haven't pulled the wool over my eyes. So stop worrying I'm going to realize who you are and be disappointed."

"I've never known anyone like you," she says, shaking her head. "Are you really mine?"

I pull her against my chest and hold her tight. "Heart and soul."

Chapter Twenty-Four

VERONICA

I've always been intimidated by lawyers. Some might assume it's because the legal system played a role in my foster care experiences, but I don't think it's that. As kids, Nicole and I talked with social workers and occasionally a friendly judge, but never a lawyer.

In truth, I think my discomfort comes from the fact that I associate lawyers with wealthy people. My mom would tell these stories about people who could afford good lawyers getting away with everything. To some degree, she wasn't totally off-base, but it made me grow up distrustful of the system and seeing it as something that's stacked against poor people. Like so many things are.

So I'm not surprised my hands are shaking when I go to meet with the lawyer Colton recommended.

"Veronica?" the woman asks, greeting me in the waiting area. She has shining brown skin and a wide smile.

I stand and wipe my sweaty hands on my skirt. "Yes. That's me."

"I'm Henrietta, but you can just call me Etta. It's nice to meet you."

"Veronica," I say, then realize she just said my name and I sound like an idiot. "Obviously. Thank you so much for taking the time to meet with me."

"Of course. That's what I'm here for. Come on back. We'll just chat in the conference room. Can I get you a drink?"

I'm afraid anything I tried to put into my body wouldn't stay down. "No. I'm good. Thanks."

"You're a friend of Colton's?" she asks, ushering me into a room with a big table surrounded by eight rolling chairs. The walls are papered in a soft pink-and-white pattern and the room is lit by old-fashioned wall sconces instead of fluorescent overheads.

"Yeah." *Friend.* What a weird word for what we are, but I'm not sure I have a better one. "We work together." I cringe as soon as the words are out of my mouth. We're more than coworkers, and I feel guilty simplifying our relationship to that, but now isn't the time to figure it out.

"Oh." She lifts her chin in a way that says my explanation isn't the one she expected, but she doesn't go into it. "Well, take a seat and fill me in on the situation."

We sit across from each other at the oval table, and she scribbles notes on a legal pad as I explain my history with Marcus and how he hasn't been involved in Jackson's life until recently.

"So he requested visitation and you've allowed that, but now he's making noise about pursuing primary physical custody—is that right?"

I nod. I wish this wobbly feeling would subside. I wish I didn't have to be here. "He has so much money, and I . . ."

She waits for me to finish that sentence, but when I can't, she gives me a gentle smile. "Well, the good news is that outside of extreme circumstances, no judge is going to jump from a parent having no rights to having primary custody. They'll first look at your son's established custodial environment, and from everything you've told me, you've provided that for your son's whole life. If there's no significant reason to remove the child from his established custodial environment, the judge is extremely unlikely to do it."

"And the bad news?"

"I suppose the bad news, as I see it from the little information that I have, is that his father does have rights, and there's nothing keeping him from continuing to pursue more custodial rights even if the judge rules in your favor initially. That can be frustrating and, if you retain counsel, expensive as well. Really, the best thing for everyone involved is if you can come up with a custody agreement everyone can live with without getting the judge involved. Do you think they'd be interested in that?"

"I could ask, but I don't think they'd be happy to hear from me right now."

"Because they know you don't plan to give them what they want?"

I clear my throat. "Because I punched Kristi, Marcus's wife."

Etta blinks, but there's no other sign of shock or disapproval.

"When did this happen?"

"On Sunday when she brought Jacks back from his weekend with them."

"And was a police report filed?"

"No. She's not pressing charges."

She nods slowly, scribbling more notes before lifting her gaze to meet mine. "Do you have any criminal record?"

"When I was a minor, I made a few mistakes."

"Anything as an adult?"

I shake my head vehemently. "No. None. That thing with Kristi was . . . it was out of character. I'm not like that anymore."

"That's good. And you said you work with Colton, so that's good. Is that a full-time position?"

"Yes. It's full-time for the summer at least, but they don't need as much help once the tourist season is over. I have a teaching degree and am hoping to get a position with the school corporation this fall. I have an interview at the end of the week."

"And what's the plan if that doesn't work out?"

I swallow hard. I'm hanging all my hopes on getting a real job doing the thing these stupid student loans paid for. "I haven't let myself think too much on what happens if that doesn't work out."

She puts down her pen. "Have you applied anywhere other than the Jackson Harbor school district?"

Embarrassment and shame creep up my neck. "Not . . . yet." I guess I should add that to my list.

"You'll need a plan. The last thing you want to do is end up unemployed when we go before the judge."

"They'd take Jackson away if I didn't have a job?"

"That's unlikely."

"But possible?"

Again, she puts her pen down. "Listen, you could probably go to court on your own and be just fine without me. You're the child's mother, and you've provided him with a good home through all the years his father's been absent. While Marcus's explanation for not being involved when he lived in Alabama seems reasonable, the fact of the matter is he *wasn't* involved, and that might be enough for the judge to refuse him any more custodial rights than he already has. But if you were happy with those odds—even as favorable as they are—you wouldn't be paying me. My job is to make sure we leave no doubt in the judge's mind as to what's best for Jackson, and judges tend to look favorably on *working* single moms."

"Of course." I bob my head, but tears are clogging my throat, threatening to overwhelm me.

"What about housing? You said Marcus has a very nice, large home, but judges don't care about fancy. Tell me about your living situation."

I swallow hard, but it does nothing to push down my rising fear. "I was subletting a room from a friend until recently. It was a really nice house. Not huge, but near the bay, so convenient for me."

"And now?"

"Well, she kicked us out suddenly, so we moved in with my sister for a while, but now we're living with my friend."

This time when Etta lifts her gaze from her legal pad, she doesn't bother trying to hide the concern in her expression. "And is this a long-term plan? Staying with your friend?"

"She's a really good person," I blurt.

She nods, but for some reason, it worries me when she doesn't pick up her pen to scribble this down. "In cases like these, your argument is *stability*. If you're hoping to avoid even a joint custody arrangement, you want to prove—through your job, your home, your car, and every other element of your life—that you're providing Jackson not just a loving home, but a stable one."

"So I need to move soon?"

She squeezes the back of her neck, and I feel like I'm back in those interviews with the social worker. They'd separate me and Nic and ask us a bunch of questions about home. I wanted to make Mom sound good, to prove she loved us so they wouldn't take us away, but no matter how hard I tried, I always felt like I was failing. "You need a long-term plan. If you want to continue living with your friend, that's not necessarily a bad thing. There may be a little bias toward the nuclear household in this part of the country, but not enough that a judge couldn't be convinced of the benefits of a more extended family living situation. What we want to avoid is painting a picture of you and Jackson hopping around from house to house—renting a room from this friend then staying with your sister for a while, then maybe renting a room from another friend. We want to demonstrate stability."

Tears spill down my cheeks. She's speaking to my darkest fears—that I can't prove the best place for my son is with me. "I'll find something. It's just hard. The housing market here is tough, and I have a lot of debt." *And now I have to pay* you, I think, but I don't say it out loud.

This time, she actually cringes. "I'm not here to give you financial advice. That's not my area of expertise, but I will say that whether or not you want this to be about money, money will play a role. I recommend you call your student loan company and ask about a deferral. If you explain your financial situation and that you're looking for steady work in your field, they'll likely grant it. If that would allow you to find stable housing, it'd be in your best interest to consider it."

Now I feel like I should be taking notes. I fumble inside my purse, looking for a piece of paper and a pen, and scribble down a reminder to myself. *Call student loan company. Deferral.*

She tilts her head. "We prepare for the worst."

"But you don't think he has a chance, right?" I ask. "He can't actually take my baby away?"

"I can't make any guarantees. Find an apartment for you and your son, cast a wide net of applications for the school year, and make sure you don't do anything stupid."

"Like get arrested for battery?" I ask, my voice monotone.

She gives me another one of her soft, sympathetic smiles. "Yeah. Let's avoid things like that. You're his mother, and there's nothing in the system to indicate you've been a neglectful one. These are points in your favor."

"Doesn't seem like much beyond the basics."

Her expression is gentle as she studies me. "When it comes to the best interests of a child, the basics are what's most important. I'll reach out to Marcus and arrange a meeting with him or through his lawyer, but the system is bogged down, so you're looking at a year at least before a judge can see your case. I'm sure once they have a chance to think it through, Marcus will agree to mediation, where we can come to an arrangement on our own."

COLTON

I pace the office until Veronica returns from her meeting with her lawyer. She's quiet when she walks in the door.

"How'd it go?" I ask.

"Fine. She's optimistic." She takes my hand and doesn't say a word as she pulls me into my office.

"So, that's good, right?" I ask as she turns the lock.

"Yeah." She slides a hand behind my neck and pulls me down, kissing me hard and full, like we've been apart for years and not hours. When she breaks the kiss, she strokes my cheek with her thumb and studies me.

"What's this about?"

"Just a kiss to thank you for not running away yet." She smiles. "Every time I realize you're still here, I'm dizzy with relief."

I settle my hands on her hips and pull her body flush with mine. "I think you're stuck with me."

Chapter Twenty-Five

VERONICA

*O*oh La La! has been my safe space since Star and I became friends, but tonight, not even the smell of fresh chocolates and coffee can put me at ease. Marcus got the call from my lawyer and texted to see if we could talk privately before involving our legal counsel. I'm hoping this is a good sign.

I've recited the lawyer's words to myself over and over again. *Come up with a custody arrangement you can live with. Keep the communications open. Nothing good comes from a contentious relationship between parents.*

Marcus and I were terrible for each other when we were together, and whether or not he's just as terrible to Kristi, I don't think he's a terrible person. If I did, I wouldn't let Jacks stay with him. I'm hoping Etta is right and that a civil, rational conversation is all it'll take to end this nightmare. If not, I'll wait for our court date and trust that my lawyer can prove Jackson needs to be with me, but I really don't want to put this in a judge's hands.

The bell above the door chimes, and Marcus strides inside the café, scanning the room before spotting me and smiling. My stomach flips. He looks so calm as he moves toward me. So casual. As if we're meeting to discuss who's going to take Jacks to soccer practice and not who he'll spend the majority of his life with.

He pulls out the chair across from mine and sits, leaning back. "You look good," he says, the corner of his mouth tugging up into a crooked grin.

This strikes me as strange. Him smiling at me when I recently bloodied his wife's nose, telling me I look good when he saw me last Friday. But that's Marcus. He can't turn off the charm. "Thanks. How's Kristi?"

He grimaces and squeezes the back of his neck. "Her face is still a little swollen, but she's fine. She considered filing a restraining order, but I convinced her it'd be harder for us to see Jacks if she did that."

I swallow. "I tried to apologize a couple of times, but she isn't taking my calls."

"She's not scrappy like you." Again that familiar smile as he looks me over. "I don't think anyone's ever raised a hand to her before."

Excuses spring to my tongue—she was trying to piss me off, it's hard for me to be rational when someone's talking about taking my son—but I swallow them all back. I made a mistake and don't want my anger toward Kristi to suggest what I did was acceptable in any way. "I'm not proud of what happened."

He arches a brow. "If you say so."

I hate that superior smirk on his face, as if he knows me better than I know myself. I force myself to look at my coffee and take two deep, cleansing breaths. "I'm glad you wanted to talk about this. My lawyer thinks it'd be best if we resolve this ourselves."

"Your *lawyer*." Marcus lifts his chin. "Fancy. You haven't been able to afford a place for yourself and Jacks to live in over a year, but you're dishing out cash for a lawyer. Interesting."

My internal temper barometer ticks up a few notches. "Kristi made it clear you'd already obtained counsel and that the two of you plan to take me to court if I don't give you the custodial rights you want."

"She just wants to take care of our boy. That's no crime, Ronnie."

Coming from him, the old nickname makes my heart ache. Not because I miss Marcus or because I have any romanticized notions of a life we could've lived together, but because it's a reminder that this man once claimed to love me. Now, he truly believes that taking my son is the right thing. I blow out a breath, determined to stay focused. "I don't have any intention of giving you primary physical or legal custody. I've been more than accommodating with your visitation requests, especially when you consider you haven't been in Jackson's life at all before this summer."

"You moved across the country when you were pregnant. How could I—"

I hold up a hand. "I don't disagree that you could be a positive force in his life, and I'm willing to work out a generous visitation schedule, but *you* are his father. I want to do this with you and not her."

He scrubs a hand over his face. "Shouldn't we let the judge figure this out?"

I cock my head to the side. "Is that what you want? We can go back to how things were with you getting no visitation until our court date. I'm sure your lawyer explained, as mine did, that we should be able to get in front of a judge in about a year. You'd miss another entire year of your son's life just so we don't have to look at a calendar together and come up with a visitation schedule we can both live with?"

"There is no visitation schedule that Kristi can live with. Trust me when I say she'll fight you until she's Jackson's primary guardian."

"No schedule *Kristi* can live with?" I ask, irritation bubbling up and threatening to wash away my civility. "This is about what she wants, then. Not about you."

He doesn't look the slightest bit ashamed or uncomfortable being called out on this. He just shrugs. "Happy wife, happy life, right?"

That barometer hitches up another notch. "That's what you say when your wife wants to remodel the kitchen or buy a new minivan. That's not a reason to take a child from his mother."

He folds his arms on the table and leans forward. "It doesn't matter what the reason is. The end result will be the same. You'll save yourself a lot of pain and money if you just drop the lawyer and the court date and do what you already know is best for Jackson. Give him to us and save yourself the heartache."

Give him. Like he's some *object* that can be passed between adults. I shake my head. "You're wrong. I'm a good mom. No judge is going to take him from me."

"How can you be so sure?"

My stomach twists in the face of his confidence.

"It's logical," I say, but I have none of his bravado.

Marcus sighs. "I'm not out to get you, Veronica. I want to do this with as little fuss as possible, but you need to understand that if you fight us on this, you'll lose."

He has something—some reason to believe that if this goes to court, they'll win. Does he know my mom's been back in town? Would a judge care about that? "If you think I'm going to give him up without a fight, you never knew me."

"Actually, I knew you *really* well," he says, and this time when he looks me over, I feel an aura of slime everywhere his eyes touch. "I knew you well enough that it was easy to tell the private investigator we hired where to look. Not that we needed to. We had enough against you without what he dug up, if you ask me. And they *will* ask me. I'll tell them everything I know about you. About your history, about your mother. About how when you were in college, you'd get high together."

"That's not who I am now." I swallow hard. He knows too much. I told him too much, and he's enough of an asshole that he'll use it all against me. *Trusting him was a mistake, and I'm paying for it over and over again.*

"No. Now you're the woman who bloodied my wife's nose when she brought Jackson home after visitation. Never mind your boyfriend."

"What about Colton?"

"He's the last person a judge is going to want to see Jackson living with." He ticks off reasons on his fingers. "He's an addict. He has a record of violence and was the primary suspect in a homicide."

"He was cleared of that." My voice breaks. I didn't think about how Colton's past might look to a judge. Henrietta didn't mention Colton being a problem.

"What about the drunk-and-disorderly charges in his file?"

I shake my head. "That was the past. It doesn't matter now. He's sober."

"So you say, but my PI took some pictures of him with some known dealers that might make a judge question your confidence. I'd sure hate for this to all go sideways and for your boyfriend to end up with a new criminal charge against him."

Bile surges into my throat. "You wouldn't. You wouldn't risk it."

"I wouldn't have to. Your boyfriend is trash, and there's a long line of people he did dirty who'd do the job for me. And you? Do you think it was *hard* to get your mom to come to town? To convince her to come sniffing around you again?"

I should've known. He probably gave her money. Or worse. Someone like me can't just escape my past. The cards have always been stacked against me, and Marcus knows just how to play them to his advantage.

"You don't want to be on my bad side, Veronica. It won't end well for you or for your boyfriend. Let me have my son."

"Why are you doing this to me?" My vision blurs as my eyes heat with tears. I hate letting him see me this vulnerable.

"Maybe you're doing it to yourself. Have you ever considered that?" He pushes back from the table and stands. "I don't want to do this the hard way, but I will if I have to. And I'll win. You remember, don't you?" He looks me over one last time. "I always get what I want."

Then he walks out the door, and I feel myself turn cold.

COLTON

I've been pacing since Veronica left an hour ago. I hate the idea of her meeting with Marcus alone, so I offered to shut down the office and go with her, but she insisted she'd be fine.

Unfortunately, when she returns, it's obvious that wasn't true.

She's pale and all her eye makeup's been wiped away, as if she's been crying.

"How'd the meeting go?"

She lowers herself into her chair and stares at the notebook on the desk in front of her. "It was okay," she says, flipping it open to a calendar page from February. "Nothing's resolved, but I'm not giving up."

"Hey." I touch her shoulder. She's still staring at the page. Hasn't looked at me even once. "What's wrong?"

She turns her chair and opens the laptop, giving me her back. "It's just a lot. I'm tired."

I know. That's why I want you to talk to me. But I need to be patient. We're at work and it's the middle of the day. It's completely understandable that she might not want to get into it here. "I bet. We can talk about it later."

"I'd like that." She swallows. "Later."

"Can I get you anything? Coffee? A snack? The heart of your enemies?"

That doesn't get me even a slight smile. "I'm fine."

She's obviously not, but I'm not going to argue the point with her right now. "I thought after we close up we could go get Jacks, pick up some fast food, and do dinner at the park."

She closes her eyes. "I can't tonight. Today's just been . . . I need to prep for my interview."

Let me help. Let me take care of you. "Okay. Maybe another time." I tuck back into my office, but I keep looking out to the reception area as Veronica helps customers and answers the phone. I plan more tours, reply to a message from Mike confirming he's sober as a judge, but my mind never strays far from Veronica. Something Marcus said shook her, and I want to know what, but maybe it's not my place to push.

Eventually, I end up out back helping Brady dock one of the boats, and Crosley comes to find me.

"Veronica okay?" he asks.

I glance toward the building and shake my head. "She had that meeting with her ex today. She's been a little off since." And since I'm not a selfish teenage boyfriend, I don't complain that she's ignoring me. "Did she say something to you?"

He wipes the sweat off his brow. "Nah, but she asked Amelia to cover for her so she could leave early, so I figured something was going on."

She left early? I pull my phone from my pocket and look for missed texts, but there's nothing there.

"She didn't tell you?"

"No." My jaw's tight, and a sick feeling settles in my stomach. "What is it?"

I pull up my texting app and Veronica's name. I hover my fingers over my phone screen for a few seconds before I decide against it and shove my phone into my back pocket. "I gotta get out of here. Can you handle helping Brady tonight?"

Crosley slaps my back. "Sure, man. I got you. I hope everything's okay with your girl."

My girl. I love those words. And I'll do whatever it takes to make everything okay with her.

Chapter Twenty-Six

VERONICA

I am in full avoidance mode. I took off work early with the excuse of needing to go look at apartments. With the help of my newly deferred student loan payments, I found a couple of places that aren't awful that I can afford without depending on child support, and then I got Jacks and brought him to the park. Star's daughter is chasing him around while I upload my resumé to online job listings in the school districts surrounding Jackson Harbor. I've even applied to some preschools, since I got my pre-K certification in undergrad, but in my experience those positions don't pay well, so I'm not holding my breath.

The most promising opportunities are in Chicago, but I'm nervous about living in the city. I moved from one small town to another, and don't know if I want to raise my kid alone in Chicago.

I'm staring at an application for a position in Gary, Indiana when the crunch of mulch sounds behind me.

Colton. I don't even have to turn to know he's there. It's like my body recognizes when he's close.

"Hey," Colton says, straddling the picnic table bench beside me. "Whatcha doing?"

I close Star's laptop and nudge it away as if I need to get rid of the evidence. I can't look at Colton, so I stare out into the lawn by the playground, where Jacks is chasing after a bright red kickball. "Nothing important."

Colton is the second-best thing that ever happened to me. Only for Jackson—the most important person in my whole world— would I give him up. And if giving him up means protecting them both? I don't have a choice.

"You feeling okay?" Colton asks, following my gaze. "Cros let me know you left early. I went to the bakery, and Star said I could find you here."

"I was apartment hunting. Gotta establish that long-term housing in case we end up going to court." Not that I can sign a lease until I know where I'll be working in the fall. This whole mess feels like a series of catch-22s.

Colton blows out a breath. "I could've gone with you."

"It's better if I do it alone, I think." I sound like a robot. That's the only way I can do this. If I cut off my feelings for anything but protecting Jacks and Colton.

"Shit, I kind of hate for you to spend your money on a place for yourself when I'm just going to want you with me all the time anyway."

My attention jerks from the lawn to the man facing me.

"What?"

He gives me a goofy smile and shrugs. "Okay, I realize it's crazy fast, but we both know we're headed there anyway, right? So why not now?"

He can't possibly mean what I think he means. "Why not . . .?"

"Why don't you and Jacks move in with me instead of signing a lease? It would save you money, and we'd get more time together, and . . ." His gaze dips to my mouth before flicking back up to meet mine. "I want you there. I know this is faster than is ideal, but it could work." He hesitates a beat then sighs. "I'm so sick of pretending I'm not already madly in love with you."

There's a piece of my heart that soars when it hears these words. *Colton loves me. Colton loves me and wants me and my son to move in with him.*

I take that giddy, blissed-out piece of me and I lock it up tight. "We can't."

He blinks at me for a minute, and I realize he's probably processing what I said—or rather, what I *didn't* say. He said he loves me and I didn't say it back. He has no idea how much I've betrayed my own heart by pretending I don't feel the same.

"Sorry," he says gruffly, his gaze darting toward the playground. "I know this is fast and I know my timing is shitty."

You have no idea.

"I don't want to rush you. I just wanted to put it out there as an option, but I totally understand you might need to be on your own for a while first."

"I need to be on my own until we're through this."

"Hey, that's fine. It's a big step."

"You don't understand," I whisper. He cups my face in his big hand, and I make myself scoot back to put some distance between us. Pulling away breaks something inside me, but it's the look on his face that makes something even bigger crumble.

"What's happening right now?"

"Jacks and I need to be on our own. Completely."

Confusion slashes across his features. "Tell me you're not breaking up with me."

I bite the inside of my cheek and redirect my focus toward Katie and Jacks.

"Veronica?"

Marcus will destroy you. He will make you lose everything you've fought so hard for, and it'll be entirely my fault. "I have to focus on being the best mother I can." I swallow, but I feel like there's glass in my throat. "You have a criminal record and a history with drugs. If we're together, Marcus could use those things against me."

Hurt flashes in his eyes before he schools his expression. "Is that what he told you during your meeting today? Is that why you were so upset when you got back?"

"I've been thinking it through."

He stands and paces in front of the picnic table, dragging both hands through his dark hair before spinning back to face me. "And you're okay with this?"

"I'll do whatever I must to keep my child." I sound cold and heartless, but the tears that stream down my cheeks are hot and feel like they come right from those bleeding chunks of my raw and aching heart.

"Have you talked to Etta? Have you asked if this is really an issue?"

"It doesn't matter. I won't risk it."

"I wouldn't question this if I was having any trouble at all staying clean or if I'd slipped." He tips his face to the sky. Agony lines those beautiful eyes when he looks at me again. "You said you didn't care about my past. You said . . ." He cuts himself off with a shake of his head. "This is really happening."

"I told you my son would always come first," I whisper.

Jackson's attention is pulled away from his ball long enough for him to spot Colton. He races to the table and wraps his little arms around Colton's leg. "Co-tin!" he squeals.

Colton drops to his haunches and pulls my son into a hug. "Love you, buddy," he whispers. When he stands, his face is red and his eyes are brimming with tears.

I did that. I took this strong, amazing man, and I hurt him. Even knowing I'm doing exactly what I have to, I'm not sure I'll be able to forgive myself.

He looks at me for a long time before nodding. "You're making the right choice. I'll . . . get out of your hair."

He walks away, and I close my eyes because it hurts too much to see.

COLTON

Six guys in penguin suits and, judging by the casual posture of the other five, I'm the only one who can't wait to take mine off. The Jackson brothers look completely comfortable in their tuxes, and here I am, the odd man out. That's the way it always is with me and the Jacksons. They've always welcomed me, but I've never quite fit in.

Because you're not a fucking Jackson.

I barely recognize the guy staring back at me from the mirror. It's not just the tux—though I can't remember the last time I wore one of these—but it's the bloodshot eyes and the face that's pale from stress, heartache, and lack of sleep. Maybe this is the face of a guy who's lost and gained everything over the last three years. I got a third and fourth chance at a decent life when I'm not sure I even deserved the second. And here I am, still standing, still sober, through another fucking heartbreak.

It's been two days. Two days since I've looked at the woman I love. Two days since she broke my heart. Two days since I realized I didn't escape my past when I got sober.

I've avoided the office completely, making Crosley and Wes cover inside and working entirely on excursions and doing the grunt work of manual labor that never seems to end.

In the mirror, I see Levi approach me from behind. He smacks me on the shoulder and smiles at my reflection. "Looking good. Who knew you could clean up so nice?"

I arch a brow. "Could say the same about you, but you've gotten pretty comfortable in the monkey suits lately."

Levi shrugs. "People change." The words are light—a cliché we could easily walk away from—but we both know he's not just talking about himself. He's talking about me. "Thanks for doing this."

"No problem." The whole eye-contact-through-the-mirror thing is awkward, so I turn and give my lifelong best friend a one-armed hug. "I'm happy for you."

Levi doesn't hesitate to return my embrace. He wraps both arms around me and squeezes me hard enough that it almost hurts. If I didn't know him so well, I'd find it awkward as fuck—I didn't grow up in a family where the guys showed each other affection, physically or with words—but Levi's a Jackson, and they're a touchy-feely bunch. He's the closest thing to a brother I've ever had, so I close my eyes and count to five before I let myself back out of it. "If you're this hard up for physical contact, I'm sure Ellie can help you out," I say.

Levi chuckles, but that tenderness is still in his eyes. "You're sure you still want to stand up for me? Because if it's weird or painful at all for you, all you have to do is—"

"I'm sure. Now shut up about it. You're making it awkward."

He laughs, but then his smile falls away. "Are you okay?"

"I'm fine."

A low whistle sounds from the front of the tailor shop, and Nic waddles toward the men's fitting room area. She's wearing a lilac bridesmaid dress and has one hand on her massively round belly. "Look at all these handsome men."

"Look at *you*," Ethan says, striding toward his wife. He drops a kiss on her lips then another on her stomach. Seeing Veronica's identical twin round with pregnancy never bothered me before, but now it's a reminder of what I don't get. What I've never truly believed I deserved.

Something twists low and painful in my gut, and I wish I could numb it without having to turn to booze or pills or the other shit that fucked up my life before. But that's the thing about being sober—it doesn't come with options for oblivion.

"What are you doing here?" Levi asks his sister-in-law. "Spying for Ellie to make sure I got the right tuxes?"

Nic shakes her head. "Hardly. You could show up in jeans and a T-shirt and she'd still marry you." She winks at him, then surprises me by turning her attention my way. "We're all trying on our dresses to make sure the alterations are right before taking them home. Well, most of us . . ." Her smile falls away. "Veronica was supposed to meet us here for the bachelorette party. Do you know where she is?"

I tug at my collar as all eyes turn to me. "Why would I know?"

Nic's eyes go wide, then she looks to her husband and back to me. "Aren't you two . . . ?"

"Sorry." I pretend to study the uncomfortable, shiny shoes on my feet. "Not anymore."

"What happened?" Ethan asks, and the protective edge to his voice pisses me off.

I scoff. "Her roommate screwed her over, and you couldn't give her a place to stay without making her feel like a second-class citizen, but now you're going to get all protective-big-brother with me because we broke up?"

Ethan winces. "I know I handled everything terribly, but I do care."

I grunt. "Hell of a way to show it."

Nic worries her bottom lip between her teeth. "When?"

I shake my head and turn back into my curtained dressing room. "I need to get out of this thing."

The whole time I'm changing, I can hear their confused whispers. By the time I'm back in my jeans and have returned the tux to its fancy hanger, I'm no more ready to answer questions about my love life than I was when I came in here.

My stomach's in knots when I exit the changing room.

"You can leave the tux there," the attendant says before I can ask. "We'll do the final adjustments when you pick it up for the wedding."

I force myself to smile. "Thanks." Then I turn to Nic, who's clearly waiting to speak with me again. "Sorry she didn't tell you, but I don't want to get into it."

"I understand," she says.

I head toward the exit.

"Just one minute. I'll walk you out." She kisses her husband, and he whispers something in her ear before she nods and pulls away, following me to the front of the store. "What happened?" she asks when we're a few feet from the group.

I close my eyes, praying for patience. "I said I don't want to get into it."

She grimaces, rubbing her back as she settles onto one of the wicker chairs. "I've been trying to give her space, but that was when I thought she had you to lean on."

The accusatory edge in her voice raises my hackles. "Well, she doesn't *want* me to lean on anymore, so there's not much I can do about it. Maybe you should talk to her and make sure she knows she can still lean on you." I glance toward the guys gathered around the fitting rooms—the ones not even trying to pretend not to look our way. "If that's even still true."

Her eyes fill with tears. Yep, I just made a pregnant lady cry. "Of course she can."

"Good to know." I walk toward the door, then stop and turn back to her. "I don't think you have any idea how hard she tries to protect you, even now."

Nic's brow creases with confusion. "From what?"

I sigh. I shouldn't get in the middle of this. Veronica's secrets are her own. "From *everything*," I say. "Now I'm getting out of here."

Chapter Twenty-Seven

VERONICA

The soft knock on the door pulls me from my half-conscious state on Star's couch. I'd ignore it, but I'm afraid whoever it is might knock louder next time and wake up Jacks.

When I see Nic through the peephole, my heart squeezes.

"Hi," I whisper, pulling the door open.

"Can I come in?"

"Yeah. Is everything okay?"

She nods. "I just wanted to check on you."

"I'm fine." I'm a liar. There's nothing about me that feels fine. Every minute I'm walking the tightrope of too many emotions. But none of that is Nic's fault. "Jacks is napping."

"I'll be quiet. I promise." She smiles at me, and the gentle love in that smile makes me marvel at how different we are despite being "identical." Nic's soft and sweet. I'm hardened and cold on my best days, straight-up bitchy on my worst. "I told the girls to get the bachelorette party started without you."

I flinch. "Oh my goodness. It totally slipped my mind, and I . . ." I blow out a breath. "I don't think I can do a bachelorette party tonight."

"Kathleen is all set to watch the kids," Nic says, referring to her amazing mother-in-law. "Jacks would be fine."

I shake my head. "I can't. I wouldn't be any fun. I'll text Ellie and let her know. Was she upset?"

"No one's upset. We were just worried. But the guys were there trying on tuxes, and Colton mentioned you two aren't together anymore?" It comes out like a question—the kind you ask when you want someone to tell you you're wrong.

"It didn't work out."

"It didn't work out, or you decided to walk away from him before he could walk away from you?"

"Don't psychoanalyze me." I close my eyes. "I'm tired and I know I'm predictable, but we both know I don't deserve Colton anyway."

"Bullshit."

"Trust me. It's not."

"Ronnie, I don't understand. I've forgiven you a hundred times over for what happened with Marcus. Hell . . ." She presses a palm to her chest. "I'm *grateful.* When I try to think about what my life would look like if I hadn't ever come up here pretending to be you, if I hadn't ever met Ethan and Lilly . . ." Tears spill down her cheeks. "You made bad choices. It's true. And at the time, those choices hurt worse than anything Marcus could've done to me." She swallows. "But it doesn't matter anymore. I've forgiven you, so when exactly are you going to forgive yourself?"

If only it were that easy. "The custody situation with Marcus is complicated. *Everything* in my life is complicated right now."

"Seems to me like that would be a nice time to have someone standing by your side. Someone you know will be there when the disappointments come and the days are hard."

I bite my bottom lip. I want to tell my sister everything, but I can't. Nic is so good—optimistic to a fault. If I tell her what Marcus threatened, she'll want to go to the police. She doesn't understand that sometimes love doesn't conquer all. Sometimes good doesn't triumph over evil. "He's a good guy," I say instead. "The best. But I can't do it right now."

She pulls me into a hug, and I let her hold me. I don't cry. I'm too dried up. But I let myself be sad and I don't try to hide it.

"Ethan wanted to come to apologize," she says after a long time. "Colton kind of called him on being a dick to you, and he realized he wasn't being rational about everything."

I step back and take a seat on the couch, pulling my feet up under me. "He doesn't owe me an apology."

Nic snorts softly and takes the seat to my right. "He absolutely does. I'd be way more pissed at him about everything if I didn't understand what he was going through."

I cock my head. "What's going on?"

She rubs her stomach. "The baby. It was after Lilly was born that Elena's depression spiraled. He knows I'm not her, but those years and how it all ended? It left a mark."

I blow out a breath. "Poor Ethan."

"Well, he's not off the hook for that apology, but I wanted you to myself tonight."

I lean my head on her shoulder. "I'm glad to see you."

She bites her lip, then pulls a brown package from her purse and sets it on my lap. "Tell me about this?"

I shake my head. "I don't know what it is."

"My friend Toni works the front desk at the public library. She called me and said a woman dropped it off for me. She told her she couldn't take it, but then she turned around to do something else, and when she looked back, the woman was gone but the package was still there."

I lift the package closer to the light on the end table and squint to read the nearly illegible print. *Nicky, please hold on to this for Ronnie. I'm afraid I'll lose it, and I owe her.* "Oh," I breathe.

"That's Mom's writing, isn't it?"

I nod so much that I probably look like a bobblehead. "She came to town, and I refused to talk to her. Refused to take this, too."

"It says she owes you."

I swallow hard. I've kept secrets from my sister to try to protect her from the painful truth—and maybe I can't tell her everything about the situation with Marcus, but I can tell her this. Maybe I should've told her this a long time ago. "Not long after you ran away from your wedding, she needed money."

"Money," Nic says flatly. "For drugs?"

I bow my head. "She'd borrowed from a loan shark in Birmingham, and when she didn't make her first payment, his guys broke her hand."

Nic closes her eyes, and I can practically feel her focusing on her breathing.

"You don't need to hear this." I put my hand on her shoulder, but she shakes her head and opens her eyes.

"Yes, I do. Tell me what happened."

"I gave her the money." I sigh. "I foolishly thought Marcus would be taking care of me, so I took a large cash advance on one of my credit cards. And then she didn't use the money to pay her debts, so I had to do it again. That was right before I came here."

"Ronnie, why didn't you tell me?"

My heart aches when I look at my sweet sister. "Because you would've given her the money. You would've tried to help. And once she figured that out, she wouldn't have left you alone."

"She's hated me since I told that social worker I didn't want to live with her anymore."

"She would've overlooked that if she figured out you had access to cash."

"Did she leave *you* alone?"

I shrug. "I'm a cold-hearted bitch, remember? I moved across the country and blocked her on my phone."

She giggles—a sound that skates the line between amusement and hysteria. "Oh, Ronnie."

I close my eyes and let myself feel that ache in my chest that comes from losing my mom. Because I did lose her. The day she decided to put me in danger so she could use my money for drugs instead of paying her debts, I lost her forever. "I wish I could help her. Really help her."

Nic's face goes somber. "I know." She nods. "I do too."

"I hope she's okay. I hope . . ." I cut off the thought. *I hope she'll get sober one day.* I haven't let myself hope for that in a long time, but when I meet my twin's eyes, I know she's thinking the same thing I am.

"I know, Ronnie. Me too."

I flip over the box and cut the brown paper all the way around the edge with a fingernail. When I lift the lid, there's a pile of cash inside. "Jesus," I whisper, shoving it away.

Nic grabs it and pulls out the thick stack of twenties. "This has to be at least a couple thousand dollars." She lifts her head, her eyes wide. "Will this pay off what you owe?"

I cough. "No. Sadly, it won't make a dent, thanks to compound interest." *But she tried.*

"Where do you think she got it?"

"Marcus," I whisper. And then, because my sister's here with me and my mother finally did something selfless, because sometimes the bad guy's plans don't work out in his favor, I finally tell her everything.

COLTON

I'm alone in my apartment on Sunday morning when a key scrapes in the lock. There are exactly two people who have a key to my place—Levi and my sister, Ava—and I don't want to see either one of them right now.

"Sitting in the dark and feeling sorry for yourself," Levi calls, then in the next second I'm squinting against the flood of light filling my living room. "If you were going for *total fucking cliché*, you nailed it."

I glare at him. "Fuck you."

"And verbally abusing your best friend. Another point for team cliché." He strides into the room, tucking his hands into the pockets of his jeans. Despite his words, I know he's here to help. Here because he's worried about me. He sinks onto the couch by my side. "Bachelor party wasn't the same without you."

I swallow hard. "Sorry about that. Everything go okay, though?"

"It was a good time. I missed you, but . . . I get it. Want to talk?"

My throat feels like it's closing up. As if I physically *can't* talk about it. "Nah. Nothing to say."

Leaning forward, he rests his elbows on his knees. "Cool. I can do the talking, then."

"Please don't."

"You're in love with her," he says as if I hadn't spoken, "even though you did everything to keep yourself from having real feelings for anyone. But she got to you, made you put your guard down and start to think that maybe you deserved happiness despite all your mistakes. You started to believe you were more than your past, but then that past became the very reason she dumped you."

I don't know who filled him in, but it doesn't matter anyway. "I didn't need a recap, but thanks."

Levi ignores me. "Now you're sitting here telling yourself you were right all along. That you don't deserve her or love or happiness or any of the other shit you'd wish for the people you love." He turns his head, meeting my gaze before arching a brow. "How'd I do?"

"Made me sound as pathetic as I feel," I mutter, but I feel too numb to put any real feeing into it.

He smacks my thigh. "Anytime."

"If you're done, you can show yourself out."

"Give it time," he says softly. "All this shit with her baby daddy and custody of her son . . ." He settles farther into the couch cushion next to me. "She's freaking out."

"I know."

"Every decision she makes right now is focused on what the judge—some stranger—might think."

"I know."

"You two . . ." He shakes his head. "I've watched you around her the last couple of months, and I don't know what it is, but I like you guys together. I liked seeing you smile the way you did with her. And once you finally got over yourselves and got together? I loved the way you looked at her."

"That's not fucked up at all," I say, trying for humor I don't feel.

He grunts. "Don't make it weird."

"You can stop. Even if Veronica dumped my ass, you and Ellie still have my blessing."

"While I appreciate that, the truth is you could tell me you were still madly in love with Ellie and it wouldn't stop me from marrying her."

I rub my temples. "Thanks a lot."

"She's the fucking love of my life, Colt. I'm saying I need and want her enough that I'd be with her right now regardless of what you thought, but I've spent years wishing and hoping you'd find the same thing for yourself, and I was glad to see it happen."

I cut my eyes to him. "Given how it ended, why don't you

save your hopes and wishes for someone else next time?"

"Nah. I want soul-deep love for you."

"Not everyone gets that shit, Levi."

"Well, you need to, because I'm marrying Ellie regardless, but the guilt kind of sucks."

I roll my eyes. "Sorry to inconvenience you."

"My point is I saw you and Veronica together last week. You two have that special something."

I fall against the back of the couch and tilt my face toward the ceiling. "*Had.* Past tense."

"Nah. It's *have.* That shit doesn't go away just because it's inconvenient. Trust me. I know."

"None of it matters. I'd never ask her to choose me over her child. Even I'm not enough of an asshole to ask her to risk it."

"Is it a risk, though? Really? You're sober. You're a business owner and a community servant. What judge is going to see you as you are now and rip a kid out of his home just because his mom's dating you?"

I shrug. I've asked myself that same question a thousand times, but the answer doesn't really matter. If Veronica thinks being with me is risky, I can't ask her to do it.

Levi sighs and smacks my thigh. "Just give it time, is all I'm saying. Give her time to get through this and have faith that she'll come back to you."

"What? In fifteen years when Jacks is off to college and the custody issue isn't a thing anymore?"

"Nah. It won't be fifteen years." He grabs my empty bottle of water off the coffee table and picks at the label. "She'll come around long before that."

"But should she? With my background and his threats to keep pursuing custody, should she ever risk it?"

Levi's quiet for a long time, the only sound in the room the soft cracking of the plastic bottle under his fingers. "I think there will come a point when there's no custody issue. This is the same guy who was MIA for the first three years of his son's life. I can't predict the future, but something tells me he will lose interest soon enough." He shrugs. "Or maybe he won't. Maybe I'm wrong and he'll keep trying, but I know you. You'll wait as long as it takes, whereas he will move on to some other new shiny."

I close my eyes. *Fifteen years. Twenty. Fifty.* I'd wait whatever it took. "The problem isn't whether or not I'd wait for her. The problem is I don't want her waiting for me."

"Because you don't believe you're worth waiting for?"

I set my jaw. He means well, but I'm not in the fucking mood for this. Every word out of his mouth just makes me want to guzzle a fifth of vodka.

"Have you called your sponsor?" Levi asks, reading me, because he's always known my mind better than I've known myself.

I close my eyes. I know he's trying to help, but the question's another rock thrown at my fragile self-regard.

Levi waits a few beats then sighs heavily. "Call your sponsor, Colton. That's what you'd tell your friends to do."

"I don't want to *need* to call my fucking sponsor." I lurch off the couch and pace the living room, dragging my hands through my hair. "Don't you get it? That's the whole problem. I'm the kind of guy who needs to call his sponsor when life goes to hell or he'll implode. And *that* is exactly why she can't be with me."

"She can't be with you because a manipulative asshole is trying to take her kid. And the fact that you're *going* to call your sponsor, that you're stronger than your addiction, that you choose sobriety day after day, is exactly why any judge who looks at this case will say your past doesn't matter."

I scoff. "Well, it definitely doesn't matter if I'm not around." I brace my arms against my kitchen island and bow my head. "I'm not in a good a place for company. Could you just get out of here?"

I hear Levi coming up behind me but I don't look. I don't move.

When he slides my phone in front of me, Etta's number is already up on my screen. Veronica's lawyer. My AA sponsor.

He squeezes my shoulder once. His steps echo through the apartment as he walks to the door.

When I hear his steps on the stairs, I pick up the phone and press call. Sometimes the act that feels weak is the one that takes the most strength.

Chapter Twenty-Eight

COLTON

I've dreaded this day since the first time I found out Ellie was falling for my best friend. Dreaded it and knew it would come. But now that it's here, I feel none of the things I thought I would.

Ellie is a woman I care about. One I loved once. And she's marrying the best guy I know.

I'm happy for them. The jealousy I feel when I look at them has nothing to do with me wanting Ellie and everything to do with me wanting to be with the woman I love now.

The ceremony was a short but sweet exchange of rings on the pier leading out to the Jackson Harbor lighthouse, and the reception is at the Jackson Brews event center. We've been busy all day with last-minute wedding duties, and the guests arrived at the reception before the wedding party, thanks to pictures and whatnot. The second I walk into the ballroom, I practically run into Veronica, who's heading in the opposite direction.

"Oh! Excuse me!" She backs away and then freezes when she meets my gaze. "Hey."

I gobble up the sight of her in a fitted navy dress that flares at her hips but hugs every inch of her ass all the way up to the halter top. Her makeup's a little heavier than usual tonight, and her hair's swept up off her graceful neck. She's wearing a pair of strappy silver heels that put ideas in my head. It's far too easy to picture her in nothing but those heels, and the sexy possibilities have nothing on how much I just want to *hold* her.

When my gaze meets hers, she blushes as if she knows exactly where my thoughts have gone.

"How are you?" I ask, the question coming out rusty and awkward, but fuck. It is. I'm not supposed to run into her at some big event to find out how she's doing. I'm supposed to know because she's part of my every day.

It's been three weeks, and I still haven't accepted that it's over. After three days, she trained a college student to cover her position at HBA because she had the opportunity to be a lead teacher and program manager at a sought-after local preschool. For any other job, I might've thought she was running away from me. But this one was exactly what she needed. Amelia said they pay their teachers well and have great benefits, and Jacks will be able to attend preschool there. It's perfect, and I've been so busy avoiding running into her that I've never gotten the chance to tell her in person how happy I am for her.

"I'm good." Her smile is gentle. "Busy. Of course. They say the first year is the toughest."

Before I can reply, a guy I don't recognize comes up beside her and drapes an arm over her shoulder. "I thought you got lost on your way to the bar," he says. He turns an easy smile on me and offers his hand. "I'm Sam."

Veronica flashes him an uneasy smile. "Sam, this is my friend, Colton."

Friend. A better man would be her friend, but no matter how hard I try, I can't be that guy. I want too much more from her to ever pretend I'm okay with friendship. Ava tells me this makes me a dick, but so be it.

I take his hand and lift my chin. "Nice to meet you."

"It was a nice ceremony, huh?" Sam asks.

I shift my weight. Are we really going to do this bullshit where we stand around and have an awkward and meaningless conversation just to prove we can be civil? My gaze lands back on Veronica, whose expression is twisted with worry. "Yeah. It was nice." I take a step back and motion over my shoulder. "I've gotta get back to the head table before they think I've gone missing."

Sam laughs good-spiritedly. This is obviously the kind of guy who puts everyone at ease. He's probably got a squeaky-clean past and coaches a Little League team or some shit too. Someone the judge would *love* to see in Jackson's life.

"It was good to see you, Colton," Veronica calls when I'm headed toward the table.

I glance over my shoulder and nod at her, not trusting my voice with the lie. This wasn't good. It was torture. *And I'd endure it over and over again if it meant getting a look at her, if it meant getting to see her happy.*

VERONICA

"**Y**ou okay?" Sam asks after Colton walks away.

I start to nod then shake my head. "No. Let's go get some wine."

I met Sam my first day at Grove Park Prep—the ridiculously officious name of the very sweet preschool where I have a new job with a fancy title. He's the art and "musical expression" teacher and one of my favorite coworkers. Not only do the kids adore their time with him, but he's a genuinely nice guy. And since his boyfriend is out of town this weekend, he was nice enough to accompany me to the wedding.

"Think I passed for straight just now?" he asks, tugging on the lapels of his suit jacket. "Or should I grab your ass to drive the point home?"

I roll my eyes then laugh despite myself. "You're here to keep me from being miserable, not to make him jealous."

"Mm-hmm, that's what you keep saying." The people in line ahead of us step away, and Sam signals for two glasses of wine.

"Why would I want to make him jealous? What would the point be?"

"You're so funny," he says, scoffing.

I shake my head and gratefully accept my wine from the bartender while Sam tucks some bills into the tip jar. "He looks good, don't you think? Like he's doing okay?"

"He looked . . . hot? I mean, if you like that bearded Zac

Efron look."

I tug my bottom lip between my teeth and shake my head. "I just want him to be okay."

"No. You want him to grovel and tell you how desperately he needs you."

I frown. I can't deny there was a part of me that was hurt he didn't fight harder for me, but I quickly shoved those feelings away, because that's not fair. I told Colton exactly what I needed, and he gave it to me. "He knows I can't risk losing Jacks."

Sam studies me for a long time, then shrugs. "I can't tell you what to do. How about we get shitfaced and become wedding reception clichés?"

I laugh again. "I think that plan has bad decisions written all over it."

He grins. "*Exactly.*"

COLTON

The meal passes in a blur. I'm so focused on not staring at Veronica and her date that I don't even remember eating my food. Brayden wanted to give the speech, so at least I'm spared fucking that up. I probably would've turned it into an excuse to make some thinly veiled plea to Veronica about how I'd wait for her forever and still love her. It would make her feel bad, and all the guests would pity me and the room would fill with awkwardness. Big brother's loving toast about family was a much better alternative.

I miss having Veronica at the office. I miss hearing her laugh from the other room, miss the way she'd subconsciously swish her hips to the music, miss her dozen notebooks and planners, and her fucking infuriating sass. All of it.

I don't know how long I've been staring off into space when Ellie sinks into the chair beside me. "Hey, you."

I straighten and look around. "Shit. Sorry. Do you need me somewhere?" I've been in enough weddings that I'm familiar with all the required parts and thought I was done for the night.

She laughs. "No. I just wanted to come over here because you look sad."

I scrub a hand over my face. "Sorry, El. I'm just tired. I'll get some coffee and perk up." I go to stand, and she grabs my arm, her eyes burning into mine.

"Talk to me a minute." Her smile is gentle. Beautiful.

I huff out a breath and settle back into the chair. "It's your wedding reception. Aren't there a thousand things you'd rather do than talk to me?"

"Right now? Not at all."

Silence stretches between us, and it's filled with the sounds of the reception. The music, the laughter, the conversation and tinkling of glasses. "You look beautiful," I finally say, because I didn't say it in the receiving line earlier when so many people were around—watching and listening.

"Thank you."

"I mean, Levi is the hotter between you, but you're not bad."

Her nose wrinkles with her laugh, and hundreds of memories wash over me, but instead of leaving me feeling lonely and full of regrets, they're just . . . *nice*. It's good to have pieces of my past that bring comfort instead of guilt or bitterness.

She glances over her shoulder toward the far side of the dance floor, where Levi is surrounded by his brothers. He must be telling a story, because he's gesturing wildly and the guys are all laughing.

"You're marrying into that," I say, nodding toward them.

She shrugs. "Yeah, but I'll be okay anyway."

"Funny."

She smirks. "I know how lucky I am. Trust me."

"You deserve it—the big family. The white picket fence. The storybook ending." I blow out a breath. Moments like this, it's really easy to miss booze, but I'm glad I don't drink. I don't want to spend Ellie and Levi's wedding blitzed out of my mind and making stupid mistakes. "I'm sorry all my selfishness kept you from having it sooner."

"Colton." She grips my forearm and squeezes. "I don't regret our time together."

"Maybe not, but I'm grateful for how it all ended—grateful you got the good guy."

Her eyes fill with tears. "Is that really how you see it? Even now?"

"I see two of my favorite people in the world building a beautiful life together. He makes you happy, right?"

"Of course."

"And you make him happy?"

Her lips twitch. "I do what I can." The DJ starts playing the Electric Slide song, and Kathleen pushes her sons onto the dance floor, then leads the pack through the moves.

After watching with a big smile for most of the song, Ellie turns her attention back to me. "I'm sorry about you and Veronica."

I lift a shoulder. "It is what it is."

"I wish she'd . . ." Her mouth twists.

"Don't," I whisper. "Don't make this about her. I made my own choices. My past is my past, and I don't get to ignore it just because it's inconvenient now."

"Did the lawyer think this was necessary?"

"Etta couldn't speak to Veronica's case specifically, of course, but as a general rule, no." I sigh. "But that's not the point."

Ellie watches her new husband and brothers-in-law do the Electric Slide. I haven't had the courage to look in that direction much tonight, too worried I'd spot Veronica dancing with her date. "I can't blame her," Ellie finally says, "but I hate it. We all hate it."

I arch a brow. "I thought you came over here to cheer me up."

"You're right." She pushes back her chair and stands, offering me her hand. "Come on, Captain Grumpypants. We're going to dance."

"We are?"

She grabs my hand and tugs me toward the dance floor, and because she's the bride, I follow, groaning.

The DJ transitions into a slow song, so I pull her into my arms like I did so many times during our years together.

"You know everyone is going to watch us dancing and overanalyze every move, right?" I ask.

She rests one hand on my shoulder and loops the other behind my neck. "Let them analyze. The people who matter most won't question it for a second."

"So true." Over her shoulder, I see Levi studying us from his post at the edge of the dance floor, and when our eyes meet, he lifts his chin. There's so much in that gesture. *I see you. I trust you. I promise I'll take good care of her.* And maybe . . . *Thank you.*

"You haven't asked what I know about Veronica's date," she says.

I cough on a laugh. "I didn't realize there was anything worth asking."

She shrugs mysteriously, and I blow out an exasperated breath.

"What do you know about Veronica's date?"

"I know they work together. He was the first person to befriend her at school, and she talks about him constantly. He makes her laugh, and—"

"You can stop. I'm sorry I asked," I mutter.

"And his boyfriend is out of town this weekend visiting his grandparents in Toronto, so Veronica made him come keep her company."

"His . . ." *Oh.* For the first time all night, I scan the room to find Veronica and find she's already watching me. My pulse skips a beat then stutters into a sprint. Across from her, Sam's in an animated conversation with Easton Connor, Shay's husband, former NFL player and local celebrity. "So you're saying there's no romantic history with them?"

"I'm saying she brought a *friend.*"

"Fuck." I tear my gaze off Veronica. "I wish that weren't as much of a relief as it is."

"I'm not trying to meddle, but I hate seeing you sad."

It doesn't change anything.

"Oh, look," she says. "My great-aunt is trying to get Levi to dirty dance with her. I'd better go save her."

I laugh. "You mean *him*?"

"I said what I said." She scurries away and throws a wink at me over her shoulder when she's halfway across the dance floor to where her great-aunt is . . . holding Levi's hand against her shoulder as they dance a very respectful distance apart.

Brat, I mouth at Ellie, but then I head to Veronica. Just like Ellie knew I would.

Chapter Twenty-Nine

COLTON

Veronica watches me walk toward her, but she still looks surprised when I stop at her table and offer my hand.

"Dance with me?"

She glances around as if someone's going to jump out and tell her she can't.

"It's all good, V," her date says. "Go on. Dance. Have *fun* for a minute."

The second she steps into my arms, I don't care that I'll regret this tomorrow. I don't care that it'll hurt like hell to let her go. All I care about is the press of her warm skin against me and the smell of her hair.

"Where's Jacks tonight?" I ask, looking around the ballroom. I spotted him earlier, but he was so busy playing with his cousins that he didn't notice me. Probably for the best. I would've lost it.

"Star picked him up about an hour ago so I could enjoy the reception."

"She's a good friend."

"The best."

"Are you still staying with her?"

"I moved into a new apartment last week. It's really nice." She laughs. "Okay, not *overlooks the bay* nice like yours, but better than I thought I could afford at the beginning of the summer."

"Child support?" Somehow, that surprises me. From everything I've heard about Marcus, he doesn't strike me as the kind of guy who pays child support without a court order if he's not getting his way with custody.

"No. I told Nic about the credit card, and . . ." She shrugs. "She insisted on helping, since I'd done it for Mom."

"I'm glad you told her. And glad you have a little relief financially."

"Me too," she whispers.

The song changes, and she steps back. I want to hold her close and tell her all the reasons she shouldn't walk away from me again, but I won't. Not as long as she thinks it's a choice between me and her son.

She glances back toward her table, and Sam circles his finger in the air. "Dance another," he calls.

Laughing, Veronica shrugs and steps into my arms again.

VERONICA

*E*very time he touches me, tingles zip up my arms and my stomach flip-flops.

Colton's smile is gentle when he pulls me back into his arms. He's so warm, and I'd somehow forgotten how small I feel when our bodies are pressed together. How protected.

The couples on the dance floor move around us, but Colton and I stay in one place, gazes locked as we sway to music I'm not sure either of us really hears.

"I have missed the hell out of you," he whispers, and my heart tugs in my chest. It's trying to jump ship. Trying to break these shackles I've put on it and take up residence with him. Where it belongs. "The office isn't the same without your bullshit."

"It must be terrible. I heard the new girl is"—I wrinkle my nose in disgust—"punctual."

The corner of his mouth quirks, then his gaze dips to my mouth. "I think . . ." He shakes his head and looks away.

"What?"

"I'm going to keep my mouth shut. I didn't ask you to dance so I could beg you to take me back."

But I wish you would. The words sit on my tongue, but I trap them. It's not fair. "I've missed you too," I admit, though I have no doubt it's written all over my face. "Jacks is asking when you'll play Spidey with him again."

"I would." He grimaces. "I mean, if you don't think that would look bad on you, I could meet you at the park or something. He's a good kid, and I don't want him to feel like I've abandoned him."

My heart aches. Colton is such a good man, and none of this

is fair. "He'd like that."

"And what about you? Is there anything you need? You got moved in okay?" He scans the room around us, the corner of his mouth hitching into a crooked grin. "I guess you have five Jackson brothers as in-laws of sorts who could help you with anything you'd need me for."

"I'm not so sure about that."

"Come on. Ethan gives you grief because he's overprotective of Nicole, but they all care about you."

My lips curl in as I fight back a smile. "I'm just saying their wives might not appreciate their husbands attending to *those* needs."

He squeezes my side. "Pest."

"I'm fine, Colton. The apartment is decent, and the job is great. I don't need anyone to move furniture, if that's what you're asking. For most things, I can take care of myself."

He throws his head back and groans. "Now I'm going to be thinking about that for the rest of the night."

I loop my arms behind his neck, stepping closer. "You thought I'd just bring someone else to my bed? That I'd let just anyone take care of my needs?"

"I didn't know what to think, Veronica. I've been focused on trying to give you what you wanted."

"And that's hard?"

His hands slide down my back until he's cupping my ass, then he pulls my body tight against his, and his erection presses against my belly. Lust slams into me and makes my breath catch. "So hard."

When he moves to put space between us again, I grab his

hand. "Come with me a minute."

Wordlessly, he follows me out of the ballroom. I take the hall around to the offices at the back of the building and tug him in the first open door I see, then shut it behind us.

Colton looks around, confused, but I don't give him a chance to ask any questions before I launch myself at him, hungry and desperate, my mouth on his, my hands on his chest.

He grunts softly and kisses me back, his hands plunging into my hair and making a mess of it as I shakily undo the buttons of his shirt.

I know this will only complicate things, know it will only make it harder to walk away from him tonight, but I don't care. I need him so badly. Need to feel him and taste him.

With the final button undone, I yank his shirt from his shoulders and shove it down his arms. It gets caught at his wrists, but he makes quick work of the buttons, and the material floats down to the floor like a white flag. He peels off his undershirt in a flash before drawing me into him again.

I'm lost in the flurry of our mouths and roaming hands. His kisses, alternating between tender and rough. Teeth and nipping followed by sweet passes of soft lips, as if he knows I need both. As if he knows I need everything in this moment, in this night.

He yanks my skirt up around my waist and cups me between my legs, and I rock into him, whimpering pleas of need and gratitude all mixed together. I'm a mess, but I'm afraid if I slow down, I'll lose this moment. Scared we'll both come to our senses, and I'll go back to having nothing. I unbuckle his belt and release him from his pants, wrapping my hand around his thick length.

His fingers delve into my panties, and he's murmuring

between kisses. *"So fucking beautiful." "Wet, so wet." "Need this. Need you." "Come home with me."*

No. I pull back and shake my head. "We can't do that."

"Do what?" His teeth scrape down the side of my neck, and when he sucks at that tender spot at the junction of my shoulder, I nearly cry out.

"Just this. Just here. So we don't blur the lines." I stroke his cock. I would drop to my knees and take him into my mouth if I weren't so greedy for the feel of his fingers inside me. "I need this."

Colton freezes, and while he's against the wall and can't back away, I feel him retreat. "Veronica." He takes my wrist and gently removes my hand from his cock before tucking himself inside his pants again. "Shit. We can't do this."

"What?" God, I can barely think straight. Is he saying we can't do this here or . . .? "I thought you wanted . . ." I look down, but he cups my face in both his hands and tilts it up so my eyes meet his.

"Of course I do. I *always* want you. I'll want you until the day I die. But a quick fuck in Levi's office isn't going to be enough." He scans my face and sighs. "Maybe it would be for you, but it would never be for me."

"I'm sorry. I misread you. I thought . . . I'm sorry."

"You're not some itch I need to scratch. You're the woman I love, and if I can't have all of you, I'm not going to torture myself by fucking you and remembering exactly how good it feels to make you come."

My cheeks heat and my eyes burn with unshed tears. "Colton, I'm—"

"Don't. Don't apologize again." He wraps his arms around me and pulls me tight against him, pressing a kiss to the top of my head. "Never apologize for being an amazing mother. Never apologize for being the woman who makes a screwup like me want to be better."

He releases me, scoops his shirts off the floor, and walks out the door.

Chapter Thirty

VERONICA

I like to spend as much of my weekend as possible with Jacks, but I've been letting Katie watch him for a couple of hours on Sunday afternoons while I work on lesson plans downstairs in the bakery. He thinks she's a magical fairy princess, and she loves getting the babysitting experience, so it's a great opportunity for me to get work done before the school week begins.

It's hard to believe this is my life. I have the teaching job I always dreamed of. I have good friends, and my sister is settled and happy with a family of her own.

I should be so happy, but the custody hearing looms over me like a storm cloud. For now, I don't even have to share my son with his father. Since he *threatened me* and there's no custody agreement holding me to our previous arrangement, I told him he can't see Jacks until we either do mediation or it's decided before a judge. I hoped this would nudge him to compromise, but he and Kristi have chosen to wait rather than give up on their demand for primary custody.

On top of all that, I miss Colton so much it hurts.

I'm in my usual booth when someone drops a manilla folder on the table in front of me, and when I look up, my heart feels funny as it tries to do too many things simultaneously. Like it's trying to race out of my chest and freeze all at once.

Colton's looking down at the folder thoughtfully. He looks so good. His beard's a little longer than usual, and I can smell him from here—a clean laundry and soap smell that's somehow unique to him.

"Hey," I say softly.

"Hey." He scans my face. I feel so damn cared for when he looks at me like this—as if he's trying to determine if I need anything or if I'm well. I wish I deserved such care. I wish I weren't such a coward.

I swallow and nod to the seat across from me. "Do you want to sit down?" I owe him an apology for what happened at the wedding two weeks ago. And about everything else. But how do I say sorry for kicking him out of my life when my own cowardice has kept me from letting him back in?

He shakes his head. "This won't take long."

Or he doesn't want to be close to me for long. God, who could blame him?

He flattens a hand against the file folder. "The first thing I want to say is the contents of this folder aren't about you and me. I didn't do this for us. I did it for Jacks. And, to be honest, I don't know if what's in here will help you at all. Personally, I think it's pretty clear what the judge will decide regardless, but I can't blame you for doing what you need to do for yourself and for Jacks."

I eye the folder but don't dare reach for it. I'm afraid if I touch him, all my resolve will fall away. "What is it?"

"You were right. Marcus hired a PI to follow us and dig up dirt."

I gasp. Not because I'm surprised, but because I forgot I'd shared those suspicions with Colton before Marcus ever confirmed them.

"I figured turnabout's fair play," he says.

"You hired a private investigator." I draw in a shaky breath, and it feels like a prayer. "What did he find?"

"Like I said, I don't know if any of this will change anything, and I don't think it'd do you any favors if you shared this with a custody judge, but it might matter to someone else." He blows out a breath and pulls his hand away.

I open the folder and slowly flip through the pictures stacked at the front. They show Marcus with not one but two different women. And neither is Kristi. "These are recent?"

"All within the last three weeks," he says. "There's nothing here that proves Marcus is an unfit parent, but . . ."

"More than enough to prove he's a shitty husband," I whisper. *More than enough to prove he's exactly the man I thought he was when I left.*

"I'm not telling you what to do with it," Colton says, "but I wanted you to have it."

I only vaguely register his words. I've been so hung up on my own shortcomings—so hung up on every bad thing I ever brought into anyone's life—that I forgot my own happiness is worth fighting for. Mom always just wanted to get by, but I've always wanted more than that for Jacks. I look at him and know I would fight *monsters* to prove to him that he matters, that his happiness matters. But what good is that if he only ever sees me surrender to the monsters when they come after *my* happiness? What kind of example am I setting for my child if I don't show him that I'm willing to fight for *myself*?

I finally tear my gaze off the pictures and meet Colton's eyes. "Why did you do this for me? After what I did to you—why?"

"Do you really have to ask?" He steps back like he's ready to leave. "I'd do anything for you, V. That never changed."

"Colton, I'm sorry."

He looks me over, sadness so clear in those dark eyes. "I already told you I don't want you apologizing for putting Jacks first."

"I would do anything for *you*." I bite my bottom lip so hard I might draw blood, but I don't care. I deserve Colton, and I'm going to prove it by being brave enough to fight. "It's not only about Jacks. Marcus made some threats. He made it clear that if I made them take me to court about Jacks, you'd find yourself with criminal drug charges. I couldn't let him destroy your life as a way to take my child."

Colton squeezes his eyes shut and mutters a string of curses. "He can't create charges against me. He doesn't have that power."

"He has money to pay people to make you look guilty. Or to plant drugs on you. Or worse." I swallow. "For years and years, I brought nothing but trouble to the people I love most. My foster families. Nic. I couldn't do the same to you."

"You should've told me." He tightens his hands into fists and releases them. "And I should've suspected that he'd threaten something like that, but I missed it."

"You assumed the mistakes from your past meant you couldn't have me. And I assumed mine meant I shouldn't have you. I don't know what tomorrow will bring, and I don't want to be the reason the life you've fought for gets taken away from you. But I shouldn't have let Marcus win so easily. I should've fought for you. For us."

"What if I told you I'm willing to risk whatever Marcus throws at me?" He pulls me from the booth, dark eyes searching mine. "I don't want to live without your love. You're worth the risk, and I swear I'll fight with every connection I have to make sure he can't take your child from you."

I look up at him, full of hope and helpless to keep my walls between us. "I love you, and I've always been yours. That never changed."

"I love you too." He lowers his mouth to mine, and I melt into him, vaguely aware of the bakery crowd turning our way and Star's whistle of approval behind the counter, but entirely aware of him. Here with me, loving me despite everything.

I was afraid Kristi wouldn't meet with me if I asked, so I drove to Grand Rapids and followed her to her favorite coffee shop. Now I'm standing on the sidewalk, gathering my courage next to Colton, who refused to let me do this alone.

"I might not like them," I say, "but I hate knowing I'm about to toss a grenade into the middle of her life."

"She did that to you," he says, "trying to take Jacks."

"That doesn't make it right."

"Careful. You're showing that ooey-gooey soft center of yours out here in front of everyone."

I nudge him with my elbow. "I don't know what you're talking about. I'm a stone-cold bitch."

"Mm-hmm." He presses a kiss to the top of my head. "We don't have to do this. We can go with Plan B."

The hope is Kristi will see these pictures and leave her husband, and without her to push him, he'll drop the custody suit. Plan B, if she doesn't, or in the unlikely event he decides he wants custody even without Kristi, is to pay Colton's PI to keep following Marcus until he does something incriminating in his efforts to sabotage Colton.

"No," I say, finding my resolve. "She deserves to know."

"If this destroys their marriage, it won't be you who did the damage. He's the one with mistresses. No matter what happens, Marcus is the one who made the bad decisions."

I take a deep breath and push into the coffee shop.

Kristi spots me immediately and walks toward us. When her eyes land on the manila folder I'm clutching to my chest, her face pales. "What's that?" Does she know already? Suspect?

Maybe.

Still, I step forward and hand it over gently, only to watch her tear it open.

Her chin quivers.

She tried to build her perfect little family by ripping mine apart, and I see it in her eyes the moment she registers it might not even be worth fighting for.

It makes me sad for her when I know the man I love would wage war for me.

Chapter Thirty-One

COLTON

*V*eronica is wearing a hole in the floor of Ethan Jackson's kitchen by pacing. She's been on the phone with Etta for five minutes, pacing back and forth the whole time.

Nic and I are hanging on every word, but there's not much meaning to be pulled from *yeahs*, *okays*, and *uh-huhs*.

"Yes, I agree," she says, nodding as if Etta is in the room and not at her office across town. "Okay. Thank you so much for all your help. Yes. Thank you." She taps her phone screen to end the call then sets the phone on the counter with a *thunk* before slowly turning to me.

"So?" I ask gently. "What's the news?"

"Marcus has officially withdrawn his custody complaint," she says.

Nic does two excited bunny hops, then winces and presses a

hand to the middle of her back.

Ethan pulls her to his side and rubs the sore spot. "So that's it?" he asks Veronica. "He's going to settle for weekends and splitting holidays?"

Veronica wraps her arms around me and leans her head on my chest. "No. His lawyer told Etta that Kristi kicked him out and he's moving back to Alabama. He'll contact me for visits a couple of weekends a year."

"The nerve of him," Nic says. "Dragging you through all this, and then he doesn't even want to see his kid a couple of times a month?"

I hold Veronica tight against my chest. "It was never about what he wanted," I say, and Veronica nods.

"Kristi was leading the charge on the visitation and then custody the whole time," Veronica says. "He was just going along with it. Turns out he'd really been enjoying that trust of hers and wanted to keep her happy by getting Jacks."

"Did he ever consider keeping her happy by keeping his dick in his pants?" Ethan asks, and Veronica and Nic respond in unison with "Not Marcus," then laugh.

Nic waddles across the kitchen and joins our hug, wrapping her arms around both me and her sister. "It's over," she whispers.

I feel Veronica take a long, deep breath. Is it the first she's taken in months?

"What are you going to do to celebrate?" Ethan asks as we all pull apart.

"Just being together is enough," Veronica says, glancing out the window toward Jacks.

"I mean, that's true," I say, "but I might've gotten us something to commemorate the occasion."

"What?" Veronica asks.

I glance out the kitchen window and to the backyard, where Jacks and Lilly are running through the sprinkler. "You should probably get Jacks out of the sprinkler and dressed. We'll need to leave in about an hour if we're going to make the show."

Veronica props her hands on her hips. "What show?"

I pull the tickets for Marvel on Ice from my back pocket and offer them to her. "It's in Chicago, so we'll stay the night too."

She squeals in excitement but shoves them back toward me. "Hide those. I want it to be a surprise when Spider-Man skates out on the ice the first time."

"That can be arranged."

She grabs me by the belt loops and presses her body to mine. "Thank you."

"Any time," I say around the emotion swelling in my throat. "I love you."

"Love you back."

Epilogue

VERONICA

I read a lot of romance novels, but until I started dating Colton McKinley, I never really understood how hot a growling man could be. I mean, I assumed the heroes in question were sexy, but my imagination had nothing on the growling man in front of me.

"You're late," he says, a mock scowl covering his features.

I toss my purse on the floor and saunter across his living room. "Thank you, Captain Obvious."

I try to squeeze past him, but he grabs me by the hips, spins me, and pins me against the wall. "I hate waiting," he says. He kisses his way down my neck while his hand slides up my side until he's cupping my breast, his thumb seeking my nipple through my dress.

"I promise it'll be worth the wait," I say.

"I never doubted that."

I pull at his shirt, untucking it from his jeans. "I needed to go shopping."

He arches a disapproving brow at me. "We have exactly two hours alone and you took time to go shopping?"

I yank his shirt over his head, and my mouth goes dry at the sight of his strong chest. So fucking hot. "I had a gift card from the girls to that cute little boutique on the square."

He finds the tie on the waistband of my dress and releases it. "What shop is more important than our first time alone in a week?"

I wiggle my shoulders and let the material fall to the ground, and his nostrils flare at the sight of my new black lace panty set. "The one that sells these."

Long seconds pass as he looks me over, his eyes growing darker. "Goddamn, you're perfect."

"Not perfect." I tug him close again. "This lingerie is hot, but it makes me no less the hot-mess bitch I was yesterday."

He skates his palms over my belly and breasts, back down, and around to cup my ass. "If you insist, but you're slacking if you want to keep up the hot-mess persona. Pretty soon, no one's going to believe it."

Because things are coming together. Finally, my life feels less like a race I'm losing and more like a challenge under which I'm thriving. The new apartment helps—we actually have space to live and play and cook. My job makes a huge difference, since I love it, and having Jacks there simplifies my day. So does not being dragged down by bills and juggling work and side hustles.

But part of it is Colton. It's not just about having someone to lean on. It's about having the right someone. Someone perfect *for me.*

"No one's going to believe you're an asshole," I say, barely getting the words out as he drops his head and sucks my nipple through the thin lace of my bra. "You hardly ever walk around like a brooding grump anymore."

"I guess people change," he says, scraping his teeth against my collarbone.

I grab a handful of his hair and pull him up to kiss me again. Our mouths meet, and my phone rings.

I scoot out from between him and the wall, and he groans. "Sorry!" I cry.

When I bend to retrieve it from my purse, he smacks my ass. "You're about to see grumpy Colton."

"It's *Nic*. She could be in labor," I say, swiping to answer. She and Ethan want the delivery to be a private affair—a request I'm sure was necessary, since there are, like, a million Jacksons in this town—but you don't ignore your phone when your twin is nine months pregnant. "Hey, sister. If this isn't an emergency or you calling to tell me you just popped out a baby, I'm gonna have to call you back."

"Neither," Nic says. She huffs like she's just run up several flights of stairs. "I'm at the hospital. Five centimeters dilated. Ethan just left to get me more ice chips, but I need you."

My stomach clenches. "I'm on my way." I'm already tying my dress back on. "What happened?"

"Nothing," she says. "But labor is terrible, and I *need* my sister. Please?"

"Five minutes," I promise.

"Thanks, Ronnie." She hangs up, and I turn to apologize to my sex-starved boyfriend.

"I'll drive you," he says, grabbing his shirt off the floor. He pulls it over his head. "Then I'll grab Jacks from school and keep him for as long as you need me to."

"Really?"

"Of course." He leans in to kiss me again, but I dodge and put space between us.

"If I let you kiss me right now, it'll take *much* longer than the promised five minutes to get there, and I don't want to be late for this."

He chuckles. "Fair."

"You're really not pissed?"

His brow creases. "Hell no. Someday, Ethan'll be the one with blue balls because you're in labor and you need Nic. He can make it up to me then."

His eyes go wide when he seems to register what he just said, but I smile. "You think?"

He steps close again and tilts my face up, brushing a gentle kiss across my lips. "I *hope*. If I'm lucky."

I bite back a smile. "You've always struck me as a pretty lucky guy."

He scans my face. "I seem to be when you're around."

"I really want to kiss you right now."

He smacks my ass again. "Don't worry. I'm worth the wait."

He really, really is.

The End

Thank you for reading *Not Without Your Love*, the final book in The Boys of Jackson Harbor series. Join me in 2022 for my new Jackson Harbor series, Jackson Harbor Heartbreakers. To receive an email when the series launches, please sign up for my newsletter: lexiryan.com/signup

I hope you enjoyed this book and will consider leaving a review. Thank you for reading. It's an honor!

Acknowledgments

First, a big thanks to my family. Brian, Jack, and Mary, thank you for giving me the time and space to write and for understanding why my books are so important to me! To my mom, dad, brothers, sisters, in-laws, aunts, uncles, various cousins and cousins-in-law, thank you for cheering me on—each in your own way.

This book is dedicated to my friend Kim Jackson (no relation to the Jackson Harbor clan), who is not only an incredible person but who was instrumental in helping me understand the most important facets of this book. I went to her for help on the legal implications of Veronica's custody battle and came away understanding Colton's character so much better. Thank you, Kim, for being so generous with your knowledge and so open about your journey. Any errors are my own.

To everyone who provided me feedback on this story along the way—especially Tina Allen, Larissa Cardozo, Heather Carver, Lisa Kuhne, Samantha Leighton, and Janice Owen— you're all awesome. Rhonda Edits and Lauren Clarke at Creating Ink, thank you for the insightful line and content edits. You both push me to be a better writer and make my stories the best they can be. Thanks to Arran McNicol at Editing720 for proofreading. Thank you to Sarah Eirew, who took the gorgeous cover photo and did the design. I'm grateful for this team!

To all of the bloggers, bookstagrammers, readers, and reviewers who help spread the word about my books, I am humbled by the time you take out of your busy lives for my stories. I can't thank you enough. You're the best.

To my agent, Dan Mandel, for believing in me and staying by my side. Whew! It's been a *year*!

Finally, a big thank-you to my fans, who couldn't get enough Jackson Harbor. I thought I was leaving after Shay's book, and when I missed my fictional little beachside town, your enthusiasm persuaded me to return. Because of you, I live my dream every day. I couldn't do it without you, and I don't take one second for granted. You're the coolest, smartest, best readers in the world. I appreciate each and every one of you!

~Lexi

Printed in Great Britain
by Amazon

76965771R00203